"You can't blame
into our own han
Sumner replied.

"We're using first names, remember?"

"Mr. Ramsey—"

"Jonah."

"Jonah, I—" Sumner paused, then found herself unable to continue. As the light of the lantern coated his features, she became aware of deep lines of weariness fanning out from his eyes and bracketing his mouth.

Perhaps it was a trick of the light, the silence of the dark Utah night or merely the fact that Jonah appeared as ill at ease in reporting the message as she did receiving it. But suddenly, she didn't want to argue.

"You look exhausted, Jonah."

Her comment clearly surprised him. "It's been a long few days."

"And I've managed to complicate them even further."

In the lamplight his eyes were darker, warmer. Almost…kind. And even though she tended to bristle in his presence, tonight she couldn't summon the energy or the animosity. Instead, a strange heat invaded her chest. She became intimately aware of the stillness of the night and the fact that the two of them were alone.

Completely and totally alone.

Lisa Bingham is the bestselling author of more than thirty historical and contemporary romantic fiction novels. She's been a teacher for more than thirty years, and has served as a costume designer for theatrical and historical reenactment enthusiasts. Currently she lives in rural northern Utah near her husband's fourth-generation family farm with her sweetheart and three beautiful children. She loves to hear from her fans at lisabinghamauthor.com or Facebook.com/lisabinghamauthor.

Books by Lisa Bingham

Love Inspired Historical

The Bachelors of Aspen Valley

Accidental Courtship

LISA BINGHAM
Accidental Courtship

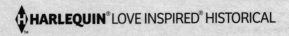

If you purchased this book without a cover you should be aware that this book is stolen property. It was reported as "unsold and destroyed" to the publisher, and neither the author nor the publisher has received any payment for this "stripped book."

Recycling programs for this product may not exist in your area.

LOVE INSPIRED BOOKS

ISBN-13: 978-1-335-36951-2

Accidental Courtship

Copyright © 2018 by Lisa Bingham

All rights reserved. Except for use in any review, the reproduction or utilization of this work in whole or in part in any form by any electronic, mechanical or other means, now known or hereinafter invented, including xerography, photocopying and recording, or in any information storage or retrieval system, is forbidden without the written permission of the editorial office, Love Inspired Books, 195 Broadway, New York, NY 10007 U.S.A.

This is a work of fiction. Names, characters, places and incidents are either the product of the author's imagination or are used fictitiously, and any resemblance to actual persons, living or dead, business establishments, events or locales is entirely coincidental.

This edition published by arrangement with Love Inspired Books.

® and TM are trademarks of Love Inspired Books, used under license. Trademarks indicated with ® are registered in the United States Patent and Trademark Office, the Canadian Intellectual Property Office and in other countries.

www.Harlequin.com

Printed in U.S.A.

I know both how to be abased, and I know how to abound: every where and in all things I am instructed both to be full and to be hungry, both to abound and to suffer need. I can do all things through Christ which strengtheneth me.
—*Philippians* 4:12–13

Dedicated to David and Esther, Leonard and Mable
and most especially to ElMont and Joyce.
Thank you for all the wonderful stories.

Chapter One

Utah Territory
Batchwell Bottoms Silver Mine
December 1873

"When's the new doc getting in?"

Jonah Ramsey looked up from the ore reports he'd been handed and sighed. "He was supposed to arrive on the U an' P passenger train last week. So…"

He took a gold watch from his vest pocket—a watch that had once belonged to his father. Absentmindedly, he brushed his thumb over the dents and scratches that proclaimed the timepiece had been through a battle or two—quite literally—then depressed the plunger so that the cover opened. It was already past noon.

"You think the doc'll be on the fool thing today?" Gus Creakle looked up from his scribbling to squint against the brilliant December sun streaming through the office windows. "Because I got me a toe that's plum mortified, I'm tellin' you. I done dropped that idiot filin' cabinet on it, an' I'm afeard it's gonna have t' be cut off if'n it don't get no doctorin'."

Although there were daily locomotives that came

through Batchwell Bottoms, a passenger train was more of a rarity. Once a week, it brought fresh miners to the valley, or took away those who were injured or who'd had enough. But even those were more infrequent now that winter was settling into the Rockies. It wouldn't be long before the pass would become completely sealed off, and the miners would have to wait until spring for any contact with the outside world.

He worried what would happen if the doctor didn't arrive before they reached that point.

Creakle scratched his chin with a stubby finger. "So what do y' think, boss? Think the man will be on this week's train?"

As if on cue, a faint whistle broke through the usual din of the mining camp, followed by the distant pant of the locomotive as it struggled to pull its cargo the last few yards of an uphill grade.

"You should have your answer within the next fifteen minutes, Creakle. Think you can hang on until then?"

Creakle considered the idea, his eyelids blinking, the tufts of hair on his balding pate poking out at odd angles until he gave the appearance of a ruminating owl. "Maybe. If'n I ain't got no other—"

Creakle's words died the same instant that a muffled *boom* echoed through the valley. Jonah felt a jolt through the soles of his boots. He threw the files onto the desk, snatched up his hat and coat and ran outside toward the yawning entrance to the mine.

From the corner of his eye, Jonah noticed he wasn't the only person racing to find the source of the shudder. But even as he did, an uneasiness slid through his veins. Any man worth his salt knew what to expect when there was a "bump" in the mine. But somehow, the vibration that had sent him running hadn't been quite right.

The other miners had come to the same conclusion. One by one, they stopped in their tracks, their breaths hovering in the frigid winter air.

From his spot a few yards ahead of them, Jonah turned in a slow circle, his eyes narrowed to near slits against the uncomfortable sheen of sunlight bouncing over newly fallen snow. From far away came the eerie whistle of the Union Pacific passenger train. Jonah could see the puffs of steam and soot as the stack of the locomotive emerged from the canyon, a pair of brightly painted passenger cars snaking along behind it.

"What's going on, boss?" one of the men called out.

Jonah shook his head. "I don't—"

But his words were drowned out by a loud crack. Then a rumble swelled up through the soles of his feet, vibrating his whole body.

"Would you look at—"

Jonah's eyes skipped from the mine entrance to the two-story office, the Miners' Hall, the livery, the company store and beyond to the row houses that were scattered like children's blocks in front of the steep mountainside, then up, up, past the snowy cornice of Seesaw Point. At that moment, an entire wall of ice separated from the precipice and snow roiled down the slopes like a tidal wave, building up steam as it raced toward the valley.

"Avalanche!" someone shouted just beyond Jonah's shoulder.

The men dived toward the shelter of the mine, the Miners' Hall, the main offices.

Jonah instinctively leaped for the cover offered by one of the ore cars. Ignoring the stab of pain in his back, he hunkered low as a cloud of snow and vapor swallowed him whole. Gasping for air, he covered his head and his face while an icy blast of wind swirled around him, kicking up dirt and sleet and pine needles that pelted his cheeks and hands with such force they drew blood.

Then, just as quickly, the noise stopped.

Jonah waited, dragging cold, wet air into his lungs. His senses, keener than they'd been only a few moments earlier, picked out the slightest sounds: a plop of snow, the crack of a branch. A whimper.

For a moment, Jonah found himself lost in a wave of memories.

Thundering cannon.

Distant drums.

And pain, so much pain...

Opening his eyes, he took quick, shallow breaths, forcing the images away and ignoring the searing pain that traced down his spine—an injury forged in battle. Then he grabbed the rim of the ore car and hauled himself to his feet.

Around him, the mining camp looked as if it had come through the back end of a blizzard. The air was heavy with a gray mist, and several inches of ice and snow covered every surface. If it weren't for the glitter of rocks and the dark green bits of broken evergreens, Jonah could have believed that they'd emerged from a storm.

Whirling, he blinked against the moisture and dust. Mine offices...*fine*. Mine opening...*fine*. Miners' Hall, row houses, blacksmith shop, cook shack...*check, check* and *check*. They'd be digging themselves out of a few drifts, but there didn't appear to be any permanent damage. As long as the timbers had held underground...

From far away, Jonah heard a plaintive, bleating whistle. It wavered, then trailed off completely.

"The train!" Jonah called out, already running toward the livery. "The snow must have pushed it off the tracks!

Grab anything you can find—pickaxes, shovels, tools. Creakle!"

The daft man must not have taken cover when the avalanche hit, because he hovered in the office doorway, completely covered in white, bits of ice sparkling from his face and beard. If not for the blinking of his eyes, he could have been a children's snowman.

"Head into the shaft, and make sure everything's okay. Let them know that the encampment is fine, but the passenger train may be in trouble."

Creakle lifted one snow-encased arm to offer a half-hearted salute. "Will do, boss!"

Jonah flung open the doors to the livery, rushing to the far stall where he kept his own dappled gelding. He didn't bother with a saddle, but slipped the bridle over his mount's head, then drew him into the center aisle.

As the men streamed in behind him, he gestured to the other stalls. "Harness all those mules. We may need them to pull the carriages out of the drifts. And get a couple of sledges hitched up, as well. God willing, there'll be plenty of passengers needing a ride back into town."

Then he was swinging onto the back of his mount and galloping toward the canyon.

Sumner Havisham blinked against the darkness, willing herself to focus on something—anything—that would reassure her that she was alive.

Dear Heavenly Father...help me...please...

Black dots swirled in front of her eyes and a wave of faintness threatened to swallow her whole, but she forced the dizziness away.

She would not pass out. She *would not*. She'd learned that lesson long ago, when she'd had a bout of scarlet fever as a girl and had collapsed in the nursery. She could still hear her step-brother's scornful words.

Only girls get the vapors, Sumner. Only good-for-nothing, silly girls. How will you ever catch a husband if you act like that?

Her hands curled into tight fists, her jaw growing tight.

She hadn't been a silly girl then, and she didn't plan on being one now. Nor had she set her sights on marriage. She was a doctor, and she needed to behave like one. Especially when people's lives might hang in the balance.

Inwardly, she took stock of herself, noting the bumps and bruises, the stinging pains. When she felt sure nothing was broken, she lifted a hand to the sticky wetness trickling down her forehead. Blood seeped from a cut near her hairline, and just below that, she found a lump on her forehead the size of a goose egg.

Go on, cry. Girls always gotta cry cuz they're weak.

But she wasn't weak. Never had been. Never would be.

"Ladies? Is everyone okay?"

Silence pressed against her, accompanied by odd creaks and groans. But finally, there was a faint cry.

"Here. I'm here."

Sumner thought she recognized the voice of Miss Willow Granger, the shy woman who'd sat in the seat behind her. She hadn't said much on their cross-country journey, but when she had, Sumner had recognized the broad vowels of Manchester's working class and it had reminded her of home. "Willow?"

"Yes, miss?"

"Are you hurt?"

It was quiet for a moment, then, "No. I don't think so. But I'm pinned by some fallen trunks."

Another wave of light-headedness threatened to overtake her, and Sumner squeezed her eyes shut. She'd been so close to her destination! Only that morning, the train had left the fertile farmlands of Utah Territory to thread through the last mountain pass. The grade had become steeper there. They'd followed that course until the canyon had abruptly opened into a narrow valley, and she'd been sure that finally she'd reached Aspen Valley.

And then...

There'd been a roaring noise. A wall of snow slammed into the car, throwing them from their seats. Then they were tumbling...

Sumner opened her eyes again. As she finally began to focus, she could make out the confines of the railway car—unfamiliar now, with blackened windows and seats hanging giddily above her. Around her lay a flotsam of bags, loose articles of clothing, books...

"Do you think you can get yourself free, Willow?"

Sumner heard a rustling noise, then, "No. I'm wedged in tight."

"Are any of the other women nearby?"

"I—I don't know. It's too dark to tell."

This time, as Sumner gazed around her, she was able to make some sense of what she was seeing. The world wasn't as dark as she had at first supposed. Instead, packed snow was preventing the light from shining inside.

Sumner tried to find the other women in the dimness, but since the railway carriage had tipped on its side, she couldn't discern anything in detail. Instead, she saw a hand here, a foot there, a ruffled flounce.

She had to help them get out.

There was no telling how tightly the snow had sealed off the car. The women would need fresh air before Sumner could assess their injuries.

Sumner rolled her head to investigate, and there, just a

few yards away, she could see a thin shaft of light piercing through the gloom.

"Willow, I don't think I can make my way back to you, but if I can get outside…"

When the avalanche had struck, Sumner had seen a quick glimpse of a town in the valley. She'd even smiled when the other women had teased her about disembarking from the train at the famed "Bachelor Bottoms"—the nickname given to the mine for its peculiar regulations: no drinking, cussing, smoking, gambling or women.

How the mining community had decided on hiring a female doctor had been the source of speculation for most of their journey from Denver—especially since the passenger train had been reserved, primarily, for a handful of small families, a few widows and a group of mail-order brides heading for Salt Lake City, San Francisco and Seattle.

"If I can get out, I can get help from the mine."

"Go, miss. The others are bound to rouse soon enough and I can tell them where you've gone."

Behind her, Sumner heard a muffled moan, and she knew that she didn't have any time to waste. The other women could be injured—perhaps seriously. But she couldn't care for them in the dim light of the ruined carriage. And if there was a possibility of the car shifting or another avalanche thundering down upon them…

"Hold on, ladies," she called out to anyone who might be conscious enough to hear her. "I'll be back soon with help."

Fighting the tangle of her skirts and the debris that littered what had once been a wall of windows, she crouched low and crawled toward that beam of light. Thankfully, she'd been seated near the front, so once she'd wriggled over the seats, she was able to brace open the ruined door and dig her way onto the mangled outer landing. Although most of the space had been compacted with snow, there was a small gap. If she could use the decorative railing to hoist herself up, she could probably push her way to the top.

Sumner rued the fact that she'd removed her mittens and heavy coat soon after boarding the train. Her fingers already throbbed with cold, but she refused to be cowed by the discomfort. As a physician, she knew that time was of the essence.

Help me, Dear Lord. Please.

Burrowing like a mole, she finally managed to maneuver her hand up to the gap above her. Biting her lip, she wedged the toe of her boot into the twisted iron railing and clawed at the ice, gradually making the aperture large enough for her head, her shoulders. Then, as she reached up, something snagged her wrist.

A squeak of surprise burst from her lips before she realized that it was another hand that gripped her. A very strong, masculine hand crisscrossed with faint scars.

She thought that a low voice called out, "Over here, boys!"

Relief swept through her. "Help is already here, everyone. Just hold on!" she called out to the gloom behind her.

A deep voice came from above. "Can you grab me with your other hand?"

"I—I think so."

She wrapped her fingers around the broad, tanned wrist.

"I'm going to try to yank you out. Don't let go."

"Yes. O-okay."

"You ready?"

"Yes, I'm—"

Sumner didn't have a chance to finish her sentence

before she was wrenched from her nest of ice. For a moment, her body seemed weightless, flying through the air, before she felt herself falling, landing over the body of her rescuer.

Sputtering, she struggled to catch her breath. Then her gaze latched on to a masculine face, dark wavy hair, a beard touched with threads of gray and eyes the same mix of brown, green and blue as the river that wound through the canyon gorge.

He regarded her with an equal measure of surprise before it became quite clear to her that he'd just figured out that she was a woman in a camp famed for its lack of females.

Sumner's cheeks grew heated and she scrambled to stand up. But with the tangle of her skirts and the slipperiness of the ice, she wedged herself more tightly into the stranger's embrace.

She could feel her cheeks growing hot, but every time she put a hand down to brace herself, she touched his arm, his shoulder, until—*finally*—two sets of fists grabbed her and pulled her upright.

She wavered for a moment, a swirl of dizziness nearly pitching her onto the ground again. In an effort to appear calm and collected, she planted her heels more firmly in the ice and stood with as much dignity as she could summon.

"Thank you, gentlemen," she murmured.

The miners on either side gaped at Sumner like a pair of landed fish.

At her feet, the stranger winced and pushed himself to a sitting position. He grabbed for a hat that had fallen into the snow, settled it over his brow, then gingerly rose to his feet.

Had she hurt him that badly?

Self-conscious, Sumner reached to smooth her hair—only to discover that the careful swirl of braids and curls had come completely unmoored. Even worse, as she tugged at her bodice, she discovered one sleeve had torn free and she'd lost a pair of buttons in a most inopportune spot. Nevertheless, other than the bump on her head, and some scratches on her hands, she appeared to be unscathed.

At least, that was what she presumed, until she looked up to find that nearly thirty men stood amid the wreckage of the train. Every single one of them was staring at her. Even the mules in the distance seemed to be giving her the eye.

"Hel-lo?" she offered hesitantly.

Except for a half-hearted bray from one of the animals, there was no response. It grew so quiet that she swore she could hear the snow crystalize beneath their feet. Her cheeks grew hotter.

She cleared her throat, gesturing to the wreckage around her. "We've had an accident…"

Honestly, Sumner. They already know that.

"An avalanche…"

They know that, too.

"There are more people in the various cars. I'd say about a half-dozen crew members, a couple of families with small children. Some more women. All totaled, I'd say…fifty or sixty of them."

Obviously, the men hadn't known that piece of information, because their impromptu game of freeze tag came to a halt and they moved, swarming toward the exposed corners of the passenger cars, shouting out orders.

Sumner hurried to help them, but a hand snagged her elbow, pulling her away from the railway carriage she'd just abandoned.

"I need to show them where to dig!" she retorted, realizing that the gentleman who held her at bay was the same one who had pulled her from the smashed railway car.

"They know what to do."

"But—"

"You'll only be in the way."

Cuz you're a girl.

The hard set of the stranger's jaw and the crease between his brow told her plainly enough that, even though the man wouldn't offer the words aloud, he was thinking them. Once again, she'd been summed up in a single glance and pigeonholed as useless, simply by virtue of her sex. And that brought a starch to her spine that the avalanche had nearly knocked from her system.

She refused to let one more man tell her what to do.

"I assure you, I won't be in the way. I'm a doctor." She flung an accusatory finger in the direction of the hole from which she'd been tugged as unceremoniously as a turnip. "There are injured women inside."

His eyes narrowed. "A doctor?" he murmured in disbelief.

Sumner shook herself free of his grip and pulled herself to full height. Unfortunately, she still barely reached his shoulder, but she wasn't about to let that fact deter her. "Yes. I'm Sumner Havisham. The mining camp is expecting me. I've been hired to serve as their company doctor for the next five years."

His brows rose, nearly disappearing beneath the brim of his hat.

"*You're*… Sumner Havisham."

"Yes, of course. I have a copy of the signed contract…" She automatically felt for her reticule, then sighed, resisting the urge to stomp her foot in frustration. "It's with my things." She waved in the direction of the train.

The stranger sighed and stared at the ground as if pained, the pad of his thumb rubbing at the crease that appeared between his brows. Then he muttered, "Give me strength," before gesturing to a wooden sledge a few yards away. "Why don't you wait over there, miss—"

"Dr. Havisham."

"*Dr.* Havisham. As the passengers are pulled free, we'll bring them to you."

When she would have argued, he held up a broad hand to stop her.

"The way things are, we've got to tread lightly over the debris path so we don't end up crashing through a window, or starting another avalanche. None of this is stable."

Sumner shivered at the thought, her gaze convulsively leaping up the slopes of the mountain where an enormous gash gouged through wind-carved whiteness. Broken trees and displaced boulders gave evidence to the churning power of the forces which had already given way.

"Please, Mi—*Dr.* Havisham. We don't have a lot of time."

Although her pride still prickled at being excluded, Sumner had to concede that this was hardly the moment to prove her strength of will, especially since Willow and the other women were awaiting rescue.

"If you think that's best."

"Oh, yes, *Dr.* Havisham. I really think it's best."

Sumner's eyes narrowed. The tone of the man's voice had held an irritating mixture of condescension and vehemence.

"And you are…"

He paused. Sighed. Then momentarily lifted his hat. "Jonah Ramsey. I'm the superintendent of the Batchwell Bottoms mine."

She'd only been in the valley for a few minutes and

she'd already managed to irritate one of the top offi-
cials—a fact she could ill afford.

Sumner wasn't foolish enough to think that the owners
of the Batchwell Bottoms mine had willingly chosen a
female doctor. Not when the rules of the community were
so strict against the gentler sex. She'd been astounded
when her letters of introduction had been answered—and
even more amazed when further correspondence had led
to an offer of employment.

*We would be honored to offer you a five-year contract
at our establishment...*

Sumner had hardly been able to believe she'd been so
blessed. She hadn't just received a job; she'd been offered
a contract for five years.

It hadn't been until after she'd sent her acceptance that
she'd begun to feel the first needling doubts.

Why on earth would a mining community so well-
known for its stringent rules—no drinking, no cussing,
no women—been willing to hire her as their doctor?

She'd tried to reassure herself that she wasn't an actual *miner* but a member of the support staff. Next, she'd
bolstered her inner argument by reminding herself that
her professors and fellow staff at Ludlow's Hospital for
Women must have offered her a glowing recommenda-
tion. There was nothing untoward about her job or her
appointment as mine doctor, despite her gender.

And then she'd remembered one salient point. Although she'd answered every question put to her by Ezra
Batchwell and Phineas Bottoms, neither one had ever
asked her if she were male or female.

They'd just assumed that Sumner Havisham was a
man.

Even now, her body filled with the same frustration
that she'd felt that day. But by then, it had been too

late to retrieve the letter or clarify the offer—even if she'd wanted to do so. It shouldn't matter whether she was male or female as long as she could do the job. It shouldn't matter if her name were Sumner or Sally or Madame X.

Weeks later, when she'd received instructions, a sum of money for supplies and the journey and her travel arrangements, Sumner had decided to give the owners of the Batchwell Bottoms mine the benefit of the doubt. Maybe it wouldn't matter. Maybe they'd be accepting of her and her skills. She would journey to Utah Territory and see what happened. True, the owners might try to force her to leave so that they could find a "more suitable male replacement." But with the weather closing in and a signed contract in her pocket, she'd hoped she could force her hand—for a few days, a few weeks, a few months. Long enough for her to find another position somewhere in America so she wouldn't have to return to England.

Where the men were even more unreasonable than those in the wild and woolly American territories.

She blinked, unable to keep herself from studying the man who stood in front of her. If anyone epitomized the rough and rugged men of the West, Jonah Ramsey fit the bill. He wore his hat low over his brow, and his hair exploded from below the brim in an unruly tangle of waves. His beard was full and needed a trim, and his eyes…

Those eyes could melt ice with their intensity.

And they were focused on her.

His gaze was so direct that it caused a prickling to skitter down her spine, but she ignored it. Instead, overlooking the fact that her appearance wasn't entirely conducive to formal introductions, she held out her hand.

Best to show the man at the very beginning that she considered herself his equal.

"I'm very pleased to meet you, Superintendent Ramsey."

The man's eyes narrowed as if she were behaving untowardly. She realized that Bachelor Bottoms had a "no women" policy, which probably meant they had a "no touching" policy.

Did that include shaking her hand?

Or was Mr. Ramsey one of those incredibly stuffy gentlemen who believed that a woman shouldn't offer introductions herself, but should wait for a male relative to do so?

If Mr. Ramsey was waiting for any kin to offer such niceties, he would wait a very long time.

He reluctantly closed her fingers in his. Her skin was icy and numb from digging through the snow, but it wasn't so cold that it didn't immediately absorb the warmth of his clasp. In that brief instant, she became intimately conscious of the calluses at his palms, the strength of his grip and the long, slender fingers that nearly swallowed hers whole.

Then, just as quickly, he released her and began tugging on his gloves.

"If you'll wait over there," he prompted.

It wasn't a complete dismissal, but it felt awfully close. Clearly, Mr. Ramsey wasn't pleased with her identity or her profession.

Her spine stiffened and her chin tilted infinitesimally. Ignoring the disarray of her clothing and her disheveled hair, she picked up her skirts and marched with as much dignity and decorum as she could muster. She'd been treated worse before and she supposed that she would be again.

But if Mr. Ramsey thought that she would be dissuaded from practicing medicine in Bachelor Bottoms by such aloofness alone...

He had another think coming.

Chapter Two

It was well past midnight when Jonah brought a halt to the rescue operation on the hill. By that time, they were able to confirm that the railroad crew, nine farmers and businessmen, a widow, two families and forty-one mail-order brides had been found—all fifty-nine of them.

No. Make that sixty.

Because there was the doctor.

Sumner Havisham.

A woman.

Thanks to the Good Lord, there had been no fatalities. But some of the injuries had been severe. There were broken bones, gashes and head wounds. Two women and the conductor were currently unconscious, and they were already running low on medical supplies—which didn't bode well for the rest of the winter. Especially since it didn't look like anyone would be leaving Bachelor Bottoms anytime soon.

"You're sure the pass is blocked?" Creakle asked for the hundredth time.

Jonah silenced him with a warning glance. "Let's not spread that piece of news around, Creakle."

"But you don't know for sure, do you? I mean, once

it's light outside, y' might see another way out," Creakle
said, his tone only minutely softer.

Obviously, Creakle was hoping that Jonah was exag-
gerating because the man's expression fell and his eyes
took on the woe of a little boy who'd been told Christmas
was canceled. Being cut off meant that there would be
no fresh supplies. No more shipments of food or goods.
Even worse, no deliveries from Creakle's beloved Montgomery Ward catalog.

"But there could be *some* other way out?" Creakle
asked again, his tone full of both hope and dread.

"Maybe," Jonah offered. But he doubted they'd find
a different means to escape the valley. The debris field
from the avalanche had filled the gap with more than
fifty feet of snow. The locomotive and the passenger cars
were destroyed, and Jonah was sure the rails would be
warped or torn free. There would be no trains coming
or going from Bachelor Bottoms until the snow melted.
Even then, it might take months to repair the line.

"Mebbe we could get a man t' hike over the top." The
suggestion was given half-heartedly.

Jonah had already entertained the same thought.
He'd even sent one of the miners to test the slopes. But
the drifts were unsettled and loose, and each step had
threatened to cause another avalanche, so Jonah had been
forced to call the fellow back. He wouldn't risk a man's
life in a foolhardy attempt to get the women out of the
valley. It could wait a day or two.

He hoped.

Unfortunately, he was beginning to see that while he
and some of the other men had spent their time on the
mountainside, the situation here in the mining camp was
growing more critical than he'd first supposed. Just as
he'd feared, the arrival of the women had upset the care-

fully regulated schedules of shifts and respites. Worse, there was a restlessness permeating the air—as if the wind itself could sense that things had changed at Bachelor Bottoms.

The men were no longer alone.

"How long have they been this way, Creakle?"

"An hour or so. 'Bout the same time Batchwell came stormin' into the office and told me to send someone t' tell you t' come back t' town fer a meeting."

Jonah grimaced. A late-night conference with the owners wasn't completely out of character. But Batchwell's exact words as quoted by the runner was for Jonah to "bring along that chit," meaning their new company doctor.

"I guess it was too much to hope that I could break the news about Sumner Havisham's gender to Ezra Batchwell and Phineas Bottoms," Jonah said ruefully.

Creakle chortled. "Word spread through the camp faster than that snow comin' off the mountain. Mebbe you didn't notice, but Batchwell and Bottoms hightailed it to the accident scene so quick I wouldn'a been surprised if the snow hadn't melted ahead of them like the Red Sea parting for Moses."

Jonah grimaced. He might not have seen the men coming, but he'd heard Batchwell shouting at the rescue party with such indignation that his bellowing had threatened to bring the rest of the mountainside down around their ears. Jonah's only consolation had been the fact that *Dr.* Havisham had left with the first group of passengers to be taken into town. Jonah had told Ike Everett, one of the mule skinners, to take the passengers to the Miners' Hall where the women could warm themselves and dry their clothes. Therefore, when Batchwell had stomped up the hillside, demanding to see the "lying, thieving, no-good charlatan," Sumner Havisham wasn't around.

Jonah might not approve of a woman parading around as a doctor, but he wouldn't subject any gentle-born female to Batchwell's anger. He had a short fuse and his temper could burn as hot as dynamite. After nearly twenty minutes of ranting about the avalanche, the mangled train and the stranded passengers, Jonah had thought the man had vented his anger once and for all. But judging from the lamplight blazing from the office windows, both Ezra Batchwell and Phineas Bottoms were waiting for round two.

Creakle snorted. "Looks like they're ready t' confront the lady doctor, and you get t' be the witness."

Right now, all Jonah wanted was a hot meal and a warm bed. He was cold and hungry and had long since lost his patience. He needed a few minutes of peace, quiet and solitude to push back the old demons that rattled inside him whenever his back seized up and burned like the blazes.

Many more days like today, and you'll be pushin' up daisies.

No.

Any moments of respite he'd hoped to have seemed far from likely. Even now, as he nudged his gelding onto the main thoroughfare, he sensed the hushed expectancy. The shivering anticipation. The need. Even worse, the air shimmered with a host of unusual noises.

Laughter.

High-pitched chatter.

Singing.

With each step his mount took, it became obvious that— while Jonah had been overseeing the rescue operation—the men who hadn't been on the slopes or on duty had seen to the needs of the stranded passengers, the bulk of whom were women. Now they didn't look inclined to leave. By the looks of it, half the men of Bachelor Bottoms stood on the road outside the Miners' Hall. All of them within full view of the mine offices.

No wonder the owners were riled up again.

"We found a few menfolk—farmers and salesmen—and two small families on the train. They've been put up in the empty miners' houses on the edge of town," Creakle said. "A few of the miners doubled up so we had enough room for everyone. But the womenfolk…"

They'd been brought to the hall as a temporary situation, but it was apparent that they would have to stay there for a little while longer. There was no other building large enough to house that many females at once. Unfortunately, that meant that the men who were used to gathering there to play darts or checkers had nowhere else to go.

Jonah followed the direction of the men's gazes toward the two-story building. Even though the evening was black as pitch, it was easy to see that the women had staked their claim on the frame structure. Soft lamplight painted the street with panes of buttery gold. Due to a lack of curtains, the women had seen fit to make do with what window coverings they could find. The openings were hung with lacy petticoats and brightly patterned shawls, scarves and dresses. Overall, the effect was warm and inviting and fanciful—and certainly more welcoming than the chilly miners' shacks or the inquisition that awaited Jonah in the main office.

Even worse, now that the men had been drawn to the hall by the feminine sounds, they weren't inclined to leave, even though there was little hope that they would ever be invited inside. Instead, dressed in their coats and hats and scarves, they pounded their boots to keep warm. But they didn't talk. There was a nervousness, a giddiness and…a *reverence* to their vigil—as if they feared the women would disappear in a puff of smoke.

"The men have been at it since they ended their shift," Creakle offered "By then, they weren't needed on the hill, so's they came to gawp at the ladies."

Which meant Batchwell and Bottoms were probably close to a fit of apoplexy.

Jonah opened his mouth to order the men to return to their quarters, but before he could speak, one of the heavy carved doors to the hall flew open, and there, backlit in the lamplight, was Miss…

No.

Dr. Havisham.

Somehow, she'd found the time to clean herself up. Her face was washed, her clothes were changed and a voluminous apron covered her from hem to neck. She stood for a moment, her hands on her hips, frowning at the shapes she could see in the darkness.

"Get away now! Scat!" She shooed at them with the hem of her apron. "These women don't need you spying on them like foxes eyeing a henhouse. Go *home*."

Finally, the miners began slipping away into the shadows. As soon as the last man had turned away, Dr. Havisham sent a stern gaze in Jonah's direction.

"Mr. Ramsey."

Jonah brought his mount up short. He hadn't been aware that Dr. Havisham could see him in the darkness. He'd been hoping to slip away unnoticed. That way, he could send someone to retrieve the woman and deliver her to the mine offices. Apparently, he wouldn't escape a confrontation so easily.

"Yes, Miss…" She frowned and he quickly corrected himself. "*Dr.* Havisham."

Her disapproving glance could have set fire to a bush at twenty paces.

"I might have expected such rude behavior from the workers, but not of their leader."

For some reason, the woman's clipped British accent and lilting cadence softened her reprimand. Jonah opened his mouth to explain that he'd just arrived and that he'd had no part in the silent vigil. But one glimpse of the spots of pink on her cheeks warned him that it would do no good. She had her dander up, that was for sure.

So he lifted his hat instead, murmuring, "Ma'am."

Her lips pursed, causing a shallow dimple to appear in her cheek. A part of him wondered if that tiny crease would deepen if she laughed.

Dr. Havisham huffed. "I hope you'll make it clear to your miners that we women aren't to be stared at like monkeys in a menagerie, Mr. Ramsey."

He tried not to laugh. She looked quite militant with her arms folded, even when she used that imperious tone and highfalutin words like *menagerie*. He wondered if she was always like this, quick to battle, eager to defend those she felt were in her care. Unfortunately, some of her bravado was negated by her obvious weariness. Dark shadows lingered under her eyes. A garish bruise made her look vulnerable and fragile. Judging by the number of people they'd pulled from the wreckage with injuries—both major and minor—Jonah wasn't the only one who'd had a trying day.

"Yes, ma'am," he drawled in what he hoped was a soothing tone of voice. "The evening Devotional was canceled due to our rescue efforts. There's a morning Devotional scheduled to take its place when the hoot-owl and the early-bird shifts switch places. I'll be sure to mention that the Miners' Hall is off-limits to all the men."

"Thank you," she said. Then, since he'd conceded so easily to her argument, some of the starch wilted out of her posture.

Leaving her looking...lost...

Exhausted.

"How are all the passengers?" Jonah asked, somehow loath to see her disappear inside again. Now that her militant stance had eased, he couldn't help thinking that Sumner Havisham might be considered a handsome woman. She wasn't pretty exactly. She wasn't sweet and dreamy with a Cupid-bow's pout. No, she was sturdy. A little tall for a woman. Unconventional.

But that didn't mean she wouldn't turn heads. Especially in the territories where a fragile ingenue wouldn't last a week.

No, this woman could hold her own.

"Now that I've had time to examine everyone pulled from the wreckage, I'm relieved to say that most of them are better off than I'd first believed. We've got a half dozen broken bones, lots of bruises and cuts, but no life-threatening injuries. Thankfully, the last of my unconscious patients roused a few minutes ago, which is a good sign. For most of the women and the few remaining crew members still housed in the hall, there's nothing that some sleep and a good, hot meal won't cure."

A good, hot meal.

"I told Stumpy at the cook shack to bring you something."

"Early this afternoon, a pair of men brought coffee and biscuits. Thank you, Mr. Ramsey. But many of the women were too dazed or upset to eat. There was no evening meal provided, probably because your...chef...was overwhelmed with the task of feeding the men who'd helped in our rescue. I'm sure the women can wait until morning. By then, I imagine their appetites will have completely returned."

Botheration. Why hadn't Stumpy sent something to the women when he'd fed the men? The last thing Jonah needed on his hands was a passel of hungry, angry women.

But quick upon the heels of that thought came another dilemma that Jonah hadn't anticipated when the pass had been blocked. Although the mine stockpiled the necessary staples to see them through the winter, their supplies were made with two hundred hungry miners in mind. If they couldn't get the stranded passengers through the canyon, their foodstuffs would need to be stretched. Jonah would have to send out a hunting party. And if they couldn't make up what was lacking that way, they would have to cut the men's daily allotment.

Which meant hungry miners.

Which meant trouble.

"And what about you, Miss Havisham? Did you take the time to eat?"

Her guilt was so obvious that he felt a tug of protectiveness. One that made him ashamed that he could be so easily swayed by a striking woman. No. Not striking. Inviting? How else would you describe a woman with such soft brown hair, brown eyes—even her dress was brown.

So why did the combination make him feel warm inside?

Jonah resolutely pushed that thought aside. He must be even more weary than he thought if he was entertaining such drivel. He'd long ago dedicated his career and his future to the Batchwell Bottoms mine. And he'd had no regret at signing an agreement to forego drinking, cussing or being in the company of women.

Which meant that it was time for him to focus on the job. And that meant summoning Dr. Havisham to the impending meeting with the mine's owners.

Straightening in his saddle, he tried his best to look authoritative and imposing—even though his back felt as if it were on fire. Pushing aside the pain, Jonah pointed toward the mine offices. "If you'll join me at that building there, the one at the end of the row, I'll see to it that Stumpy brings you a plate."

"I don't think it would be appropriate for me to—"

He sighed, lifting a hand to stop her.

"You misunderstand, Miss Havisham. I wasn't offering a social invitation." He hesitated before saying, "You've been summoned to a meeting with the owners of the mine—your so-called employers. I've been told to ensure that you get there as soon as possible. They want to have a word with you before you retire." He waited one second, two, sure that she would object. When she didn't budge, he prompted, "If you wouldn't mind."

When she finally spoke, she all but pushed the words through her clenched jaw. "If you'll give me a moment, I'll fetch a wrap."

He hadn't meant to imply that he would squire her to the offices himself.

As soon as the thought appeared, Jonah realized he was being churlish—and shortsighted. If Dr. Sumner Havisham were to march up the boardwalk without an escort…

Resisting a groan, he turned to Creakle, the only man brave enough to disobey Jonah's orders to hotfoot it back to the row houses.

"Ya want me t' take yer horse t' the livery?"

It was the last thing Jonah wanted—because he wasn't sure if he'd be able to stand up, let alone walk.

"If you wouldn't mind."

Creakle made a cackling noise. "I got no problem missin' the fireworks that're 'bout to go off in the office."

"What do you mean?" Jonah handed the older man his reins.

"Yer forgettin'. They hired Dr. Havisham on the understanding that *she* was a *he*. She's got a boy's name, don't she? So they're probably thinkin' she was up to some shenanigans in getting the job. Problem is…she's got a five-year contract."

"And?"

"And I don't think she's of a mind t' give up an' go home just cuz they tell her to." He nodded in Dr. Havisham's direction. "An' she's not likely to give in anytime soon. Not with a signed agreement. Don't know whether they've thought of that. Seems to me, she prob'ly has the law on her side."

Jonah winced at the thought. Then, knowing that there was no way around it, he swung his leg over the saddle and lowered himself to the ground. The pain that radiated through his body was enough to make him rethink the "no cussing" portion of his employment contract.

"Don't s'pose there's any way you could just go home an' put yer feet up, is there?" Creakle asked once Jonah had managed to hold himself up under his own steam.

"No," he grunted through clenched teeth.

Creakle grinned. "Then I'll be leavin' ye with my best wishes." When the door to the hall opened and Dr. Havisham sailed out, Creakle added, "Yer gonna need it."

Sumner didn't need her ears to burn for her to know that Jonah Ramsey and the wizened Mr. Creakle had been talking about her. Their guilty looks were all the confirmation she required as she stepped outside.

"Evenin' t' ye, ma'am," Creakle said—a vein of hidden mirth evident in his tone.

Before she could comment, he reined his mule in the opposite direction to the mine offices, pulling Mr. Ramsey's horse behind him.

"Mr. Creakle won't be joining us?" she murmured as the man disappeared.

"No. He'll be needed at first light for the morning Devotional."

"As will you," she pointed out.

The man moved slowly, joining her on the boardwalk. In the lamplight that streamed from the hall windows, Sumner was able to see sharp lines of weariness bracketing his lips.

"True. But I'm used to an all-day shift, now and again."

She wanted to point out that he'd had an all-day, all-night shift, but she feared that such a remark would allow a...*personal* note to enter into their conversation, and she supposed that wouldn't be the wisest course of action.

"Shall we?" Jonah gestured to the office and she fell into step next to him.

She was surprised to find that, despite the rough-and-tumble surroundings, the boardwalk was wide and completely devoid of snow. The buildings—which had obviously been constructed with some haste—had been made to withstand the elements. On each building, a placard proclaimed the building's purpose: Cook Shack, Barber Shop, Company Store. Bachelor Bottoms had the comforts of a real town, if in miniature.

However, the more she gazed around her, the more Sumner became aware of a lack of a feminine touch.

There were no displays at the store, no curtains in the windows, no library, no schoolhouse—not that an all-male encampment would have children to educate. But it left an impression of starkness. Impermanence. As if the town knew that such austerity could not be tolerated for an extended amount of time.

"How long has the mine been here?" she asked.

"Seven years."

She gaped at Mr. Ramsey. "Really? Everything looks so...new."

Jonah nodded and she became aware of the way he moved with a gingerness that belied his powerful frame.

"The first five or six years...this was a tent city. Most of the buildings are less than a year old."

"But how could you live here in the winter without some kind of shelter?" The air around her bit through her clothing and her breath hung in front of her face like a silver cloud. Why would anyone endure such conditions with only a tent for protection?

"I suppose a man can get used to anything if the job is right."

She couldn't prevent the way that her mouth gaped—and Mr. Ramsey must have taken exception to her disbelief because he said, "Most of the miners are immigrants from England, Scotland and Wales. There are some from Europe, and a few from the coal mines back east. All of them came here with empty pockets, hollow bellies or dreams for a better future. They can make twice at Batchwell Bottoms than they could at their old jobs. That's a powerful incentive to any man."

"And what was *your* incentive, Mr. Ramsey?"

He looked at her, meeting her gaze with an expression that was as fathomless as the shadows that surrounded them. In the light of the lanterns posted at intervals on the buildings they passed, she thought she saw a flash of pain, a loneliness. But just as quickly, the emotions were gone.

"That's a conversation for another time." His curt refusal set her firmly in her place. After all, she was a woman in a man's world.

The unfairness of it all caused an old, familiar defensiveness to bubble up inside her.

She stopped him with a hand on his arm, then snatched it back again when he stared down at it.

"You don't like me very much, do you, Mr. Ramsey?"

His gaze was impatient. "I haven't formed an opinion one way or the other, Dr. Havisham. I haven't had time."

"But you don't like the idea of a woman doctor in your town, do you?"

He considered his words before saying, "No, ma'am, I don't."

"Haven't I demonstrated that I'm more than qualified?" She waved a hand in the direction of the Miners' Hall. "I'm highly trained and good at what I do. Shouldn't that be the only factor in my employment?"

"No."

"And why not?"

"Because you're a woman."

"Obviously."

"And as a woman, you'll cause trouble."

"Do you think me so lacking in self-control? Or is it your men who can't keep themselves in line?"

He huffed, clearly unwilling to enter into her argument, but she refused to let him dodge it—a fact she made clear by refusing to budge until he answered her question.

"I don't think you or my men are morally weak, Dr.

Havisham. I'm merely being realistic. Men will be men, and women will be women."

"Meaning what? That a woman must be, by definition, weak?"

"No. Meaning that a man and a woman cannot be together without certain…situations coming into play."

She huffed softly.

"Then there's the fact that, so far, your only doctoring has been on women. I've seen the correspondence you've had with the owners. All your experience was completed at a charity hospital in Bristol."

"A fact that has little relevance."

"It will have a great deal of relevance when the next injured miner refuses to let you treat him. And if that's the case, what use are you to any of us?"

The words shivered in the cold, echoing into the darkness.

You're just a girl.

"We shall see about that, Mr. Ramsey."

He shook his head, pausing a few feet from the door of the office. "Look, you asked me what I thought, and I told you the truth. I've been at this mine from the moment the first stick of dynamite was lit and the first timbers were put into place. I know these men like I know my own family. There's a reason why no women have been allowed on the premises, and those reasons aren't going to change just because you managed to get a contract under false pretenses."

"False pretenses!"

"It's pretty obvious that you misled the owners, falsifying your credentials—"

"My credentials are in perfect order!"

"Then falsifying your name. Come on, Dr. Havisham.

Admit it. Your Christian name couldn't possibly be 'Sumner.'"

Indignation bubbled up in her chest so strongly that Sumner couldn't prevent the words from spilling free. "For your information, at my christening, I was named Sumner Edmund Havisham. *S-u-m-n-e-r.* My father wanted his first son to be named after his father. So when I arrived, and my mother died soon thereafter, he was too disheartened to bother changing his mind."

The words reverberated in the darkness, revealing far more than she'd ever intended. But now that they were uttered, she couldn't withdraw them.

"Dr. Havisham, I presume."

The stern voice came from a spot behind her, and when she turned, Sumner found the grim countenance of Ezra Batchwell regarding her from the open door of the office. She recognized his balding pate and dark curly hair from an article called "Entrepreneurs of the American West" in the *Christian Observer*, the same periodical which had drawn her to this remote place.

"I believe this conversation would be more suited to the privacy of our offices rather than the street, don't you?"

Just when she'd hoped to impress the men of Bachelor Bottoms with her strength and dignity, she'd been caught hollering in the dark like a fishwife.

She thought she saw Jonah Ramsey's lips twitch in amusement—and in that moment, she wanted nothing more than to stamp her foot in frustration. But that would never do. Not if she hoped to repair the damage she'd already done.

"After you, Miss Havisham," Jonah drawled, sweeping a hand in front of him to indicate that she should enter first.

"Doctor," she reminded him.

"*Dr.* Havisham," he corrected himself.

But he wasn't able to completely stifle his amusement at her plight.

Chapter Three

It was well into the wee hours of the morning when Jonah stomped the snow off his boots, then let himself into the row house he'd been assigned when the buildings had first been erected.

As superintendent, he'd been given first pick of the living quarters and permission to be the sole occupant. But Jonah had seen no need for privacy or more space than he could handle, so he'd taken one of the smaller houses closest to the mine, then invited Creakle to room with him. The arrangement was practical, since Creakle spent as much time at the office as Jonah did. This way, he and Jonah could carry on their discussions in the off-hours, if they had a mind to do so.

Aware that Creakle would be asleep upstairs, Jonah moved quietly. He poked at the coals in the squat box stove in the corner, noting that Creakle had left a dented pot on the burner. A peek inside and a quick sniff made Jonah smile. Most of the miners had a preference for coffee—the blacker, the better. But Creakle had a fondness for cocoa. Where the man got the precious stuff, Jonah had no idea. Nevertheless, he was grateful that the older man had left him enough for a few cups.

Limping to the table, Jonah lifted a napkin from the tin plate, and found a hunk of bread, a large piece of cheese and slices of cold ham.

The sight of the food caused his stomach to rumble, and Jonah realized that he couldn't remember the last time he'd eaten. Thankfully, Creakle tended to look after him with the devotion of a maiden aunt.

Jonah threw his hat on the table and hung his jacket on the hook by the door. As he made the lamp brighter, he couldn't remember ever being so tired. His body ached and his hands were raw from digging in the snow— even though Creakle had appeared at the avalanche site to distribute fresh gloves to everyone several times during the day.

Testing the bucket of water left near the stove, Jonah splashed a healthy measure into a basin, plunged his hands in to the wrists, then washed his face. Hissing at the sting of his wind-burned skin, he glanced at the clock on the far wall. Only three hours remained before he was scheduled to return for the morning Devotional where the men would indulge in an hour of worship before descending into the mine. He wasn't sure if the ache in his back would let him nod off, but he sure meant to try.

His gaze slid to the stairs, knowing that a comfortable feather bed awaited him. But the steps looked like a sheer slope a hundred miles high, so...

He wiped his face off with an old towel, then sat on the edge of an old hickory rocker that had once belonged to his mother. Hissing, he nudged his boots off with his toes. A folded blanket lay on the table nearby. Next to it lay a bottle of liniment and a flannel.

Who needed a wife when Creakle was around?

He moved gingerly, mentally assessing new aches and old wounds. He wiggled his toes, then his feet, then allowed himself to breathe a little easier. Near as he could tell, he had no numbness or tingling other than that caused by the cold.

Safe for another day.

Jonah was about to settle back—even if it meant foregoing the warm cup of cocoa and the plateful of food—when there was a sharp rap at the door.

Now what?

Barring the entire mine collapsing, he wasn't in the mood for company. But late-night interruptions were part of the job.

Hauling himself to his feet, he padded to the door, whipped it open and offered a curt, "What is it?"

He immediately regretted his harsh tone when he saw Miss Havisham standing on his doorstep, her hand poised to knock again.

"Dr. Havisham," Jonah drawled. They'd parted company less than an hour earlier, and he would have thought that her pride would still be too dented to warrant a confrontation with Jonah. Yet, here she was, standing on his doorstep at an ungodly hour.

She lowered her hand and shifted uncomfortably.

"Mr. Ramsey. I…uh… I hope you'll pardon my interrupting your night like this."

So formal. So… British.

She chafed her hands together, but he was betting it had more to do with nerves than the cold.

When she didn't speak, he peered behind her and said, "Actually, I think we've left *night* far behind us and we're well on to *morning*."

She grimaced, but didn't appear inclined to leave. "Be that as it may, what I have to say won't wait."

He was beginning to understand why Batchwell and Bottoms had insisted on the "no women" clause. He sighed, holding the door wider. "Then you may as well come in."

Her lips thinned. Which was a shame.

"I don't think that would be...appropriate, Mr. Ramsey."

"Miss—"

She scowled.

"*Dr.* Havisham," he corrected himself quickly. "I think we sailed past *appropriate* hours ago. And I, for one, don't intend to stand in the cold waiting for a formal invitation. So you can either come in where it's warm, or you can hold your peace until morning."

A crease appeared between her brows, but she didn't move.

"If it will make you feel better, Gus Creakle lives here, as well. He's as good a chaperone as you're going to get in these parts, especially in the wee hours. I promise. Neither he, nor I, will bite."

She finally offered a grudging, "Very well, then."

He held the door open, allowing her to step inside, then closed it before the winter air could taint the warmth of the kitchen.

"Would you like a cup of cocoa?"

Her brows lifted.

"Creakle has a fondness for the stuff, and he's left me half a pot." He hooked a finger through a pair of tin mugs stacked on the open shelf above the dry sink.

She shook her head, but when he poured a healthy measure into one of the cups, he saw the way she breathed deeply of its heady scent.

"I insist, Dr. Havisham. A nice cup of cocoa will warm you up before you have to brave the cold again."

Miss Havisham hesitated, but finally took it, wrapping her hands tightly around the mug.

Too late, Jonah realized that Dr. Havisham, for all her bravado, didn't have a coat—and the dress she wore offered no real protection against the elements.

"Have a seat over there near the stove."

He gestured to the worn, overstuffed chair that Creakle had ordered all the way from Boston nearly a half dozen years ago. It was old and scarred and had begun to conform to the shape of Creakle's backside, but, other than Jonah's rocker, it was the only comfortable chair in the house.

"Oh, I couldn't. I—"

"Miss... *Dr.* Havisham," he said, a trifle impatiently. "I've been on my feet all day, and good manners forbid me from sitting until you do."

She looked instantly ashamed. "Oh, of course."

Dr. Havisham brushed by him in a wave of something that smelled like...orange blossoms? Then she sank into the chair in a flutter of skirts. Funny how he hadn't noticed until now that her dress was a good six inches too short. And the bust was a little too large. Had she borrowed it to replace the wet and torn suit she'd worn while tending to the wounded? Although the simple brown garment was serviceable enough, especially with the overwhelming apron, it couldn't have offered her much warmth.

The thought made Jonah feel unaccountably...guilty.

"Would you like a blanket to put around your shoulders?"

She stiffened—as if the very idea was a mark of weakness, or worse, a sign that she'd strayed into the realms of impropriety.

"No. Thank you."

He gestured to the food Creakle had left on the table.

"Did Stumpy bring you a plate like I requested? Creakle's left me more than I could eat."

"I'm fine. But you should have your dinner, Mr. Ramsey. You must be starving."

Her pronouncement was firm, but he saw the way her eyes skipped from him, to the plate, then back again. Ever so subtly, she moistened her lips.

Which told Jonah that Stumpy, cantankerous man that he was, probably hadn't roused out of his bed long enough to send her anything.

"Please. I insist you have your dinner, Mr. Ramsey. We can talk while you eat."

Jonah didn't bother to ask her again. Instead, he grabbed another plate from the cupboard, then two knives and forks. After dividing the generous portions in half, he handed her the food and a set of utensils.

"Dig in," he said curtly. "Or we don't talk."

She opened her mouth—and he was sure she meant to argue—but she finally offered a soft, "Thank you."

Taking his own meal, Jonah settled into the rocker, wincing slightly.

"Do you want to say grace, or shall I?" he asked.

"Oh, I...uh—"

Obviously, she thought he was a complete heathen because his suggestion startled her. So Jonah bowed his head, closed his eyes and offered, "For this and all we are about to receive, we are truly grateful. Amen."

"Amen."

For the first time that night, Jonah was able to sink back into the rocking chair and allow the tension to flow from his tired muscles. But something about his expression must have alerted the doctor, because she eyed him with concern, and her close scrutiny had the power to set his teeth on edge. He'd seen that look often enough in the last ten years. It smacked of pity—and if there was one thing he couldn't abide, it was pity. But he managed to avoid her gaze by concentrating on tearing his biscuit in half and piling it with ham and cheese.

"Were you injured today?" she asked gently.

The woman was observant. He had to give her that at least.

"No."

"You seem to be favoring your back. Have you pulled a muscle?"

"No, ma'am. It's merely an aggravation of an old wound."

She looked unconvinced.

"Honest, Doc."

"Perhaps there's something I can do to help."

He shook his head.

"Because I'd be happy to take a look at you if you'd like."

"No!" The protest burst from his lips with such vehemence that he quickly added, "I'm more than capable of applying liniment all on my own."

Her eyes grew dark, causing a curious twisting sensation in his chest, but he pushed the reaction aside. He'd been to enough doctors and quacks to last a lifetime—and he certainly wasn't about to add a female surgeon to the mix.

Even so, it was clear that Dr. Havisham was intent on gnawing the issue like a dog with a bone.

"But even if this complaint is one you've experienced before, you may have truly injured yourself today."

He knew the last thing he needed was this woman pulling up his shirt to poke and prod at the scars on his back. Hadn't he already seen what the sight did to the gentler sex?

Becca hadn't been able to stomach the sight, even when the wounds had healed to pinkish scars. Jonah would be hanged before he'd allow another woman to get close enough to see them ever again.

"No. Thank you, Dr. Havisham," he said with a firmness that bordered on rudeness. "Look, it's late and I'm tired. Maybe you should tell me why you're here."

She didn't immediately speak. Instead, she regarded him with narrowed eyes. Brown, brown eyes.

"You are a very stubborn man, Mr. Ramsey. I might be able to help you. My schooling included a course in the latest advances in surgery and—"

He sighed. "I think we already went through your many qualifications during your interview with Batchwell and Bottoms."

"As you well know, I left that discussion without managing to impress upon either gentleman the full extent of my education."

He knew she was reliving each harsh word that had been uttered in the mining office. Although Phineas Bottoms had seen fit to listen in placid silence, Ezra Batchwell had not been so reticent. He'd accused Dr. Havisham of fraud, dismissed her competence and had even questioned her sanity. Then he'd vowed to ruin her if she didn't leave the valley as soon as humanly possible.

Although Jonah would have been the first to admit that the mine was no place for a woman, he thought that Batchwell had been a little harsh. As one of the fairer sex, she should have been offered a gentler dismissal.

"Dr. Havisham, why are you here in Aspen Valley?" he asked, dodging her question with one of his own. "What on earth possessed you to sign up for employment at a silver mine?"

She met his gaze with a directness he wasn't accustomed to receiving from a woman.

"Why should I confide in you, Mr. Ramsey? I asked you the same question mere hours ago and you refused to answer."

There was a note of challenge in those melodic tones, and old memories threatened to swamp him. He was transported to another life...the company of another woman. But all that was gone now. In the space of a heartbeat, the thunder of cannon and men's screams, he'd been stripped of that future—as well as his ability to ever feel so deeply about another woman again.

Jerking his gaze away, Ramsey offered, "Like most of the men here, I came in search of a new start. And you, Dr. Havisham?"

She poked the edge of her biscuit with her fork. "I wanted to go where I could do some good."

"But why here? You admitted to the owners that most of your actual doctoring was at a women's hospital." When she didn't explain, he added, "To put it bluntly, you've spent the last few years of your career as a *baby* doctor. Why would you come to the only community that would have no need of such services?"

She made a show of cutting a piece of meat, and loading her fork. Then she slipped the food into her mouth and chewed with great thoroughness before saying, "There was nothing in the advertisement that stated women weren't allowed to apply."

"I would have thought the 'no women' clause that this mine is well known for having would have been a huge clue."

"The miners are forbidden to have emotional entanglements. There was no mention of the support staff having a similar rule."

She was purposely taking the conversation in circles, and they'd been through all that with Batchwell and Bottoms, so Jonah decided to cut to the chase. "But why do you want to work *here*, Dr. Havisham?"

She placed her plate on the table. She hadn't eaten everything, but she'd come close.

"You spoke of the men coming to Batchwell Bottoms to better themselves, Mr. Ramsey. Am I to be excluded of the opportunity because of my sex?"

"Come now, Miss Havisham. Why would you come to a mining community famous for its exclusion of women?"

She finally met him in the eye. "I've spent my life knocking down fences, Mr. Ramsey. Perhaps I saw it as another fence."

Jonah could tell from the soft flash of her eyes and the thread of steel in her tone that she was telling him the truth—at least a part of it. From what little he knew of her already, he supposed that she'd been rebelling against the narrow confines of her gender since the moment that her father had seen fit to give her a boy's name. Had the man held it against her that she hadn't been born male? Or had he blamed her somehow for her mother's demise?

There was obviously more to her motives than a simple act of rebellion, but the tilt of her chin made it clear that she wouldn't be telling him anytime soon, because she took a quick sip of her cocoa, then asked, "I came here tonight because I was wondering when you and your men would be returning to the wreckage."

His brows rose. "*That* was your emergency?"

"Yes. When will you be going back?"

"Near as I can tell…next spring."

"But you can't! You and your men have to go back tomorrow!"

Jonah took a deep swig of the cocoa, nearly burning his tongue. "Why's that?"

"We…the women…we need our things."

He offered a bark of laughter. "I'm afraid that some dresses and petticoats aren't worth the lives of my men."

"It's not just dresses and petticoats, Mr. Ramsey. The women were rescued wearing only the most basic of clothing. If we're to be marooned here for days—possibly weeks—we'll need those bags."

"Why? According to Batchwell, none of you will be allowed beyond the hall steps until such time as we can convey all of you to the nearest town."

Her eyes sparkled in the dim light of the lamp. For all intents and purposes, *Dr.* Havisham had been told that—contract or no contract—at the first possible convenience, she'd be sent packing.

"You and I both know that such an arrangement is unfeasible. At some point, the women will need to take the air."

"They can take all the air they want. All they have to do is open a window."

She shook her head. "That will never do. These women aren't prisoners, Mr. Ramsey."

"They aren't exactly invited guests."

"So they're to be punished? From what I can see, the other passengers—the crew, the stranded farmers and businessmen, even the families—aren't being held to the same constraints."

Hoping to avoid a full-fledged argument, Jonah chose his words with care. "Not *punished*. Consider it…protected."

"Protected? From what? Life?"

"This is a mining community, Dr. Havisham. By definition, that means that it is inhabited by a bunch of men."

"Are your employees convicts? Of ill-repute?"

"No."

"Then you hold them in so little esteem that you believe they will…what? Explode? If they get too close to an unattached woman?"

"Not at all, Miss Havisham."

"Doctor."

"Look… Sumner—may I call you Sumner?"

"No." Her look was obstinate, but she finally relented. "Oh, very well."

"All right… Sumner. The men here are tasked with a difficult and dangerous job—"

"The women have no designs on going into the mine, Mr. Ramsey."

"If I'm to call you Sumner, then you must call me Jonah," he offered impatiently.

It was clear that she was loath to embrace such informality, but he waited until she finally conceded.

"Very well. *Jonah.*" She took another sip of her cocoa. "The women will confine their activities to the town proper."

"No."

"No?"

"As I was saying, the men of Batchwell Bottoms have been chosen with great care. In order to even apply for a job here, they have to prove that they already have a good deal of mining experience. But that's not the only measure of whether or not they'll get a position. These miners have to prove that they are God-fearing men of good character—"

She opened her mouth to say something, but he stopped her with an upraised hand.

"—and then, they have to agree to certain stipulations—"

"I know, I know. No drinking, cussing, smoking, gambling and no womanizing."

Clearly, she'd read the advertisement for employment carefully, even if she'd omitted mentioning that she was a woman applying for a man's job.

"If you will remember, the advertisements state 'no women.' They do not use the term *womanizing*."

"I simply assumed—"

"Then you assumed wrong. These men have given up a lot to be here—including tailoring their behavior to a certain code of conduct. But that's not the most significant sacrifice they've made, Sumner. Most of these miners come from back east, the British Isles, Italy and Greece. In order to pay for their passages to the wilds of Utah, the vast majority of them have signed an agreement to work for five years to pay off the debt. Despite the nickname this place has earned, not all of them came to us as bachelors."

He pointed to the window where the sky was already beginning to turn to gray. "Out there are fathers, brothers, husbands and sweethearts who have agreed to spend years away from their loved ones in order to make a new future, not just for themselves, but for their families. They're willing to do the job and live with untold privations so that, one day, they can send for them."

"I hardly think that our group would—"

"They will be a temptation."

"One we can rebuff."

"But worse," Jonah continued, "they'll be a reminder, Sumner. And sometimes, simply seeing a reminder of what you're missing can be the cruelest form of torture."

To her credit, she finally fell silent. For several minutes, she ruminated on his words.

"Are *you* missing someone, Jonah?"

The question was so unexpected—and far too personal for their short acquaintance—that for a moment, Jonah was taken aback.

Rebecca.

No.

She wasn't his to miss. She hadn't been for a very long time.

Jonah could have commented on Sumner's lack of tact—not to mention her impudence. But he answered honestly.

"No. I'm here for the long haul."

The words held grim finality when spoken aloud, but he couldn't take them back. It was the truth. Rebecca, his former fiancée, had found a new man to share her life with. One who was free from unsightly scars. One whose body wouldn't betray him one day, as Jonah's was bound to do.

Sumner sighed and said, "Be that as it may, Mr. Ramsey—"

"Jonah."

She grimaced. "Jonah. The women will still need their belongings."

He couldn't prevent a short bark of laughter. "And what's so important that I should risk the lives of my men on unstable packs of snow less than a day after we've already suffered one avalanche?"

She lowered her mug, and he couldn't account for the way it pleased him when he found that it was empty.

"You've spoken of the sacrifices of your miners. But what you haven't yet acknowledged is that your employees aren't the only ones sacrificing a great deal. Most of those women were on that train as a group of mail-order brides heading west, and they've paid just as dearly for their passages. They have no way to notify anyone about the delay they've encountered—so, who knows if they will have husbands waiting for them when they finally arrive at their destinations? Furthermore, the women brought all of their belongings with them—some of them valuable heirlooms and household goods needed to start their lives as married women. The longer their trunks lie moldering in the snow, the more the women will have lost precious ties to families and homes they've left behind. I think that even you would have to admit that being stranded here could hold untold ramifications."

She paused, but it was clear that she wasn't finished.

"Therefore, I think that it's only reasonable for you and your men to provide these women with their belongings. As it is, most of them have little more than the clothes on their backs. Indeed, since you force me to be blunt, they have no extra…undergarments to tide them through until washing day. Very few of them have coats or scarves or mittens. And despite this valley's fondness for its Miners' Hall, there is a draft. Especially in the upper rooms. Added to that, these ladies will need combs, brushes and other personal items. The sooner, the better."

"Or…"

"Or the women may find it necessary to protest by marching down Main Street." She set her cup aside and rose to her feet. "And since many of them now have garments that are completely unwearable, your men may get more of a reminder of what they're missing than you'd ever anticipated."

With that, she sailed from the room, slamming the door behind her.

Leaving Jonah wondering what would Miss Havisham be left wearing if she decided to make good on her threat?

* * *

"Sumner!"

Sumner moaned as the voice pierced her consciousness.

"Miss!"

She blinked, vainly trying to focus. But since she'd spent hours mulling over her conversation with Jonah Ramsey—reviewing every word the man had said—she'd wound herself tighter than a spring and sleep had become nearly impossible.

Her eyes drifted shut.

"Dr. Havisham, please!"

A hand shook her shoulder and Sumner's eyes opened again. This time, she came face-to-face with Willow Granger.

"Willow?" she croaked. "How's the leg?"

"Fine, fine. I've got a bruise big as a dinner plate, but most of the swelling has gone down."

Willow was one of the reasons why Sumner had felt it necessary to approach Jonah at such an unreasonable hour. After tending to the woman's leg, Sumner had found the girl crying in one of the rear supply closets. While the other mail-order brides had slipped out of their torn, wet clothing and hung their frocks to dry, Willow had clutched at the shapeless dress she wore. After divining that Willow had spent most of her adolescence in a strict charity school, Sumner had realized that the young woman had been unable to bring herself to strip down to her "shimmies" even if it was only in the presence of other women. Sumner had helped her to fashion a robe of sorts out of a pair of blankets so that Willow could rinse the mud from her hems and allow her dress to dry. For that, Sumner had earned herself a loyal assistant.

Willow regarded her with glittering blue eyes. In the

early-morning glare, her skin was pale and spattered with freckles, and her curly red hair hung around her heart-shaped face like a wild mane.

Sumner cleared her throat, then rasped, "What is it, Willow?"

"There's a man at the door. He says he'll only talk to you."

Jonah?

She scrambled up from the pallet on the floor. Automatically, her hands flew to her hair, and she squeaked when she realized that it was a mass of tangles.

"You'd better hurry. He said he didn't have much time."

Sumner glanced down at herself and fought the urge to squeal in protest. Besides being ill-fitting, her borrowed day dress was wrinkled, the print faded from years of wear. And there was absolutely nothing she could do about the way the hem nearly topped her boots.

She supposed she should be thankful she wasn't answering the door in her all-togethers.

Nevertheless, she opened the door only a few inches and peered out, hoping it would prove unnecessary to step into the cold.

She sagged in relief when she found Creakle grinning at her, his hat in his hands. But she couldn't help looking past him to see if Jonah was there, as well.

"Morning, missy!"

"Mr. Creakle."

"This here's Willoughby Smalls."

Creakle pointed to his companion, who had to be at least seven feet tall with a squared-off jaw and a body as big and broad as a mountain.

"Mr. Smalls."

"Willoughby don't talk none, on account of how he

was hit in the throat by a falling beam. But if you ever need some heavy liftin', he's your man."

"Thank you, Mr. Smalls. I appreciate that kind offer."

She thought the man might have blushed as he continued to stare at her, his grin growing wider with each passing moment. But when he didn't speak, she finally prompted, "Did you men need something?"

"Oh. Oh, yes!" Creakle stepped back and made a flourishing sweep of his hand to something beyond her range of sight. "I'd ferget my head if'n it weren't screwed on. Jonah asked me t' make sure you got this."

She slipped through the door and shut it tightly behind her. But when she saw the neat stacks of trunks and valises piled on the boardwalk, she couldn't help gasping in delight.

"How on earth did Mr. Ramsey manage to do all this so quickly?"

Creakle snickered. "He offered the men two bits fer every trunk they managed t' deliver before noon." He nudged Smalls in the side with his elbow. "Willoughby an' me have already made ourselves more'n five bucks a piece." He glanced down at a watch he pulled from his vest. "I 'spect you'll have the rest of it delivered by lunchtime." He nodded and jammed his hat over his head. "Now, I know how you womenfolk like to have things just so, so's I'm leaving Willoughby here t' tote them trunks and boxes wherever you want them t' go. Keep him with you as long as you like. He's not due down in the mine until this evening."

Creakle slid a glance in Smalls's direction and the man nodded. Then, offering a hefty sigh, Creakle said, "Wish I could stay an' help, but I'm needed at the office." He touched a finger to the brim of his hat. "Good mornin' t' you, ma'am." Then he began marching in the direction of the mine offices.

It was only then that Sumner became aware of several men in black wool coats posted near the main door and at either end of the Miners' Hall.

"Mr. Creakle!"

He turned, squinting in her direction. "Yes, ma'am?"

Sumner couldn't think of a discreet way of asking, so she decided to be direct. "Who are these other gentlemen?"

The men in question turned, revealing that they had holsters strapped to their hips and carried rifles in addition to their revolvers.

"They're the company Pinkertons, ma'am."

Her gaze bounced over the Pinkertons, one by one. In addition to their identical wool coats, they wore dark navy tunics with shiny badges.

"Pinkertons? But why are they here?"

"This here's a silver mine, Dr. Havisham. Y' gotta have security in a place like this."

She shook her head. "No, Mr. Creakle. That's not what I meant. Why are these men *here*?"

She gestured with her finger to the Miners' Hall.

Creakle shifted uncomfortably. "Mr. Ramsey ordered it."

Her eyes narrowed. "Why?"

Creakle began backing away from her.

"He said it was fer y'all's protection."

Protection?

Sumner stiffened, an old familiar resentment filling her like white-hot steam. Of all the low-down, sneaky, conniving tricks. A trio of armed Pinkertons had been stationed outside a building filled with women who were injured, traumatized and at the complete mercy of their unwilling hosts? And Mr. Ramsey wanted them all to believe that it was for their *protection*?

Apparently, she and Mr. Ramsey needed to have another talk.

Chapter Four

"Lord, give me strength," Sumner murmured to herself as she slapped her best bonnet on her head.

"What are you going to do?" Willow asked, reluctantly holding up a hand mirror so that Sumner could check her reflection.

Sumner had tried her best to keep the news of the Pinkertons a secret, but she hadn't been very successful. Although many of the mail-order brides had been diverted with checking the contents of their trunks, changing into fresh frocks and setting up a washing station, a few of them had noticed the armed men posted outside their door. As Sumner shrugged into her coat, she spoke softly to the small knot of women who stood with her.

Besides Willow Granger, there was Iona Skye, a widow in her sixties who had traveled with them since New York City. Unable to make ends meet on her own, she was destined for her sister's farm in California. Beside her stood Lydia Tomlinson, an effervescent blonde from Boston, who, along with Iona, were the only women not contracted to become mail-order brides. Lydia was en route to San Francisco, where she would embark on a lecture tour to spread the word about women's suffrage and temperance. The last few members of the group hovering around Sumner were a trio of brides-to-be, Ruth Hubbard, Stefania Nicos and Marie Rousseau.

"What are you going to say to the man?" Stefania whispered.

Lydia scowled. "She's going to tell Mr. Ramsey that we aren't convicts, we're stranded travelers."

The conversation washed over Sumner as she checked her hair and gown as much as the small mirror would allow. Thankfully, among the trunks and valises that Mr. Smalls had carried into the hall, she'd managed to find her own things—and therefore, a change of clothing, her brush and a fresh stock of hairpins. Through it all, she'd tried her best to maintain a semblance of calm, but inwardly...

Inwardly, she'd been seething.

"Please don't let me lose my temper," she whispered under her breath.

Lydia Tomlinson must have heard her because she cocked her head to the side and offered, "Nonsense. You need to go into the office with guns blazing, Sumner. Don't hide your emotions behind that unflappable English charm. Otherwise, they'll be locking us in soon. And I, for one, am already stir-crazy."

The other women nodded in agreement.

"We all know that the arrival of the Pinkertons—and the weak excuse of their being here for our *protection*—is nothing more than an opening volley in a declaration of war."

Sumner supposed the other women were right. After conversing with Jonah Ramsey, she'd deluded herself into thinking that the man could be pragmatic, perhaps even a bit empathetic toward the women's plight. And for one brief second, when she'd seen their belongings on the boardwalk, she'd believed the man might be persuaded to look at the situation from the women's point of view.

She'd obviously been mistaken. Sadly mistaken. Apparently, Jonah Ramsey was cut from the same cloth as her father, her stepbrother, her professors and all of the other opinionated males she'd encountered over the past few years. Clearly, Sumner seemed doomed to butt heads with men who were determined to squash women into what they felt was "their place," and the superintendent of the Batchwell Bottoms mine was no different.

But this time, it wasn't just Sumner who was being repressed. It was all of the women who were in her care. And it was time to set the record straight.

"How do I look?" she breathed, realizing that she'd already fussed over her preparations long enough.

Iona reached out to squeeze her hand. "You appear very calm, cool and collected. Every inch a lady."

If only that were true.

"You'll do fine, Sumner," Willow offered quietly.

Sumner nodded, then opened the door and slipped outside while the rest of the brides were distracted with instructing Mr. Smalls where to move their trunks.

The frigid air against her hot cheeks was welcome as she turned toward the mine offices. But she'd only taken a few steps when she was halted by one of the Pinkertons. He even had the utter *gall* to brandish his weapon in warning.

"Ma'am, I'm sorry, but I've been asked to keep you here."

"Your name?" she asked abruptly.

"Lester Dobbs."

"Am I under arrest, Mr. Dobbs?"

The guard's brows creased, his mustache twitching in confusion.

"Ma'am?"

"Am I under arrest?"

"No, ma'am."

"Then you can get out of my way or you can trail along behind me. But those are your only two choices because I intend to talk to Mr. Ramsey." When the man didn't budge, Sumner allowed a portion of her frustration to tinge her tone. *"Now."*

To his credit, the Pinkerton tried to stand his ground—he even attempted to meet the blazing intensity in her gaze. Before long, Dobbs sighed, lowered his rifle and allowed her to pass. Even so, as she stormed toward the mining offices, he trailed along behind her, clearly embarrassed with the assignment he'd been given.

Sumner balled her hands into fists and increased her speed. What fueled her anger wasn't the fact that she'd had to fight—tooth and nail—to gain an education and a career, that she'd been thrown the scraps of opportunities lavished on men with half the talent and dedication that she'd displayed in her chosen profession. No, what infuriated her was that these women—women who had been injured, stranded and placed in her protection—were to be so cavalierly mistreated just because someone had deemed them "inconvenient."

No, no, no.

Since obtaining her diploma and emancipating herself from her father's overbearing rule, she'd pledged that she would never allow a man to control her again—and that she would fight for the same rights for other women, as well.

But even as the frigid gusts of wind stung her cheeks, common sense managed to wriggle its way into her brain.

After last night's confrontation with the owners, Sumner knew she was walking a fine line. As much as she might rail against the men in charge, there was also a part of her that wanted—*needed*—to make a good impression.

After completing her medical training, she'd found it nearly impossible to find a position. The best she'd managed to scrape up was a midwife's assistant's job at a woman's hospital in Bristol. She'd spent over a year scouring every advertisement she could find for work. So, when, on a whim, she'd applied to the Batchwell Bottoms mine and they'd offered a five-year contract, it hadn't occurred to her that a mistake might have been made. She'd wanted this job so badly. When she'd realized the owners had assumed she was a man, she'd been so sure that she could impress the owners with her skills and make a place for herself in the wilds of the US Territories.

Unfortunately, during her first real meeting with Batchwell and Bottoms, they'd made it clear that she would never work as the company doctor.

But Sumner wasn't about to give up without a fight. First, she had a signed, notarized, five-year contract. That had to mean something, didn't it? Even more importantly, now that the avalanche had marooned her in the valley, she was the only physician available. All she needed was a little time to prove her talent for medicine.

As she clutched the doorknob to the office, her heart pounded, her knees trembled and all the energy drained from her.

She couldn't storm into Mr. Ramsey's office in a fit of pique.

Closing her eyes, she offered a quick prayer for guidance. *Lord, please show me how to proceed. Help me to help others.*

Feeling calmer, she took a deep breath of icy air.

Tact. That's what the situation required. Tact and diplomacy.

Sumner glanced behind her to see that Pinkerton Dobbs had kept pace with her the entire way.

Lord, help me stay calm.

Knowing that if she waited another moment she might lose her nerve, as well, Sumner twisted the knob and plunged into the warmth of the mining offices.

In an instant, she was inundated with the scents of hot coffee, wood smoke and pine shavings. Homey, manly smells that swirled around her along with half-forgotten memories of her grandfather.

There had been a time when she'd been accepted for who she was, when Poppy had let her climb on his knee and chatter about her dreams of being a doctor. She'd been ten when Poppy had bought her a book with anatomical drawings. To her, the muscles and bones had been more beautiful than the fashion drawings found in the periodicals her stepmother tried to get her to read. But when her father had discovered the book hidden beneath her bed, he'd thrown it in the fire, then had made her stand and watch it burn.

Behind her, the latch snapped back into place and a brass bell offered a muted jingle. In that instant, all eyes swung in her direction and the three men in the office froze.

If the reaction hadn't been so disheartening, Sumner might have laughed at the trio of comical expressions. Mr. Creakle, the only man she recognized from the previous day, sat slack-jawed from behind his desk. Another gentleman with sad, basset-hound eyes and jowls, was half-bent toward the fire, a chunk of wood held toward the blaze. The third fellow—who was little more than a gangly teenager—stood blinking at her from where he sat on a high stool, a collection of miner's lanterns laid out on a table in front of him in various stages of completion.

The combined weight of their gazes was nearly overwhelming, but she managed to say, "I'd like to see Mr. Ramsey, please."

They didn't move, and Sumner resisted the urge to sigh in frustration. Honestly, she didn't see a need for the Pinkertons. So far, what few miners she'd encountered at Bachelor Bottoms appeared completely tongue-tied in the presence of a female.

The young man suddenly sneezed, and that seemed to break the odd trance because the two other gentlemen shouted out simultaneously, "Boss!"

A moment later, Sumner heard boots clattering down the steps on the other end of the building. Then Jonah stepped into view.

Sumner had forgotten how tall he was. Tall and broad-shouldered. He filled the doorframe. In the sunlight streaming through the mullion windows, she could see the circular impression in his hair where his hat had been. The bright rays picked out threads of silver at his temples and in his beard. He wore a dark leather vest with a soft linen shirt beneath.

After so many years spent in schools and hospitals where men took great pains with their grooming, there was something almost…*wild*…about his appearance. Nevertheless, Sumner couldn't fault Jonah's casual disregard for current fashion. If anything, his lack of formality echoed the ruggedness of the terrain that surrounded them.

Sumner tipped her chin at an angle. "Mr. Ramsey, may I have a word, please?"

His lips thinned. "Miss… *Dr.* Havisham. There's no need to thank me for your belongings."

She *had* been about to thank him, regardless of the fact that it had taken an ultimatum to get him to oblige. But his tone was so...so...dismissive that she choked on the words, her spine stiffening to a rod of iron.

"A *private* word," she rushed on.

She watched as one of his brows rose. Yet again, she was struck by the man's unusual eyes. They were a mixture of brown and blue and green. But there was more to them than that. They were keen and probing. At the same time, they offered no clue to his own thoughts or emotions.

He heaved a sigh.

"Dr. Havisham, can this wait? Perhaps tonight I could find a few minutes to speak with you."

"No!" she burst in without thinking. It wasn't as if she were asking for an audience with the king. She just needed a few moments to talk to him about...

Oh, my, she'd forgotten why she'd been so determined to corner him in the first place!

Her gaze bounced from Creakle to the wide-eyed teenager to the droopy-jowled office worker to the door. And the dark shape that waited there.

The Pinkertons.

"No, Mr. Ramsey. It can't wait. And if you can't spare me a private word, then I'd be more than happy to air our grievances in front of you and your men."

Ramsey sighed, straightening from the doorway. For a moment, she saw the way his features were lined with weariness, and she was reminded of the fact that he couldn't have had more than a few hours' sleep. That, combined with the strenuous work of freeing the passengers and the back injury he'd refused to discuss, caused a prickling of guilt. Even worse, she realized that her impetuousness may have led to her confronting the man when he would be least likely to heed her concerns.

But before she could speak, Jonah reached toward a hall tree laden with coats, hats and scarves. Snagging a battered black hat that she remembered him wearing the night before and a shearling jacket, he gestured toward the door.

"Very well, Dr. Havisham. I was just on my way to the cook shack to grab a bite to eat. If you'd care to join me, we can both have our breakfast and I can give you about fifteen minutes of my morning."

She doubted she would be able to press her case in such a short amount of time, let alone finish a meal. But the rigid set of his shoulders warned her that it would be futile to bargain with him on this point.

"Very well. Good day to you, gentlemen. Mr. Creakle."

"Ma'am," Creakle said with a wide grin.

The other two men dived toward the door to open it for her.

As they stepped from the office, Jonah clenched his jaw to keep from saying something to his employees. They'd nearly tripped over themselves to assist Dr. Havisham, and now the two of them had wedged themselves in the doorway as if they intended to follow Sumner and him to the cook shack.

Jonah shot them a glance. They began squabbling with one another as they untangled themselves, stepped back into the office and slammed the door.

Jamming his hat more firmly on his head, Jonah strode toward the cook shack, but after only a few steps, he realized that he was making the trip alone. Glancing behind him, he found Dr. Havisham with her hands on her hips, her feet planted firmly on the boardwalk.

Maybe Jonah had been too hasty in his original insistence that the women didn't need their baggage. His gaze skipped over her form, taking in the saucy hat she'd pinned to the top of her head, and the tailored greatcoat that clung to her frame. He had to admit that, this morning, Sumner Havisham looked much more appropriate, more *professional*, than she had in the too-short dress the night before. In fact, if he were honest, he'd have to say that the fur collar framed the slender line of her throat in a way that was quite...*fetching*.

At least, it would be fetching if her chin hadn't returned to that obstinate angle again.

Her brown eyes flashed, darting from Jonah to the Pinkerton who trailed her.

She speared the man with a withering glance. "Go away."

When the guard didn't budge, Jonah could feel the frustration sizzling through her slender frame. He wasn't sure, but he thought she stamped her foot beneath the hems of her skirts.

"Send him away," she said to Jonah.

Realizing that he'd probably pushed Sumner's patience about as far as he dared, Jonah nodded in the man's direction. Immediately, the Pinkerton returned to the Miners' Hall.

Sumner opened her mouth, but before she could begin her diatribe, Jonah held up a hand.

"Please. Not until I've had some coffee and something hot to eat."

She offered a curt nod and fell into step beside him.

They walked a few feet in silence before she asked, "How are you feeling this morning?"

He shot her a quick glance, but there didn't seem to

be anything behind her question other than polite conversation.

"I'm doing well, Dr. Havisham."

She didn't look convinced. "You don't appear to be moving as gingerly. Are you sure that you don't want me to look at your back?"

"No!" After he realized that his interruption had been rather forceful, he adopted a lightness to his tone that he didn't really feel, and offered, "I'm fine." He opened the door to the cook shack and gestured for her to precede him, then murmured, "Coffee first, Dr. Havisham. Please."

To her credit, she heeded his none-too-subtle reminder. After one more narrow-eyed glance, she swept into the building.

Jonah wasn't sure if she'd decided to bite her tongue or if she'd guessed at the headache that pounded at his temples like a blacksmith on an anvil. Even worse, the heavy scents of black coffee, scorched beans and overcooked eggs hung thick in the room, causing even his stomach to clench. But to her credit, Sumner remained silent as he led her through the building with its rows of tables and benches toward the serving area at the back.

Too late, Jonah realized that if the two of them wanted a private word, this was the last place he should have brought her. Men who'd finished the night shift were still lingering over breakfast. As they moved through the room, a hush washed over them like a wave and all eyes turned in their direction—causing even Jonah's hair to prickle at the scrutiny.

When they reached the warmth of the counter that separated the kitchens from the dining area, Jonah leaned in and called out to Stumpy, a miner who'd been drafted into running the cook shack after a runaway ore car had crushed his foot, forcing an amputation of his toes. The man had never really forgiven Jonah for switching him from mine duties to the cook shack. But the injury had left him with a lurching limp that was dangerous for mine work, and moving him to the cook shack had been the only way to save Stumpy's paycheck at the time.

"Have the owners been in this morning?" Jonah asked.

"Been and gone," Stumpy groused.

"Bring some coffee and a couple of plates to the private room. Dr. Havisham and I have a few things to discuss."

Stumpy offered a low grumble that could have been an agreement or a complaint. Jonah didn't wait for the man to make up his mind.

"This way, Dr. Havisham."

He pointed down a narrow hall to a single door. Sweeping it open, he gestured for Sumner to precede him.

As she gingerly made her way past, Jonah was forced to look at the room with new eyes. A single window on the opposite wall offered far too much light to conceal the cubicle's flaws. Although it was the only place in the cook shack that offered a place to eat with a real dining room table and chairs, there was no disguising the fact that the floor hadn't been swept in some time—and who knew when the surfaces had been cleaned. Dirty glasses were stacked in teetering towers, the owners' breakfast dishes scattered the scarred surface and maps and schematic drawings had long since taken the place of any linens.

Unaccountably, Jonah felt his ears grow hot with embarrassment, even though the cleanliness of the room didn't fall beneath his purview.

"Here, let me…"

He pushed everything to one side, then used his hat to brush the crumbs and dust aside.

Dr. Havisham gingerly took her place just as Stumpy burst through the door carrying a wide tray with two plates, a pair of tin mugs and an enameled pot of coffee. He shoved the tray into Jonah's arms, then limped from the room again without a word.

To her credit, Sumner offered a soft sound that was very close to a giggle. Then she reached up to take the tray.

"Here. Let me help."

Before Jonah could respond, she'd begun setting the food and utensils on the table like a practiced dealer at a poker game. By the time he'd taken his seat opposite, she'd placed all of the silverware in their proper places and poured both of them a cup of hot coffee.

"Milk? Sugar?"

He shook his head, then watched as she added both to her cup so that the liquid was a caramel brown next to his own cup's tar black.

Jonah took a quick swig of the liquid, then grimaced when it hit his tongue and the back of his throat like a brand.

"Shall I say grace this time?" Sumner asked, her eyes twinkling when she discerned his pain.

He nodded, slamming his eyes shut against the way they watered.

"Dear Lord above…we thank Thee for all of the many blessings which Thou has bestowed on us this day," she began. "We thank Thee for Thy protection and deliverance and for our safe haven here in Bachelor Bottoms…"

Jonah couldn't help cracking one eye open, but Sumner's expression was one of rapt sincerity.

"We thank Thee for the men who have come to our

aid. We thank Thee for the warmth of our shelter and the…sincere compassion and sincerity of our hosts."

Again, he shot her a quick glance under his lashes.

"We pray, O Lord, that Thou will continue to bless us all with *kindness* and *understanding*. That Thou will help us to exist together in this valley as *friends* rather than *adversaries*. We pray that Thou will bless us with the means to help one another until Thou sees fit to free us from this…*unfortunate* situation."

Jonah had both eyes open now, and was ready to offer his own two cents' worth—as well as a hearty amen—but Sumner quickly added, "And please bless Mr. Ramsey most of all, that he might feel of Thy love, guidance and compassion. For this and the food before us which Thou hast provided, we are grateful. Amen."

She opened her eyes, and smiled at Jonah with a sweet blankness to her expression, and Jonah was reminded of one of his mother's sayings.

Butter wouldn't melt in her mouth, that one.

But he wasn't fooled.

Sumner Havisham had given him as much time as she planned on doing. Coffee or no coffee, she was now ready to begin her verbal exchange.

Jonah mentally steeled himself for her arguments, aware that the good doctor planned to challenge his use of the Pinkertons. He'd known when he'd issued the orders that the women would eventually object. But the owners had insisted, and Jonah had agreed that such measures would keep interaction with the men at a minimum. Even so, there'd been a part of him that had regretted treating the women as little more than prisoners.

Knowing that it would be easier to counter Sumner's arguments if he didn't meet her eyes head-on, he began spearing chunks of fried potatoes onto his fork. Even so, he couldn't miss the way that Dr. Havisham settled her napkin carefully over her lap, then stared down at her plate. He saw a flash of something that looked very much like horror.

"Is something wrong?"

"No." She lifted her fork, gingerly prodding her food. "Your meals are...hearty."

"Mining is hard work."

Dr. Havisham continued to stare at her plate with such ferocity that Jonah took another look himself. He was forced to admit that the food wouldn't win any prizes. The portions were large, not pretty. Because Stumpy and his men were often needed in other areas of the Batchwell Bottoms enterprise, they'd taken to cooking all the food once a day, then serving things warmed up until the pots were empty. This often meant that the men were forced to eat leftovers until the food was completely gone. Then Stumpy and his crew would begin preparations all over again.

Unfortunately, Stumpy didn't have a wide repertoire of menus, so after a time, the meals all started to look the same. This morning, overcooked beans had been slopped next to a mound of scorched eggs and a greasy pile of fried potatoes. The fare didn't taste much better than it looked, but it was hot and filling and stuck to a man's ribs during a hard day's work.

"It must be difficult to feed all your men."

"The shifts break things up so we don't have to accommodate all of the miners at once. They're given a hot meal at daybreak, another in the evening, then cold meats and biscuits in their buckets midway through the workday."

She nodded, poking at the beans, which had begun to congeal into a lumpy brown pudding. Then she looked up, concern gleaming from the depths of her eyes. "We women will tax your winter stores of food, won't we?"

Jonah considered offering her a blithe denial, but he knew she would see through his subterfuge. "We prepared for the men on hand until the end of April. Perhaps, we'll have an early spring."

"And if we don't?"

"I've already appointed a hunting party. We'll enhance our supplies with whatever meat they can obtain—rabbit, venison, elk. Hopefully, it will tide us through. If not, we'll have to cut the rations."

"Which means that if enough game can't be acquired, your men may end up going to work hungry."

Hungry and ornery, Jonah thought. But he didn't bother to say the words aloud. He could only pray that the winter would be milder than usual or that spring would arrive before expected. He didn't want to think about the tensions that could arise if their rations became critical.

"These men on the hunting party," Dr. Havisham said slowly. "Is that their usual job?"

Jonah shook his head, concentrating on his food again, knowing that he had only a few minutes' time to eat before someone came looking for him.

"No."

She sighed. "So we have inconvenienced all of you yet again."

He wasn't sure what he was supposed to say to that, so he shrugged. "Part of living successfully in the Uinta Mountains is making the best of the hand you're dealt."

Her lips thinned and that little shadow of a dimple briefly reappeared. "I'm sorry. I hadn't thought far enough ahead to realize what a burden we would all become."

The word *burden* stuck in Jonah's craw more than it would have done even a few hours earlier.

"With the Good Lord's help, we'll find a way to make do."

Dr. Havisham eyed him before saying, "You're a God-fearing man, Mr. Ramsey."

He'd been in the process of scooping food into his mouth and her remark surprised him so much that his fork hovered in the air. But her keen gaze made him uncomfortable so he mumbled, "I try to do my best."

She nodded, shuffling her potatoes from one side of her plate to the other.

"And the other men…are they of a similar mind?"

"I believe so."

He thought he heard Sumner's stomach grumble in hunger, but she had yet to take a bite.

"Do you have clergy here on the premises?" she asked.

"Not currently. We have a meetinghouse on the hill. For a time, we had a formal preacher, but he left us a few months ago for a posting in California. As of yet, we haven't managed to find a paid preacher willing to mix mining with ministry. But we have a lay pastor we rely on. Charles Wanlass. He's a good man with an understanding heart. He leads us in a daily Devotional, which is held in the evenings between shifts, then in a shorter morning prayer service, as well."

"Would it be possible for him to tend to the needs of the women?"

"I could ask him to drop by the Miners' Hall."

"Thank you. I'm relieved that you won't stand in the way of their spiritual needs."

"Dr. Havisham. Although we may not have seen eye to eye on every point so far, I would never deny anyone the opportunity to worship."

Her brown eyes softened and a sweet smile touched her lips. "Thank you for that reassurance, Mr. Ramsey. I'll pass that on to the other women." She placed her napkin next to her plate and stood. "Now, if you'll excuse me, I think it's time I get back to my patients."

He frowned. "I thought you had something you wanted to discuss?"

She nodded. "I did. But I think you already know how…*loathsome* your Pinkertons are to us. I'm leaving it up to you to do the right thing."

Her gaze, when it fell on him, was full of meaning—and for some reason, it reminded him of the way his mother could level a glance on him and make him squirm when he'd been caught doing something he oughtn't. Then Sumner slipped from the room in the soft rustle of skirts, leaving the faint scent of orange blossoms hanging in the air behind her.

Jonah stared down at his plate, his appetite completely gone. The food was horrible and there was no disguising the fact. But that wasn't the reason why he felt as if a giant hand had reached in to squeeze his stomach.

I'm leaving it up to you to do the right thing.

Jonah recognized the remark for what it was: an attempt to get him to cave in to the women's demands and allow them to run willy-nilly around Bachelor Bottoms. But what they couldn't see was that Jonah was already doing what was best for everyone involved. The Batchwell Bottoms mine was one of the most successful silver enterprises in the territory. Productivity and morale at Bachelor Bottoms were high—due to the rules that were in place. To allow the women free rein would set a precedent that would be difficult to erase once they were gone. Because of that, keeping the sexes separate was of vital importance.

Even if it meant a show of force.

Chapter Five

By the time Sumner returned to the Miners' Hall, a knot of women had already gathered on the boardwalk. Somehow, in the scant hour that Sumner had been gone, the number of guards had grown from four to nearly ten. With their rifles held diagonally across their chests, they attempted to herd the women back into the building, without much success.

From the corner of her eye, Sumner could see Mr. Batchwell and Mr. Bottoms exiting the mining offices, so she quickened her step. The last thing she needed was for the owners to use this incident as proof that the women should be kept to their quarters.

Unfortunately, as soon as they saw Sumner hurrying toward them, the women sensed an ally. They turned toward her, gesturing wildly and talking all at once—garnering even more attention from the miners walking to and from the cook shack.

"Dr. Havisham!"

"Can you believe the gall!"

"It's outrageous. Simply outrageous!"

Sensing that Batchwell was about to lose his temper, Sumner called out, "Ladies, ladies!" After a few mo-

ments, the noise died down. "As you can see, the owners of the Batchwell Bottoms mine have provided a few
men for our…protection."

Unfortunately, that had been the wrong thing to say,
because they all began talking at once again. Over the
din, Lydia Tomlinson shouted, "Our *imprisonment*, you
mean!"

Sumner shot a look toward Batchwell and Bottoms,
knowing that the next few minutes would prove vital to
the women's cause. As much as Sumner might like to lead
the women in a march on the mining offices, she sensed
that such an action would be disastrous. She needed to
talk to the ladies first, to allow them to air their grievances. Only then would it be possible to look at this problem in a clear, levelheaded manner.

"Ladies, I know that you're upset. Rightly so. But I
also know how trying the past few days have been for
you. So before we do anything rash—" she paused, meeting each of their gazes, trying to silently cue them into
her line of thinking "—I believe we should take a few
moments to talk among ourselves, get to know one another. Our hosts will be delivering our breakfast soon,
so let's step inside. I have a few things I've talked over
with Mr. Ramsey that I need to pass on to you."

To their credit, Willow and Iona, Lydia, Stefania, Ruth
and Marie appeared to understand at least a portion of
what she was trying to convey and they quickly began
to shepherd the other women inside. Although Sumner
heard some grumbling, they began to move toward the
hall, disappearing inside, one by one.

Nevertheless, as soon as Sumner stepped through the
door and closed it behind her, the shouts rose up again
and it took several minutes for Sumner to calm them
enough to make it clear that she wasn't folding under

the pressure of the armed guards, but that she was urging a cautious retreat.

"Gather 'round, please. Find whatever chairs you can, or sit here on the staircase. We need to have a civilized discussion."

The hall echoed with the sounds of female voices, the rustle of skirts and the scraping of chairs, but finally, the women all seemed to find a seat and an uneasy silence shimmered in the drafty room.

"We have such a large group here—and many of us haven't had a chance for a proper introduction, so I'd like to keep this meeting as orderly as possible. If you'll raise your hands, I'll call on you one at a time. Please be so kind as to give us your name and a little bit about yourself, then continue with whatever comment or question that you might have. Agreed?"

There were murmurs of assent and several women echoed, "Agreed." Then the room grew quiet again.

"Is there anyone present who is still missing belongings from the train?"

A few hands lifted and Sumner bent toward Lydia, who was seated to her left. "Do you think that you could find paper and pencil and write down their names?"

"Of course. I have a correspondence portfolio in my belongings."

"While Miss Tomlinson is taking notes, if any of you require something above and beyond your own supplies, let me know. Once we've finished with our chat, we can send a request to Mr. Ramsey. We already know that we'll need hip baths, pots for heating water to bathe and to wash clothes, but I'm sure we'll think of other things along the way."

For a time, the original intent of the meeting was waylaid as the brides introduced themselves and discussed the items they needed to feel more comfortable. She discovered that Willow Granger had traveled all the way from Manchester. She was supposed to marry a widower with twelve children once she arrived in San Francisco.

Jenny Reichman had traveled all the way from London to reunite with the husband she'd only known for a few weeks. He had traveled ahead of her to San Francisco, and the rounded shape of her stomach conveyed that she would not be arriving there alone, but would have a babe in arms sometime soon.

Most of the women had similar stories of a hopeful future, of meeting up with husbands-to-be that many of them had never met. Sumner tried her best to remember all their names—Louisa Wilkes, with her soft, golden hair; Emmarissa Elliot with the unfortunate hooked nose; Greta Heigl, who spoke no English but had a big booming laugh. Soon, their identities began to run together in her brain and she had to reassure herself that she would eventually get to know them all.

By the time the introductions had been made, it was obvious that the women came from all levels of society— factory girls looking for a life in the country; farmers' daughters looking for a home in the city; women from large families; or those with no family at all. Their one common point was a hope for a better future.

And all those plans had been placed on hold—could even be completely wiped out—because of the avalanche.

As she listened to each story, Sumner felt a growing kinship with them. She wasn't the only one who had fought for her goals and now found them threatened, and that idea merely reinforced her desire to help.

Finally, the conversation turned back toward their cramped quarters, their longing for a breath of fresh air and the attitudes of the men in charge of the mining community.

"I'm sure they're all trying their best to handle a difficult situation," Iona offered half-heartedly.

"But we're being guarded by *Pinkertons*!" Emmarissa Elliot complained.

"Yes, that's true," Sumner inserted before the other women could drown her out. "And I find that fact as odious as you do. I don't condone what they've done, but you have to understand the climate of this community. In order to work here, these men have agreed to follow some stringent rules."

"But it's not our fault that we're here! We shouldn't be treated like criminals because of an avalanche."

"I know that, and I've tried to explain that fact to Mr. Ramsey. But the owners feel that your mere presence could remind these men of the wives and sweethearts that they've left behind."

"Ridiculous!" Iona said with a sniff, causing Greta Heigl to laugh.

Thankfully, the Bavarian woman's mirth seemed to dissipate some of the anger, and after their humor subsided, Sumner raised her hands to summon their attention again. "I know that things are difficult right now. You've been through a traumatic accident, and let's face it, we're all exhausted and hungry. But I want you to consider the fact that if we are unable to leave until the pass melts, we will also be putting untold strains on the resources of the camp. Their food stores will have to be spread farther, along with kerosene, coal and firewood."

The women exchanged worried glances.

"These men came to our aid when we needed it, and I'd wager—judging by the food we've sampled so far— that they are just as exhausted and hungry as we are."

The women laughed again, and this time, the brittleness seemed to have melted away.

"I've explained our views and our need for freedom, fresh air and sunshine, and I left him with a challenge to do the right thing."

"Hear, hear," Lydia murmured in approval.

"Let's give things a few days."

A few of the women tried to object, but Sumner appealed to them. "Please. Just a few days. It will take us that long to wash and mend our clothing and recover from the shock we've all experienced. By that time, they will have seen we're no threat to their precious rules." Sumner paused. "Will you agree to that much?"

There was a tense beat of silence, then Lydia stood. "All those in favor, say 'aye.'"

Those in agreement began to offer their "ayes."

"And those who disagree may state it with a 'nay.'"

Again, the quiet seemed to thrum with anticipation, but when no one offered a negative vote, Lydia called out, "The 'ayes' have it. Now, ladies. Shall we gather our supplies together and see if we can come up with some strong tea?"

With so much possible time on their hands—endless, empty days and long, black nights until spring could melt the pass—the women decided that their first order of business would be making the hall more habitable.

While Iona and Willow took turns sitting with the wounded, Sumner helped to divide the rest of the women into groups. Donning whatever protective gear they could find—aprons, sheets and dishcloths—they began ridding the space of years of dust, broken furniture, and overflowing waste baskets. While they worked, Sumner kept a list of supplies that the women would need within the next few days: linens, bedding, cots, food and milk. She wasn't sure how many of the items would be available in Bachelor Bottoms, but she would do her best.

It was well into midday, rather than morning, when a knock at the hall door signaled the arrival of their first meal. Pots of food were laid out on the large center table along with a pile of plates and utensils. Napkins, cups and coffee, Sumner noted, had not been provided. She heard the women begin to grumble again when they formed a line to help themselves to what was obviously the over-cooked dregs from the miners' breakfast. Most of the women refused to eat, deciding that they would wait to see what the next meal might have in store for them.

But things did not improve.

Days later, Sumner was irritated beyond belief.

"Any sign of Mr. Ramsey?" Lydia asked when she found Sumner hovering near the window.

Sumner shook her head. "I know it's silly, but I've kept one ear cocked toward the door in the off chance that Mr. Ramsey might show up—or the Pinkertons would withdraw."

Unfortunately, rather than a relaxing of the rules, the opposite was true. As she and the other women tried to focus on obtaining water for bathing and washing, linens and mattresses, it became clear that none of them would be allowed to leave the hall, not even to make their re-quests for supplies.

Lydia's eyes twinkled. "Maybe you should write him a letter."

"I've done that already. Several times."

The missives began cordially enough, but when the supplies they needed trickled in at an impossibly slow rate, Sumner's temper began to build. By the end of the week, she'd dispensed with formalities altogether and began drafting curt lists.

Mr. Ramsey,
We still need water to bathe properly.
    And food. The women are unaccustomed to eating one meal a day.
SEH

"I'm beginning to believe that the men in charge are ignoring us."

Lydia's lips pressed into a thin line. "We're all getting restless. If we're cooped up much longer, we could have trouble on our hands. Some of the women are beginning to squabble over petty issues. It's only a matter of time before someone really loses her temper."

Sumner nodded—but short of ordering the women to climb through a window, she didn't have many options. Unless…

"When I spoke to Mr. Ramsey, he mentioned that he would send the company's lay preacher to tend to the women's spiritual needs."

Lydia snorted. "We haven't seen hide nor hair of the man."

Which meant that both their temporal and spiritual needs were being shunted to the rear of the line, despite Jonah Ramsey's assurances.

Sumner's spine stiffened. "As far as I'm concerned, we've given Jonah Ramsey more than enough time to do the right thing. I think it's time for us to stand up for ourselves."

"Hear, hear," Lydia agreed wholeheartedly. "What do you have in mind?"

Sumner strode to the center of the room, clapping her hands to gather everyone's attention.

"Ladies!"

Gradually, the chatter ceased and the women turned to face her.

It was amazing what a little hard work had done to the Miners' Hall. Although the quarters were still cramped and the means to heat water and wash were primitive at best, at least the floors gleamed from a fresh scrubbing and the air had lost the stink of wood smoke, and the mustiness of being closed up for far too long.

"We've been in Bachelor Bottoms for nearly a week, and I think we've made great inroads into making our situation as comfortable as possible."

There were murmurs of agreement and a soft, "Amen to that!"

"However, I feel that there has been one portion of our stay here that has been sorely neglected. And even more than the need for fresh air and sunshine, I believe that the means to worship and draw upon our Heavenly Father's Spirit is vital to our well-being."

A hush settled over the room. Although they had tried to hold a nightly reading from the Bible, they all longed for the sense of community and devotion to be found in more formal worship.

"I don't know about all of you, but I find myself at a point where I need the opportunity to revel in the strength of the Lord. As you are well aware, the miners hold an evening Devotional as part of their shift changes. For those of you who wish to attend, we will walk to the meetinghouse together at—" she glanced down at the fob watch pinned to her shirtwaist "—five forty-five."

The women glanced at one another in confusion. "How are we going to manage that? The Pinkertons won't allow us to go to the necessary without an armed escort, let alone the Devotional."

Sumner nodded. "Yes, that's true. But I have Mr. Ramsey's word that he will not interfere with anyone's wish to worship, and I think it's time that we hold him to his promise."

In truth, Mr. Ramsey had made that promise with the understanding that the lay preacher, Charles Wanlass, would come to them rather than the other way around. But she was counting on the fact that the man wouldn't make a scene in a house of God.

Because if these women didn't have some fresh air and spiritual sustenance soon…

The men of Bachelor Bottoms could have an all-out brawl on their hands.

By the time the evening shadows began to creep into the hall, Sumner knew that the women were tired, hungry and out-of-sorts. But they also appeared resolved. And a little excited. They were about to venture outside.

Never had a frozen winter's evening looked so inviting.

"Is everyone ready?" Sumner asked at the door.

She received a chorus of affirmative answers.

The women had spent the last hour tugging on corset strings, arranging their hair and helping one another to change into their Sunday-best attire. Then, in anticipation of the cold, they'd donned their coats, scarves and mittens. Except for Jenny Reichman, who had volunteered to stay with the injured who couldn't venture out, every woman was in attendance.

"Remember, there may be some resistance to our presence at the Devotional. But our intent is to worship. Don't let anyone provoke you into behavior that you wouldn't display in your churches at home. We need to show the men that their precautions are unnecessary. We are upstanding women of faith, and the men have nothing to fear from allowing us to mingle with their group."

She turned to sweep open the door.

Immediately, a cold rush of air swirled into the hall. Almost as quickly, a pair of Pinkertons moved to block her way. However, a quick glance assured Sumner that the rest of the brigade was absent. Perhaps they had been sent to dinner.

"Good evening, gentlemen."

She was answered by the taller of the two, a man with dark muttonchop whiskers and a mustache that drooped halfway to his Adam's apple. "Dr. Havisham."

"Good evening, Mr...."

"Winslow, ma'am."

"Mr. Winslow. I believe it's time for the evening Devotional."

The man's brow creased. "Yes, ma'am, but—"

"I obtained permission for us to attend when I met with Mr. Ramsey earlier this week. Indeed, his exact words were, 'I would never deny anyone the opportunity to worship.'"

Before the man could respond, Sumner pressed forward and the rest of the women followed suit. Although the Pinkertons rushed to stop them, the force of several dozen women couldn't be held back by so few men, and within a few minutes, the Pinkertons were overwhelmed. Sumner couldn't contain a smile as she saw the Pinkertons trailing in their wake like a confused pair of lapdogs.

Although Sumner knew little more than the meetinghouse was on the hill somewhere, it wasn't hard to find. A steady tide of men was heading that way—some with freshly washed faces and hands, and others who were muddy and dirty, probably because they'd come directly from the mine. As soon as they saw the women, they stepped into the slushy street, allowing the females to clatter over the boardwalks unhindered.

Within a few blocks, their goal came into sight. The meetinghouse was a whitewashed structure with an elaborate spire that looked like it had been welded together from curled and hammered pieces of metal. Although Sumner suspected that the materials were made of leftover mining hardware, the effect was so delicate that the spire looked like fine lace against the vibrant red-and-gold sunset.

From inside, the wheezing gasps of a pump organ broke the silence. The unknown organist seemed to be attacking the melody with determined vigor. But his enthusiasm was marred by a distinct lack of skill. So much so that Sumner couldn't pinpoint the hymn.

At the foot of the stairs, Sumner paused for a moment. "Remember, ladies, as onerous as our last few days have been, this is not the time to air our grievances. We are here to partake of the Spirit so that we can be strengthened by the Lord's love."

A soft murmur of agreement flowed around Sumner, giving her the courage she needed to move up the shallow flight of stairs and through the double doors beyond. As she stepped inside, making space for the other women, a cool gust of wind swirled around her ankles and into the chapel beyond, bringing a welcome relief from the overheated air that shimmered around the potbellied stove in the center of the room.

The interior was simple. The rectangular room held long benches that marched up either side from a center aisle. At the far end, there was a raised dais with a lectern, a pair of padded chairs and, beyond that, more benches that were presumably reserved for a choir.

Taking a bracing breath, Sumner squared her shoulders and searched for spare seats where she and the other women could sit. But most of the places had been filled with men of all shapes, sizes and ages.

Despite the prelude of sorts being pounded out on the organ, the meeting hall was filled with the low murmur of men's voices. But as Sumner and the other women traversed the length of the aisle, the low rumble of conversation stilled and the occupants turned en masse to stare.

The weight of their gazes was so intense and heavy that Sumner felt her skin prickle, and she could feel the heat seep into her cheeks. But she refused to meet their gazes head-on or allow even the slightest sign of discomfort. The next few minutes would prove to be vital for the women. Sumner wasn't sure what would happen if they couldn't have some form of fresh air—or the prospect of leaving the hall on occasion—to look forward to.

Sweet Father in Heaven, please find a way to soften their hearts so that we can stay. We all need to feel of Thy love during these trying times.

Forcing herself to remain cool and calm—despite the pounding of her heart—Sumner nodded vaguely toward the men on either side of the aisle. She was able to pick out Mr. Creakle and Mr. Smalls, and the two men from the mining offices. There were faces she remembered from their sporadic deliveries, and a few of the men who passed their window each day on their way to the mine.

Sumner's knees began to tremble, knowing that if the group decided to force them back to the hall, there wouldn't be much the women could do to prevent them. So, adopting a benign, placid expression, she pretended that she was stepping into one of her stepmother's much-hated social-climbing garden parties, folded her hands meekly together and closed the distance to the empty pews.

"So far, so good," Lydia murmured near her shoulder.

If only Sumner felt as cool and collected as her friend seemed to be. While Lydia looked as if she'd stepped from the pages of a fashion plate, Sumner wasn't nearly so calm. Her throat grew dry and her fingers began to tremble because she knew that this daring invasion into the miners' territory would not remain unchallenged. It simply remained to be seen if they would be allowed to partake of the Word first.

Lord, please help me hold my temper whatever may follow.

After what seemed like miles, she led the women to the first four rows, stepping to one side. Lydia ushered the women into the pews, taking her place at the far end. Then Iona, Stefania and Marie helped the rest of the group find a place to sit.

Sumner allowed herself a small sigh of relief. So far, there had been no real resistance to their presence, and for that she was grateful. But even as the thought entered her head, she looked up to find Jonah Ramsey glowering at her from the doorway.

A jolt raced through her body when she met his narrowed gaze—and she couldn't help noting the way his fingers curled and relaxed in open frustration. When he stalked toward her, his eyes intent, his body tensed, she was reminded of her grandmother's old tomcat. The creature was more wild animal than domesticated feline and it used to lie in wait among the daisies, waiting for a bird or mouse to appear before it would creep close enough to pounce.

"*Dr.* Havisham."

She was beginning to detest the way he pronounced her title.

He took her elbow, pulling her slightly to one side as the rest of the women settled into their places.

"Yes, Mr. Ramsey."

"May I ask why you and your women are here, rather than safely ensconced in the Miners' Hall under the watchful eye of your guards?"

"Oh, we are more than adequately guarded, Mr. Ramsey." She pointed to the Pinkertons, who were sheepishly standing at the rear of the church.

"I asked you to keep your women in the Miners' Hall for the time being."

"My women have been through quite an ordeal, Mr. Ramsey, and they have expressed a wish to worship."

"And I sent word to Charles Wanlass to visit you each evening."

"You may have sent word to the man, but he has yet to appear. After several days, we decided that it wasn't necessary to burden your lay pastor with extra duties when we can walk a few scant blocks to offer our prayers. Or were you spinning me a pretty tale when you stated that you would never deny anyone the opportunity to worship?"

She'd ensnared him with his own words, and he knew it—and she feared that he might insist that the women leave, but at that moment a clean-shaven gentleman stepped onto the podium, lifted his hands and said, "If we could all take our seats."

When she met Jonah's gaze, it was clear that he would like to pull her out of the meeting hall to continue their discussion, but to his credit, he released her, then gestured for her to take the last empty seat next to Willow Granger. Then he moved a few rows away to take his own place.

As Charles Wanlass waited, a hush fell over the spacious building. The meetinghouse was filled to bursting with all of the people who had come for the evening services, but somehow, they all managed to find a place to sit. Nevertheless, as the last of the men moved inside, they chose to sandwich themselves tightly together, leaving a full empty row between the women and the miners. Sumner wasn't sure if the gesture was meant to demonstrate their adherence to company rules, to shun the women altogether or because they feared the women might bite.

However, the gentleman at the pulpit didn't share the other men's reticence. Instead, he offered the women a wide smile and gripped the lectern on either side with strong, slender fingers.

"Good evening, everyone. Thank you for joining our services. For those who don't know me, my name is Charles Wanlass, and I've been asked to conduct our meeting."

Wanlass was by no means an imposing figure. He was probably a few inches shorter than Jonah Ramsey, and so slim and rawboned that he could use a good feeding. But his blue-gray eyes were piercing and his voice low and commanding in a way that demanded instant attention, even as a faint Scottish burr added a note of gentleness.

"We would like to welcome our guests to our worship services," Wanlass said, gesturing to the women. "Please ensure that you make them feel at home among us."

Sumner shot a glance in Jonah's direction, wondering if he would jump to his feet and negate everything Wanlass had said, but he sat with his gaze pinned to the floor so she couldn't read his reaction.

"Before we offer up a word of prayer, we would like to begin our meeting with a song. Please turn to page twelve in your hymnals. 'Blessed Be the Tie That Binds.' George, if you please."

The man seated behind the organ began to pump furiously. But as the man pounded out a discordant semblance of a melody, the women glanced at one another in confusion.

Offering a pained sigh, Lydia suddenly stood and hurried to shoo the man aside. Then, taking his place, she took only a moment to glance at the music before playing.

A hush fell over the room as the familiar strains filled the meetinghouse. Indeed, the miners were so stunned that only the women sang the first few measures. But soon they were joined by tenors and basses until the structure resonated with the sounds.

In that moment, the tone of the Devotional was struck—so much so, Sumner knew that even Jonah would be unable to fault the women's presence or their sincerity. She watched beneath her lashes as his shoulders eased from their rigid line and he sank deeper into his seat.

For the first time, Sumner was able to breathe more freely. But she soon discovered that she'd relaxed too soon. As they began the last chorus, Batchwell and Bottoms appeared at a side door.

"Oh, dear," Willow whispered.

Sumner tensed, regarding the men from beneath her lashes as she feigned interest in the hymnal. Her voice wavered and her pulse pounded. Batchwell opened his mouth—probably to demand their expulsion. But at the same moment, Bottoms grasped his partner's arm and leaned to murmur something in the portly man's ear.

Instantly, Batchwell's lips snapped shut, and although his eyes burned like two dark coals as they scoured the pews filled with the women from the train, he and his partner moved to settle into the two ornately upholstered chairs that were located to the side of the podium.

Thank You, Heavenly Father, thank You.

Sumner's eyes flickered closed and she sang the final measures of the hymn with renewed fervor, knowing that, at least for now, the women would be allowed to stay. Perhaps, they could make their worship a nightly occurrence.

Willow squeezed her hand, offering Sumner a small smile.

Finally, finally, Sumner felt the tension seep from her body like sand draining from an hourglass, and she was able to enjoy the meeting.

After the song was finished, a prayer was offered by a miner named Theo Caruso. Then Charles Wanlass returned to the lectern where he spoke briefly about the importance of humility.

The words pricked Sumner's conscience and her gaze shot toward Jonah, then away again. She really hadn't put her best foot forward where he was concerned. She'd been quite proud, even boastful. But for some reason, it had been important to her that he knew the depth of her training and her willingness to work hard. It shouldn't matter to anyone that she was a woman as long as she did her job properly, and he needed to know that.

She shied away from the reason why it was so important to her. She didn't need Mr. Ramsey's approval of her character, only her professional capacity. He was a fellow employee, the superintendent of the mine. Other than that, their paths didn't need to cross.

If only things were that simple.

Yanking her gaze and her thoughts back to Charles Wanlass, Sumner caught the tail end of the man's sermon. He was underscoring the importance of showing gratitude to God by serving one's fellow man.

The words struck Sumner to the core. All her life, she'd longed to be the kind of person who could make a difference in the world. But most of the roles available to women had felt so limiting. She didn't have the temperament for teaching. The thought of being a shop clerk or a woman's companion had bored her to tears. And she had no desire to marry a man and provide him with a brood of children for no other reason than to have something to do.

No. She'd wanted—*needed*—to offer the world something more. That's why she'd gravitated toward medicine.

Her eyes skipped toward Jonah Ramsey again. He sat with his knees on his elbows, his fingers laced together, his head bowed. His eyes were half-closed, as if he were concentrating on the words and allowing them to fill his heart as they had her own. For some reason, the sight was more touching than she could have ever anticipated. She sensed that he was a good man—one who was trying to follow his orders and his conscience to the best of his ability. She mustn't lose sight of that fact when they skirmished again—because she had no doubt that they would find something else to disagree upon. Probably quite soon.

Closing her eyes, Sumner listened raptly as a passage from Luke in the Bible was read aloud.

"'Give, and it will be given unto you; good measure, pressed down, and shaken together and running over, shall men give into your bosom. For with the same measure that ye mete withal, it shall be measured to you again.'"

With the verse reverberating in her heart, Sumner joined in the singing of another hymn and listened to the sweet words of a final prayer that asked for the safety of all the men who would soon be descending into the mine. Then, all too soon, the Devotional was over.

"What should we do now?" Willow whispered.

"Let's stay in our seats. Then they can't accuse us of fraternizing."

Willow quickly passed the message down the line. Although the women whispered among themselves and cast glances at the miners heading for the back door, they didn't move.

"How long should we sit here?" Willow murmured, surreptitiously peeking over her shoulder.

"Until most of the men have left."

Sumner didn't know about the others, but she wasn't anxious to return to their imposed isolation, and the music being played by their impromptu organist was a balm to weary, frazzled nerves.

At one point, it looked like Batchwell might descend upon them, his face as thunderous as a storm cloud. But surprisingly, Jonah intercepted him and exchanged a few words. Whatever he said must have been important because the men strode from the building, heading toward the mine.

After the church was nearly empty, Sumner reluctantly stood, signaling to the women that their return to the Miners' Hall was inevitable. Even so, Lydia lingered over the last few notes before her feet stilled and the organ's sweet voice disappeared in a sigh.

"Come along, ladies," Sumner called out. "Hopefully, we'll have some food waiting for us on our return."

The women stood and began moving toward the exits.

Willow and Iona lingered with Sumner, the older woman saying, "I don't know if we should be grateful or fearful. Seems to me, they've been feeding us the scrapings from the mush pot for most of the week. I don't know how much more of that our constitutions can take."

"We're eating the men's winter supplies," Willow said. "In light of their generosity, we probably shouldn't complain."

Lydia shrugged into her coat. "In my opinion, what they've sent us isn't fit for hogs. I don't know how the men get any work done if that's what they're used to eating."

A host of ideas began to spin in Sumner's brain, inspired by Wanlass's sermon and the events of the past week. If she could only grasp the threads and weave them together.

"We've already survived an avalanche," Iona offered as she tightened the ribbons of her bonnet. "We should be able to come up with a way to offer some suggestions without appearing ungrateful."

"After all, the miners came to our rescue."

"*And* retrieved our things."

Sumner's lips lifted into a smile.

"Perhaps that's what we should do." The women regarded her curiously, so she added, "We should show them our gratitude."

"Have you lost your senses?" Lydia asked. "Since the avalanche, they've locked us up like criminals."

"Which is why we're going to smother them with kindness. We'll show them just how *thankful* we are. We'll be sweet as honey and ever so helpful."

"Because…" Lydia prompted.

"They might not know it, but these men are in dire need of the more…*refined* effects that the fairer sex brings to a society. We'll show Batchwell and Bottoms that they don't have anything to fear from allowing us to associate with their residents. They might even discover that, when the time comes, they won't want us to leave."

Chapter Six

Sumner's brain was still whirling with ideas when they arrived at their temporary home. There had to be a way to ease the women into the mining camp's routine.

"Maybe we shouldn't push things yet," Willow said, her voice so soft that Sumner doubted anyone else could have heard. "We've managed to go to the Devotional—which is already against their orders. Maybe we should leave things as they are for the time being."

"Perhaps. But I've never been much good at following orders," Sumner mused.

"Dr. Havisham."

She started, a frisson of sensation skittering down her spine when Jonah Ramsey's voice slid out of the darkness. She turned to find him standing not too far behind her, a low-burning lantern swinging loosely from his fingers.

She waited until all of the women had disappeared inside the hall before acknowledging him. "Mr. Ramsey."

The corner of his mouth twitched in a hint of a smile.

"Come now… *Sumner*. We agreed that, in private, we would call each other by our first names."

She glanced around the boardwalk, noting for the first

time that Mr. Ramsey was the only man in sight. Even the Pinkertons were absent.

"Don't get too excited. They'll be back," Jonah murmured. "Since the Devotional is over, Stumpy and his men will be run off their feet feeding the men who have just finished their shift. I asked your guards to take charge of bringing the food to the other ladies."

"I'm sure the women will be delighted to have more than one meal today," she grumbled under her breath.

Jonah's eyes narrowed. "Pardon?"

"Come now, Mr. Ramsey. I'm sure you're more than aware of the miniscule amount of nourishment we've been receiving. I've sent you at least several dozen notes to the effect."

There was a beat of silence. Then two.

"You've sent me notes?"

"Yes. Via those Pinkertons. Probably a dozen or more a day."

His brows creased and he eyed her with such a blank expression that she wondered how on earth he could summon such a sincere look of puzzlement.

"You sent them to me. Personally."

"Yes! They were taken by the Pinkertons to the mine offices."

He sighed suddenly, staring down at the toes of his boots.

"Miss Havisham. *Sumner.* I've spent the past few days working belowground in the mine. We've been opening up a new tunnel and…" He broke off, then shook his head. "Tomorrow morning, I'll get to the bottom of this. In the meantime, I fear that—since I wasn't in the office—your letters may have gone directly to Mr. Batchwell."

Sumner's frustration swelled at the owner's interference, but it was quickly followed by a wave of relief. Over the past few days, Jonah's seeming indifference had filled her with such…disappointment that she'd known she wouldn't be able to look him in the eye the next time. Not without being tempted to say something she shouldn't. And now, all that resentment rushed from her soul with a soft, "Oh."

"I assure you, I haven't seen any of your letters."

He lifted his arm and the lantern cast a warm puddle of light onto the frosty boardwalk.

"If you have the time, I wondered if you'd walk with me."

Her brows rose.

"This isn't a social call, Sumner. Merely a means to a mutual understanding."

She'd been expecting a confrontation, so she decided to give him the benefit of the doubt.

She fell into step beside him, breathing easier when they moved away from the mine offices. She might have forgiven Jonah for the issue with the letters, but she didn't know if she could be so generous with Ezra Batchwell.

The night air was crisp and cold, causing their breaths to hang in front of them in gossamer clouds.

"I apologize for not being more mindful of your needs. I assumed that you'd been taken care of and the little luxuries could be seen to later."

She opened her mouth to insist that the items she'd requested were far from frivolous, but he stopped her.

"I now understand that I should have checked with you in person."

Sumner thought back on the snippy progression of her letters and her cheeks flamed in embarrassment. It was bad enough that Batchwell had been privy to them. But she prayed that Jonah would never read them.

He frowned.

"Have you really only received one meal a day?"

"Most days." She hesitated before saying, "If I were to hazard a guess, I would think we're offered whatever remains after the miners have finished eating."

Jonah's jaw clenched. When he spoke, his voice cut through the night like a blade. "Tomorrow morning, I'll assign a couple of men to gather what you need. I can't guarantee that we'll be able to supply everything on your list, but we'll do what we can."

"I appreciate that."

"In the meantime…" He withdrew a set of keys from his vest pocket and paused in front of an unadorned squat building. Holding the lantern higher, he unlocked the door, then swept it wide. "This is the infirmary. Our previous doctor lived and worked out of here."

She stepped inside, eager to explore. If things had been different, she would have been shown to this place on the first day. It would have been *her* living quarters, *her* infirmary. Her patients could have been made comfortable on the half dozen cots she could see in a room to the left, rather than the pallets in the Miners' Hall.

"There's an examining room through there." Jonah gestured to an area on the right. "Back there are the doctor's private rooms." He pointed to the rear of the building. "I'm not sure what kinds of medicines and such the previous doc left when he moved on. If you'd like to have a look around and identify what you can use, I'll have things moved to the Miners' Hall some time tomorrow afternoon."

Discouragement caused Sumner's excitement to flag. Despite being shown the building, she wouldn't be able to work here. She would merely be allowed to collect items from the shelves and return them to her jail.

Her chin tilted. "Wouldn't it be simpler to move the wounded here?"

Jonah met her gaze, his expression glinting with a thread of steel. "Perhaps. But it's not going to happen. The owners insist that you stay with the other women. That means that you'll need to work from the Miners' Hall."

"But—"

"Don't push it, Sumner. Your little stunt tonight wasn't appreciated by Mr. Batchwell and Mr. Bottoms."

She stiffened. "Stunt? Our appearance at the Devotional wasn't meant to be a protest. You gave me your assurances, Jonah, that the women would be allowed to worship. You even promised to help us in that regard by sending Mr. Wanlass to the hall."

"And that oversight was my fault," Jonah hastened to explain. "I thought I'd sent him a note, but after speaking with you tonight, I realized that I'd meant to talk to him in person. When we had problems with the new tunnel… I'm afraid I didn't follow things through."

His mouth tightened and her fingers twitched with the need to smooth them into a softer line.

"You promised, Jonah." The words emerged as little more than a whisper. "You can't blame us if we took matters into our own hands."

His head dipped. He was willing to concede that point. "Be that as it may, you directly defied the owners' wishes about leaving the hall. And I've been asked to relay their…*displeasure*, along with a warning that any further resistance to their orders could result in more… serious consequences."

Her brow furrowed. "Is that a threat, Mr. Ramsey?"

He shook his head. "Not at all. I am merely repeating their message."

"Am I permitted a rebuttal?"

"Somehow I don't think I could stop you. But we're using first names, remember?"

"Mr. Ramsey—"

"Jonah."

"Mr.—"

"Jonah."

"Jonah, I—" She paused, then found herself unable to continue. As the light of the lantern coated his features, she became aware of deep lines of weariness fanning out from his eyes and bracketing his mouth.

Perhaps it was a trick of the lighting, the silence of the dark Uinta night, or merely the fact that Jonah appeared as ill at ease in reporting the message as she did receiving it. But suddenly, she didn't want to argue.

"You look exhausted, Jonah."

Her comment clearly surprised him. "It's been a long few days."

"And I've managed to complicate them even further."

In the lamplight his eyes were darker, warmer. Almost…kind. And even though she tended to bristle in his presence, tonight she couldn't summon the energy or the animosity. Instead, she became aware of the stillness of the night and the fact that the two of them were alone.

Completely and totally alone.

Jonah watched as the fire seeped from Sumner's expression, leaving something softer, gentler and so much harder to decipher.

"You work too hard," she murmured.

Jonah could have sworn that the sweet huskiness of her tone brushed down his spine like a silken finger.

"Some days are like that. But not all of them. There

are other days when the work is slow and we've got too much time on our hands."

"What do you do then?"

"I...uh... I like to read. I do a little carving."

He could tell that he'd surprised her. Not so much with the reading, but with his carving. He wondered what she would say if he told her that he'd once poured his energies into making beautiful furniture. He'd even built a snug little house and filled it with the handcrafted pieces.

For Rebecca.

But it hadn't been enough for her to consider taking a chance on him.

Jonah broke away from those dark thoughts, dragging his attention back to the present and a different woman.

Rebecca would have been shocked by Sumner's pursuit of an education—and even more appalled by Sumner's choice of career. Rebecca had always been one of those overtly feminine types who dressed in ruffles and wore her hair in ringlets. To her, a lost glove was a tragedy and a good meal a triumph. He'd been so sure that she would make the perfect wife and mother.

And she had.

Just not with him.

But as he unconsciously compared his former betrothed to Sumner, he couldn't find fault with the different path that this woman had taken. She glowed from her sense of dedication and the passion she felt for her causes. If anything...

He admired her for that.

Knowing that to stay any longer, alone with her, in the dark, would open the evening to a temptation that he couldn't allow himself, so he set the lantern on a nearby table.

"I'll leave the lamp with you. Take whatever time you

want and inventory what you can use. In the meantime, I'll let the Pinkertons know that you may need to make several trips in the coming days. Don't worry about locking up tonight. I'll send Creakle by with a key in a few hours, then have him unlock it again early in the morning."

She nodded. "Thank you, Jonah."

He'd nearly made it to the door when she spoke again. "Jonah?"

He couldn't resist turning to look at her one more time. She was wearing the same coat and hat that she'd worn earlier that week when they'd shared a meal. In the dim lamplight, her face was framed by a delicate halo of fur.

"Make sure you get some sleep tonight."

Jonah couldn't remember the last time he'd slept more than a few fitful hours. It had been even longer since someone had cared about his welfare. Sure, Creakle tended to nag. But that was a male fussiness that had more to do with making sure that the "boss man" could do the job rather than anything else.

But Sumner Havisham's concern seemed more…real.

"I'll do my best." He lifted a finger to the brim of his hat. "You make sure to do the same."

Then he strode from the office knowing that it was past time that he beat a hasty retreat.

Sumner listened to the sound of Jonah's footfalls as they disappeared into the night. Strong. Sure. Steady. His gait told her as much about the man as the man himself.

She waited for some time, wondering if he'd pause or come back. But it soon became clear that she'd been left alone with her thoughts—a luxury of sorts, after the women had all been living in one another's pockets.

Taking the lantern from the table, she held it high, allowing the buttery glow to seep into the corners of the room. In the waiting area, there were a half dozen chairs and a small writing desk. In her mind's eye, she could imagine what it would look like bustling with patients.

She moved into the examining area where she found a proper physician's chair made of oak with an adjustable headboard and little drawers and cubbies underneath where she could have stored her instruments. Along one entire wall, there were more bookshelves and drawers, and a glass-fronted display cabinet with an apothecary scale and a half dozen bottles of various compounds that could be mixed into medicines. Unfortunately, most of the vials were nearly empty—which meant that the previous physician had probably taken everything of value.

As she finished her inspection of the rest of the building, she began to believe that her assumptions were true. Other than a few ether cones, some prepared splints and rolls of bandages, there wasn't a whole lot for her to haul back to the Miners' Hall. A large basket should do the trick.

Sumner wasn't entirely surprised at the meager supplies. It was customary for most doctors to supply whatever equipment and medicines they might need. Her own trunks held as many tools and compounds as she could gather with the advance wages that were provided for her passage. Even so, she'd hoped against hope that she would arrive to find that the infirmary was well-stocked.

With her inventory complete, she hesitated at the door leading into the private quarters. A part of her bubbled with curiosity. But she also feared that knowing too much of "what might have been" would be tantamount to poking an open wound with a sharp stick. If everything had worked out as she'd hoped, she would have been ushered into these rooms the first day. As it was, she could be forced from Aspen Valley without ever having the chance to prove how well she could provide the miners with their medical needs.

The temptation proved to be too great and she swung the door wide to reveal a small room with a drop-leaf table and a pair of chairs, a dry sink, a box stove and a narrow tester bed. Judging by its size, the builder hadn't thought that the mine doctor would have much of a personal life; therefore, he wouldn't need much space.

But to Sumner, it looked like a palace. A place of her own. A clinic of her own.

Just as she'd feared, she felt a pang of regret, but swift on its heels came a rushing wave of determination. This place needed a doctor—so why shouldn't it be her?

Locating an empty crate near the back door, she gathered up all of the supplies that she could find. She was able to fill it to the brim, but it proved to be too heavy for her to carry back to the hall herself. Despite its weight, the collection held a woeful lack of treatments for a community with more than two hundred people. She would have to ask one of the miners to come fetch it in the morning—or a Pinkerton. If they were going to shadow the women, they may as well prove useful.

She bolted from the doctor's office, striding down the boardwalk in frustration. The entire situation was maddening. She'd become a doctor to help others, but even when it was obvious that her skills were needed, she was kept from doing her job.

So, what was she going to do about it?

Her stride grew calmer—especially when the hall came into sight and she realized that she would soon be imprisoned behind its walls once again. Unbidden, the words of Charles Wanlass's sermon came to her mind.

True gratitude is shown by serving one's fellow man.

A wave of frustration washed over her. She wanted to help this community. The fact that she was alive and healthy were two overwhelming reasons why she should be grateful to the men who lived here. She and the other women could have been killed in the avalanche. If not for the miners, there might have been a need for graves rather than an overwhelming need for freedom.

If she could just think of a way for the women to ingratiate themselves into the community, maybe then, the men wouldn't be so scared of them.

As she neared the hall, a Pinkerton—Mr. Winslow—stepped from the shadows and opened the door for her.

"Good evening, Miss Havisham."

"Mr. Winslow. Mr. Dobbs."

The lock had barely snapped into place behind her when Sumner became aware of a most peculiar stench.

Willow hurried forward to take the lantern from Sumner's hands.

"What on earth is that smell?"

Willow grimaced. "It's our dinner."

"What are they serving us?"

Willow shrugged, helping Sumner to slip out of her coat. "We aren't quite sure. It was too burned to make out. There was plenty of corn bread, even if it was dry as a desert. Some of the women are beginning to grumble that the men of Bachelor Bottoms mean to starve us to death."

Sumner's stomach chose that moment to rumble, but peering at the serving plates laid out on the table, she shuddered. No wonder the men of Bachelor Bottoms were so ornery.

But then, what could one expect from a bunch of bachelors?

A slow smile lifted her lips and her spirits rose as all of the loose threads of thought suddenly coalesced into a single, stupendous idea. For a moment, she cast her eyes heavenward, offering a soft, "Thank You."

Then she called for the women to gather near.

Jonah jerked awake to the noise of ferocious pounding and Creakle's muttered "What the…"

Cracking one eye open, Jonah glanced at the clock nailed to the far wall of the shack that was part office, part infirmary for the men in the mine. Located halfway down the first tunnel, the structure provided some protection from the noise and the damp, and offered a quiet place to grab a few minutes of sleep.

Jonah scrubbed his face with his hands, trying to gather his wits. "What's going on, Creakle?"

Creakle blinked at him from the desk in the corner. "Don't rightly know. Y' want me to check it out?"

Moaning, Jonah pushed himself upright, waving Creakle back into his seat.

"I'll do it."

With all the trouble they'd had with their newest tunnel, neither Creakle or Jonah had bothered to go home. Instead, Jonah had kicked off his boots and allowed himself an hour to rest while Creakle finished the schematics outlining a new system of beams and timbers that should help to shore up the weak spots in tunnel six. According to the clock, he'd been asleep for less than half that.

With all that racket, the mine itself had better be ablaze.

As soon as the thought was formed, he pushed it aside. Like many miners, he was a God-fearing man, but that didn't mean that he didn't have his superstitious quirks—especially where the safety of his men was concerned. He'd lived through enough mining accidents not to tempt fate with his wayward thoughts.

Dropping his feet over the side of the cot, he searched for his boots, hauling them on even as more banging assaulted his ears. Shrugging into his coat, he whipped open the door.

Stumpy Miller stood with his arm upraised. Since the man hadn't been paying attention, he came close to rapping Jonah on the chest. True to his name, the man was as short as he was stout. And with his fists balled up and his jaw clenched, he seemed even squatter. In the faint, early-morning light, his face was florid and he looked as if he were about to suffer a fit of apoplexy.

"The cook shack," he panted. "Hurry!"

Without another word, Stumpy ran down the tunnel to the main entrance.

Jonah bellowed to Creakle. "Sound the alarm! There's a problem at the cook shack!"

Several new inches of snow had fallen during the night, so Jonah's boots slipped and slid as he raced out of the mine to the main road where the kitchens were located. As he rounded the corner, he searched for a telltale pinkish glow that might signal a fire or smoke roiling from the roof. But even though the windows glowed from within, the yellow puddles appeared to be the product of lamplight rather than an inferno.

The alarm bell was just beginning to toll as Jonah pounded onto the boardwalk and whipped open the door. But rather than smoke assaulting his nose, he was nearly overwhelmed by the scent of lye and carbolic. Though his eyes stung, his gaze swept the room, taking in Stumpy, who stood with his arms akimbo. Around him stood a group of women who had obviously been interrupted in various chores—dusting shelves, wiping down tables, scrubbing floors. Beyond them, in the kitchen, Jonah could see a second group of females preparing food—peeling potatoes, kneading bread and cracking eggs.

"See? See!" Stumpy exclaimed, jabbing an accused finger into the air.

Behind him, Jonah could hear the clamor of men as they rushed toward the staging point in front of the Miners' Hall. But for the life of him, Jonah still couldn't figure out why they'd been summoned.

"What's the matter?"

"*They're* the matter." Stumpy's arm gestured to the women. "They shouldn't be here. They're supposed to stay in the Miners' Hall."

For the first time, Jonah hesitated. True, the owners had demanded that the women stay in the building across the street. Sometimes, it felt to Jonah that Batchwell had enforced a quarantine of sorts—as if their femininity were as catching like measles. But after last night, Jonah had begun to realize that the ladies would not be so easily contained. Even a group of Pinkertons had proven to be less than successful in keeping them from traipsing through town to the Devotional.

Of course, their act of defiance had been partially Jonah's fault. In spending so much time in the mine, he'd secretly hoped that the problem would work itself out and the women would come to the conclusion that they were better off secluded from the other inhabitants of Aspen Valley. Barring that, Jonah had hoped that, once he'd had a chance to think things over, he could come up with a more feasible way to compel the women to stay put. One that didn't make him feel like a tyrant.

But in that moment, as he breathed deeply of the cold fresh air sweeping in from the open door, saw the gleam of polished wood and sparkling glass and became aware of the tantalizing scents of bacon and biscuits and bread pushing aside the strong stink of cleaner…

He couldn't think of a single reason why the women shouldn't remain where they were.

As if on cue, his stomach grumbled. And for the first time in months, he found himself actually looking forward to a meal. He wasn't sure what had inspired the woman to commandeer the cook shack, but he was drawing a blank on why he should curtail their actions.

At that moment, Sumner Havisham swept from the back room. It was obvious from the color tinging her cheeks that she expected a battle because she immediately offered, "Mr. Ramsey…"

He was beginning to hate the way she said the formal title. For some reason, he wished she would draw him aside for a more intimate discussion so that she would call him by his first name again.

A part of him registered that she was beginning to voice her objections, but he was momentarily distracted by the snap of her dark eyes. She and the other women must have been working for some time because strands of hair had escaped the tight knot at her nape and the frizzled strands gave the soft appearance of a halo around her face.

Too late, Jonah became aware of a silent pause and realized that she must have asked him a question. But he was saved from having to admit his inattention when a group of men pressed through the door, all of them talking at once.

Sighing, Jonah placed a thumb and finger between his lips and offered a sharp, piercing whistle—the same sound that he'd once used to summon horses from the far pastures of his family's farm.

The sudden silence was nearly as deafening as the outburst of noise had been. Jonah waited a moment before gesturing to Sumner.

"You were saying?"

Her shoulders straightened, making him keenly aware that she was wearing a shirtwaist that he hadn't seen, one that was severe and tailored—and probably meant to hide her femininity. But a delicate strip of hand-tatted lace at her collar fluttered beneath her jaw, emphasizing the slim line of her neck.

"I was trying to explain that the women would like to show their gratitude to the men for coming to our rescue. We realize that our arrival has caused some…inconvenience. And we are keenly aware that our presence will strain your food stores, necessitating a hunting party. We felt that if we could help in the preparation of the meals, that would ease the burden and free up manpower to look for game to see us through the winter."

Jonah knew that he should object—if only because that was what Ezra Batchwell would insist he do. But as his gaze swung around the dozen or so women who were easing closer to one another for moral support, and the scent of bacon grew heady and strong, Jonah found himself saying, "Your efforts are all appreciated. I'm sure that Stumpy and his crew would welcome your help so that they could organize several trips into the woods to look for deer and elk."

He cut a glance to the man in question, and for a moment, Stumpy looked as if he was about to chew his mustache off in frustration. But then the intent of Jonah's words pierced the cloud of his anger. Jonah knew the exact moment when the stout man realized that he and his men were being given permission to abandon the cook shack and spend the day outside, unencumbered, hunting for game. The chore was tantamount to a vacation for a man who'd been chained to a stove for the better part of two years.

"You're sure about that?" the man grumped. "We don't gotta do nothing but hunt?"

"I'm sure that the women can make do for the next week or so. I know I'd feel easier if we had some meat to stretch our supplies. And if we were able to send out a full party each day rather than one or two men…"

Stumpy's chest swelled with renewed importance. "Yes…well… That would be a fine idea. A mighty fine idea."

Jonah turned back to Sumner, expecting to see the light of victory in her eyes. Instead, the coffee-like depths warmed with amusement.

"Dr. Havisham, I'll leave it to you to arrange matters with the women under your care. Explain to them that we serve two hot meals a day and supply cold meat and bread for the meal buckets. Stumpy, here, will give you all the particulars before he and his men leave."

A ghost of a smile touched the corners of her lips.

"Thank you, Mr. Ramsey."

Since he'd left his hat in the mine, Jonah touched a finger to his brow. "No. Thank you and your ladies." Then he gestured for the men to move into the cold. "All of you need to get out of their way for now. Breakfast isn't for another hour or more, so give the women some room to get things ready."

Chapter Seven

Long before the cook shack opened its doors, a line began forming and soon wound around the block.

From his vantage point on the second floor of the mining offices, Jonah couldn't blame them. An enticing aroma had begun to waft through Aspen Valley, announcing the menu long before word could spread about a change in staff.

Creakle sidled up beside him, then cackled softly under his breath. "Will you be headin' to breakfast soon, boss?"

Normally, Jonah wasn't in a hurry to eat. He tended to get a few hours of work under his belt until his hunger or the cold drove him to the cook shack for a quick meal and a hot cup of coffee.

But this morning…well, he was as eager as the other men to taste the source of the delicious smells. Unfortunately, there was still one minor detail that he should attend to first. He knew that news of the new female cooks would rush through the encampment like wildfire. From there, it was only a matter of time before the owners got wind of it. And since they were still fuming about the women showing up at the Devotional, they wouldn't be too happy to see them mingling in the community, regardless of the wonderful smells.

"Creakle, would you be so kind to send a message to Mr. Batchwell and Mr. Bottoms inviting them to join me at the cook shack for a meeting. Tell them that I've got something important to discuss about the welfare of the men, but that I'd rather do it over our meal, if they're agreeable. Tell them that I'm hoping to avoid any interruptions, so for them to come in the side door."

A slow smile spread over Creakle's features, growing so wide that Jonah could see the flash of a gold filling.

"Yes, sir! I'll deliver them there myself."

Jonah waited until he'd seen Creakle head for the pair of homes that perched high on the hill over the mine. Batchwell and Bottoms had been business partners for more than fifty years, but their personalities—and homes—couldn't be more different. When construction crews had been tasked with building the offices, warehouses and row houses, Phineas had hired a few of the men to make a small rock cottage similar to the one he'd lived in as a boy. Ezra, on the other hand...

Well, Ezra had brought in a bevy of craftsmen from back east, and had erected a huge imposing edifice designed by Ezra Batchwell himself. Some said he'd copied the building from a stately manor house in England, and Jonah was inclined to believe it. The structure was several stories high, built of limestone, and adorned with gargoyles and statuary. In Jonah's opinion, the whole thing was a bit ostentatious, but Ezra swelled with pride anytime it was mentioned.

Pulling the watch from his pocket, Jonah watched as the second hand swept around its tiny dial once...twice... three times. Then he snapped it shut with a soft chime.

After gathering his coat and hat, he crossed to the

cook shack. The front door had been flung wide and men were jostling for position as they gathered their utensils and tin trays and began working their way down the line. Avoiding the crowd, Jonah dodged down the alley to the side door and let himself in.

It took a few moments for his eyes to adjust to the dimness of the corridor. When they did, he noticed a small group of women standing at the entrance to the kitchen. They spoke in low voices, gesturing to the men and the eating area beyond. When one of the ladies returned to the kitchen, Jonah had a straight view of Dr. Sumner Havisham.

Unaccountably, he found himself rooted to the floor. He'd seen Dr. Havisham—*Sumner*—in a variety of modes and poses. Militant, when she'd insisted on tending to the wounded at the train; defiant, when she'd railed against him for involving the Pinkertons; thoughtful, when she'd accompanied him to the medical office.

But today, he was encountering a different woman, one who was in disarray and slightly harried, who saw the problem of too many miners to feed and too little room to seat them. Her cheeks were flushed and her hair had come loose from the braid wound at her nape. There was a dusting of flour on her nose and what looked like icing smeared on her cheek. She'd rolled the sleeves of her shirtwaist up to her elbows and allowed herself to unbutton one tiny fastener at her throat.

Jonah was sure that Sumner would have been horrified if she could have seen herself in a mirror. She'd always been so…professional around him. But in this moment, she appeared flustered and agitated, and completely…

Adorable.

"She's a looker, isn't she?"

He started, realizing too late that the door behind him

had opened. He frowned when he saw that Gideon Gault was watching Sumner, as well.

"Hello, Gideon. How's the head?"

Normally, Gideon was in charge of the Pinkertons guarding the silver shipments. But he'd been one of the men injured when a portion of the roof had given way in tunnel six, so he'd been confined to his quarters with a concussion for more than a week.

"It's fine." Gideon grinned. "I'd heard that we had some new scenery in the camp, but I can see now that the stories didn't do the women justice. Which one is the doctor?"

Jonah reluctantly pointed in Sumner's direction, then wished he hadn't.

Gideon offered a low whistle. "I can see why she's caused such a stir."

Jonah's jaw clenched. It shouldn't matter to him if Gideon admired Sumner. Jonah had no claims on the woman—and he had no intention whatsoever in allowing anything *personal* to come between him and the good doctor.

"The women are only here until the pass is clear. Then everything will return to normal."

Gideon's only response was, "Maybe." Then he moved into the main room to take his place in the line.

Jonah was about to back away when Sumner suddenly glanced up. A flush crept up her cheeks and she reached to smooth her hair. But in the warmth of the kitchen, the tendrils immediately sprang into tight little curls again.

Unbidden, he wondered what the tresses would look like if the pins were removed and the chestnut waves were allowed to spill down her back.

No.

He couldn't think like that. He couldn't allow himself to think of Dr. Havisham as anything but a colleague.

And a temporary one at that.

"Mr. Ramsey." She moved toward him.

He noted that two of her companions watched them with open curiosity. He rued the fact that they weren't alone so she couldn't call him by his Christian name.

"Dr. Havisham."

"Have you come in search of breakfast?"

"No. I mean…yes. I—"

Around her he lost the ability to think straight. "Actually, I've invited Mr. Bottoms and Mr. Batchwell to meet me here."

Her brow creased and some of the light in her eyes dimmed. "Oh, I see. They still haven't been told about our…arrangement."

"I figured I'd break it to them easy." He paused before adding, "After breakfast."

To his delight, her brown eyes grew warm again. "Why, Mr. Ramsey, I do believe that there's a bit of mischief buried deep in your soul."

"Not mischief. But I've handled one or two negotiations in my time and I like to stack the deck in my favor whenever possible. If you wouldn't mind, I'd like you to arrange for one of the men to deliver the plates. There's no sense getting the owners' dander up until they've tasted the food."

"Very well."

"But once they're done… I don't know, maybe you could send one of the women in to warm up their coffee."

She smiled, and how he loved her smile. She spent so much time being stern in order to persuade those around her that she was competent. But when she gave in to the joy within her, he could see that he wasn't the only one with a "bit of mischief" in his soul.

"I think that's a fine idea."

"Good."

Although he didn't have anything more to say, he couldn't bring himself to end the conversation. So he scrambled to think of something—*anything*—that would keep her standing there a little longer.

"Were you and the other women able to find everything you needed?"

She nodded. "Considering what you told me about the way your stores for the winter were limited, we tried to be as conservative as possible in our estimates. I'm afraid we're having to cook more than we'd originally thought."

"I'm sure the men will be delighted with whatever you and the other ladies have prepared. Later today, I'll show you our storehouse where everything is kept, just to make sure that you have anything you need."

"We'll take a detailed inventory. That way, we'll know how best to ration things. Then, once your hunting parties are able to supply us with more meat, we'll stretch things as far as possible by making more soups and stews. No doubt, with the weather growing colder, the hot food will be welcome."

"You'll spoil us all, Dr. Havisham. It's been a long time since my men have had a home-cooked meal. I don't know how we'll be able to return to Stumpy's cooking once spring comes."

And you're gone.

He didn't say the words, but they hung there in the silence.

Jonah could have kicked himself. He hadn't wanted to say anything to displease her. But he'd managed to remind her that her position here at Bachelor Bottoms was tenuous at best. She immediately stiffened, some of the starch returning to her posture. He instantly regretted spoiling the moment and saying something that built the barriers between them again.

But wouldn't it be far crueler to lead her to believe that things could ever be different? Regardless of the enticing aromas emanating from the kitchen, Batchwell and Bottoms would never agree to allowing women to live in the valley. Mining was dangerous work, and no matter how well-intentioned they might be, women were a distraction. Anything that pulled a man's mind away from his job could get him hurt or killed. It was a fact of life. One that couldn't be changed.

Jonah met her gaze, intending to put his thoughts into words, but the moment his eyes met hers, he knew they didn't need to be said. She'd managed to read his mind, and for some reason, the thought made him squirm inside with something akin to guilt—even though he knew that he hadn't done anything wrong.

"If you'll let us know when you're ready to eat," she said softly, a tightness to her tone that hadn't been there before.

He offered a curt nod, but his response was unnecessary. She'd already turned to disappear into the kitchens again, her friends accompanying her—and none too soon. Mere seconds after their skirts had disappeared from view, the side door opened, letting in a gust of frigid air.

Ezra Batchwell was the first to enter, stamping his snowy boots.

"What was so important that you found it necessary to call an early meeting, Ramsey?"

"Some staffing issues, sir."

Batchwell opened his mouth as if to continue his tirade, but at that moment, he must have caught a whiff of the tantalizing aromas, so he merely grunted.

Bottoms, with his halo of pure white, candy-floss hair, sidled past Batchwell, his nose already twitching.

"What's that I smell?"

"Breakfast," Ramsey said, leaning to open the door to the private dining room. "Stumpy made a few changes this morning."

Bottoms rubbed his hands together and chortled. "'Bout time, I'd say."

He disappeared inside, and Batchwell, still making soft grumbling noises under his breath, followed.

Jonah leaned close to Creakle. "Go to the kitchen and get the plates. I don't want them catching sight of the women until *after* they've eaten."

Creakle grinned and saluted. "Sounds good to me."

As Creakle hurried down the hall in his arthritic, uneven gait, Jonah turned to join them. But as soon as he cleared the threshold, he feared that the secret may have already been revealed. The room had been cleaned and polished to the brilliance of the Pearly Gates. A linen cloth had been placed over the table and all the cutlery, glasses and mugs had been arranged to perfection. A platter of muffins waited from a nest made by a crisp linen napkin, and a crock of sweet butter was by its side. There was even an old cracked pitcher filled with fragrant pine branches gracing the center of the table.

Bottoms appeared oblivious to the improvements, but Batchwell eyed it all with open suspicion.

"Stumpy's changed his crew," Jonah said, not quite meeting the man's eyes. He gestured for the man to sit. Then, before the other man could ask any questions, he said, "Have you given any more thought to tunnel three?

I think it's about played out, but I want your opinion before I start reassigning the men to other areas."

"I think that we should all be congratulated," Iona remarked as the line of miners finally gave way to a few stragglers looking for a meal.

Lydia laughed, wiping a hand over her brow. "We still have some flaws to our system, but overall, I'd say the morning was a smashing success!"

While Stefania and Marie handled the last few plates of food, Sumner and the other women huddled nervously near the doorway.

"I can't believe I'm about to say this," Lydia said wryly, "but I'm almost looking forward to a few quiet hours in the hall."

"Ideally, we should be getting a start on the lunchtime preparations," Iona said, plunking wearily onto a nearby stool." She leaned forward to speak in a conspiratorial whisper. "Any word from the men in charge?"

Sumner shook her head. For the past hour, they'd kept an ear turned toward the doorway to the private dining room, hoping that their efforts would be rewarded. True, it was hard work preparing food for that many men. They'd barely begun to wind down the breakfast service, and it was time to begin cutting the cold meats and cheeses that would be supplied for the miners' work buckets.

"They'd be foolish not to accept our help," Willow murmured. "We've done a good job this morning—and most of the other brides have already volunteered for the different shifts."

"A sampling of your biscuits should be enough to persuade them," Sumner said, making the shy woman blush.

Lydia grinned. "And judging by the number of men

who've thanked us, the entire adventure has been a rousing success. I don't know about you all, but I don't like being indebted to someone. And since we're using the company stores, I feel a lot better having contributed." She chuckled. "As well as getting out of that dreary hall for a few hours."

Sumner glanced impatiently at her fob watch. Her duties as a doctor were still needed by those who'd suffered more serious injuries, and she was keeping her eye on Jenny Reichman and another pregnant woman. But she was so anxious about the conversation being held in the private dining room that she couldn't bring herself to leave.

As if on cue, Creakle appeared. "Mr. Batchwell and Mr. Bottoms are needing more coffee, if you've got some." He grinned. "Mr. Ramsey told me to give you the go-ahead to come do it yerself, Miss Havisham, if you've a mind to do so."

"Of course."

She rushed to the enamel pots on the stove, nearly burning herself in her haste to comply. Wrapping the handle with a dishcloth, she grabbed the heavy vessel and followed Creakle.

As soon as she entered the room, she could feel Batchwell's gaze on her like a brand. He sucked in a slow breath, his face growing mottled. If Sumner didn't know such a thing was anatomically impossible, she would have expected steam to emerge from his ears. Bottoms, on the other hand, leaned back in his chair, his eyes half-closed, his fingers laced over his stomach.

Nerves swirled in her chest like a colony of startled bats. As she leaned forward to fill the mugs, her hands were shaking so hard that she feared she would spill most of it on the table. But at that moment, she glanced up, and although Ramsey remained stone-faced, she thought she saw him wink.

Once she'd topped the cups, she hesitated, wondering if she was just meant to show herself, or if she were required to say something. But it was Batchwell who spoke.

"I suppose that you're responsible for these machinations."

"Machinations?" she echoed, deciding that there was no point in admitting that for a moment she'd considered the fact that the kitchens might be the best way to curry favor.

"I suppose you thought this would be a means for you and your women to wriggle their way past the Pinkertons."

Sumner knew that it wouldn't pay to admit that the women had managed to get past the Pinkertons once before, so she merely widened her eyes in feigned innocence.

"Sir?"

"Come, Miss Havisham. Don't be coy. I've no doubt that you and your women intend to use your time in the cook shack to finagle a proposal out of a bunch of hapless miners."

Sumner couldn't help herself. She laughed. "Believe it or not, Mr. Batchwell. 'My women' as you call them, have no designs on your miners." He scowled in open disbelief, so she continued. "Most of the women who volunteered to help today are already engaged to men farther west."

He snorted. "Really, Miss Havisham. A bird in the hand…"

"Mr. Batchwell," she interjected. "These women came here today with little more on their minds than to thank your men for the way they came to our rescue after the avalanche. They realize that our being stranded here has put a strain on your resources. To put it succinctly, the women felt beholden to your hospitality, no matter how grudgingly it might have been offered."

At that, Batchwell shifted uncomfortably, but she thought the sleepy Bottoms's lips twitched ever so slightly in amusement.

"I don't know about you, but most people don't like being indebted to someone else. So, the women decided to find a way to offer something back."

She paused, knowing she was straying into dangerous territory, but she wouldn't allow their actions to be misconstrued as some sort of…amorous manipulation.

"To be quite blunt, Mr. Batchwell, the samples we had of your men's cooking were…awful. We thought you might appreciate it if we could remedy that fact."

"Hear, hear!"

The soft agreement came from Bottoms. His eyes blinked open. This time there was no disguising the twinkle in his eyes and the lilt to his voice.

"I, for one, am grateful to the women for their fine Christian sentiments. Stumpy's a hard worker, but he's never been much of a cook—and there isn't a man who works with him who can claim anything different." Bottoms stretched, then pushed himself to his feet. "Thank you, Miss Havisham. And thank the other ladies. If you're willing to help us, it would be miserly indeed to refuse that help."

Batchwell began to sputter, but Bottoms turned his attention to his partner. "Enough of your complaining. I can't remember when I've had a better meal—certainly not in this valley. And since I'm part owner of this mining property, I say they can continue to cook as long as they have a mind to do so. Really, Ezra. They'll be so busy that they won't have time to say 'boo' to anyone. Now get up and quit yer bellyachin'. We've got work to do."

Batchwell continued to grumble, but he didn't bother to speak directly to Sumner—which she supposed meant that she and the other women would be allowed to continue what they'd begun.

Batchwell stomped from the room, throwing open the side door and allowing a swirl of cold air to whirl around Sumner's ankles. But before he left, Bottoms took some time to settle his hat over his white head with great deliberation. Then he looked up, his eyes twinkling with inner glee.

"Miss Havisham, will you pass on my thanks to your companions?"

"Of course, Mr. Bottoms."

"And if you think of it, you might want to mention to them that I'm fond of pie."

She smiled. "Any particular kind?"

"The sweet kind," he whispered conspiratorially.

Jonah waited until he heard the door close behind Bottoms before standing himself. As he reached for his hat, he felt as if he'd just won a race and a celebration was in order. If anything, having the women at the cook shack would complicate matters even more. Despite Dr. Havisham's reassurances that the women had no designs on the miners' affections, he'd already been told to increase the number of Pinkertons serving as their guards. "For their protection," Batchwell insisted.

Jonah fought the urge to snort. From what he'd gathered so far, it wasn't the women who needed the protecting. They were proving that they could take care of themselves.

Sumner's breath escaped in a whoosh and her shoulders lost some of their steel.

"I don't know if I should congratulate you or not," he said. "You and the other women have signed up for a challenging chore."

Her gaze was soft and uninhibited when she looked at him—and he was struck by her unguarded joy. "Yes, but it's a fulfilling task."

Jonah couldn't help working the brim of his hat with his hands. "Is that the way you think of your doctoring, as well?"

She nodded. "It *means* something."

"I'm sure that there are women who would say the same thing about being a wife and mother."

Her eyes widened. "I didn't mean for you to think that I thought running a home wasn't important and satisfying. All in all, those roles are probably more important in many ways. But…"

He waited as she gathered her thoughts.

"You know that Scripture, 'To every thing there is a season'?"

He nodded. It was one of his favorite passages.

"I strongly believe that sentiment to be true. And I think that, if we are mindful, the Lord will help us know how to use the gifts He's given us."

"So you're not against being a wife and mother yourself?"

The moment the words were uttered, he wished he could retrieve them. Not only was the question incredibly personal, but they brought an intimate warmth to the room that hadn't been there before.

Silence floated around them before she said, "I would dearly love to be a wife and mother." She paused before adding, "Someday. But…"

"But?"

She sighed, looking down at the pot that she still held in her hands.

"Not all of us are given that blessing. Some of us are destined to live alone."

Somehow, he knew that the statement held unfathomable depths. Did that mean that she didn't think that she would ever be given the opportunity? Or that it wasn't something she would welcome.

"And your doctoring…would you give it up?"

Again, he was sure that he'd said the wrong thing because her eyes became stormy. "Will you give up your mining once you decide to marry, Mr. Ramsey?"

Knowing he had to diffuse what was obviously a tender subject to her, he offered her a quick smile. "Of course. At least here in Aspen Valley. No women are allowed, remember?"

Thankfully, her touchiness subsided and she returned his smile with a rueful grimace. "I suppose you're right. I'd forgotten for a moment where I was."

Once again, the room lapsed into silence, and for once, Jonah wished he were the kind of man who knew how to engage a woman in casual conversation. But he'd never been that good at small talk. Even Rebecca had despaired of his silences, thinking that when he grew quiet, she'd somehow displeased him.

But nothing could have been farther from the truth.

He'd loved Rebecca.

But his love hadn't been enough.

Jerking his mind away from that train of thought, he settled his hat onto his head with great care, then said, "Will you be staying here at the cook shack much longer?"

She shook her head. "I need to see to the wounded at the hall."

He nodded. "I've got my own work to get back to, as well." He cleared his throat. "If it's agreeable to you, I'll drop by in a few hours and take you to see the storehouse."

Silence.

But then she nodded, saying softly, "I think that would be very agreeable, Mr. Ramsey." She glanced at the doorway, saw that they were still alone and said, "Jonah."

How he loved the way she said his name!

"Your ankles are a bit more swollen than I'd like them to be, Jenny." Sumner touched the woman's hand. "I want you to rest today and keep your feet up. I've collected some broth from the cook shack, and I'd like you to have a cup every hour. We want to give your baby plenty of nourishment."

"Thank you, Doctor."

Jenny's fingers fiddled with the fabric of her day gown, drawing even more attention to the swell of her stomach.

Sumner eyed the woman in concern. Although Jenny showed no signs of labor yet, the baby was bound to be quite large.

"Relax and enjoy your leisure. You have plenty of women to wait on you, and you'll be busy with that baby soon enough."

Jenny offered her a weak smile and closed her eyes.

Sumner crept from the room. She'd spent more than an hour with her patients, changing bandages, adjusting splints and simply taking the time to talk and listen to each person's concerns. But with her early start at the cook shack, her energy was flagging.

She paused in front of a small hand mirror that someone had hung over a washbasin and pitcher. The moment she saw her reflection she groaned in embarrassment. Why hadn't anyone told her that she looked such a sight? Had she really faced Batchwell and Bottoms with her face dusted with flour and a streak of icing across her cheek?

Knowing that Jonah could arrive at any moment, she quickly washed her face. Then she unpinned her hair, combed it, then arranged an elaborate coil of braids to the back of her head. Unfortunately, after checking her reflection one last time, she decided that the skirt and blouse she wore looked rumpled, so she dived into the depths of her trunk to choose another gown.

Twenty minutes later, she emerged from one of the upper rooms that she shared with Iona, Lydia, Willow and the twins, Myra and Miriam Claussen. Not wishing to give Mr. Ramsey the wrong impression, she'd chosen a maroon woolen skirt and basque bodice—one that covered her from neck to wrists to floor.

"Very nice," Lydia commented when Sumner appeared at the top of the stairs.

"Mr. Ramsey said he would be taking me to see the storehouse," Sumner offered. She didn't want the women to think she'd changed for Jonah. "Once he does, we can start making lists of possible menus."

"The information will be helpful." Lydia paused before adding, "You look very…professional."

There was a note of humor to Lydia's tone that made Sumner wonder if she'd gone too far. She'd taken great care to ensure that there was nothing about her toilette that could give the impression that she intended "to lead a man on" as Batchwell had accused the women of doing. Maybe she should have worn one of her work dresses instead.

Iona looked up from her needlepoint. "You look beautiful. The braid trim is very fetching."

Drat.

She was going to have to change.

But before she could turn around, there was a knock on the main door and Marie Rousseau rushed to open it.

Even though Sumner could see little more than Jonah's silhouette against the brightness, she knew the moment that he saw her. She felt the power of his gaze. She fought to remain calm.

No.

She'd never been a woman who was prone to fits of fancy—or even the giggling whispers that some ladies exchanged when a handsome man entered the room. She'd always been too practical and focused on her education and goals to give such nonsense any heed. But she suddenly felt as light-headed and twitter-pated as an ingenue at a ball.

And she hated balls.

What was happening to her? Was this a by-product of being told that she couldn't officially practice medicine?

No. That couldn't be the case. Even though she'd been forbidden to take care of the miners, she'd spent the past few days tending to those who had been injured in the avalanche.

So why couldn't she put these odd feelings to rest?

Knowing that she'd stood rooted in place for far too long to appear casual, Sumner forced her limbs to move. But her knees continued to tremble far too tellingly.

As she approached the door, Jonah seemed to remember himself and scooped his hat from his head. The glare danced over the tousled waves of his hair, and Sumner wondered what he would do if she reached to smooth them into place.

"Is this a convenient time for you to check the storehouse, Dr. Havisham?"

"Yes. Thank you."

A pile of coats and hats had been left on a narrow bench by the door, and Sumner quickly found her own. She pinned her bonnet to the braids on her head and tied the ribbon beneath her chin. But when she would have reached for her coat, Jonah took it first, holding it up for her.

The gesture was gentlemanly, but hardly personal. So why did she become so incredibly conscious of the brush of his fingers before he stepped away and gestured to the bright patch of sunshine?

"After you," he murmured. Then he offered a nod to the other women. "Ladies. Have a good afternoon."

"Good afternoon to you, too, Mr. Ramsey!" Lydia called out cheekily.

As they strode down the boardwalk, Sumner took deep gulps of the frosty air. Honestly, she couldn't fathom what was wrong with her. Maybe the bump she'd received on the head during the accident had been more serious than she'd at first supposed. Already, the bruise around the gash was beginning to fade, turning from a mottled shade of black to a sickly yellow. She'd been so sure that she would escape the avalanche with nothing more than a tiny scar to show for it. But she was beginning to believe that maybe something had been jostled loose in her brain.

"You've had quite an effect on the men."

"What?" She blinked at Jonah in confusion.

"You and the other women. I've heard nothing but praise for you and the food you cooked."

"I'm so glad."

"Early reports for today are saying that production in the mine is up slightly. I would wager that the good food has been a major contributor. That should help to support your position that the women are providing a real service."

If only it would also bolster her argument about being allowed to serve as mine physician.

"Maybe now he'll agree to get rid of our Pinkerton guards."

Jonah grimaced. "Don't count on it. I've been told that a pair of Pinkertons are supposed to stay at the cook shack whenever any of you are there."

Sumner stopped in her tracks to gape at him. "You've got to be joking."

He shook his head—and it was obvious that he regretted the fact that he'd said anything. "They've already been given their orders—and not by me. Batchwell went straight over my head and made the arrangements with Gideon Gault himself."

An old familiar frustration began to twine in Sumner's chest. "Honestly. If he'd bothered to watch any of them work, he would have seen that the women don't have time to do anything but cook. And clean. Some of your men have forgotten their manners after being on their own for so long."

To her surprise, Jonah didn't argue. Instead, he nodded. "That, without a doubt, is a true statement. We've all been away from the…gentler influences of society."

His admission had the uncanny effect of draining away her anger, leaving her…unnerved.

"So you admit that the lack of women in the community does have its costs?"

He paused a moment before saying, "Of course. Women have the ability to soften life's rough edges, to encourage civility, to…make some of its tragedies more bearable."

"So why do you all insist on such an antiquated rule?"

"Because—as glorious as those effects can be—none of them are worth a human life. Mining is dark, dirty and dangerous work. A man's got to keep his wits about him every second he's down there. Women are a distraction. You may not like that fact—you might not even want to admit that such a statement is true. But I've seen enough men die in my life that I'm determined not to let another one go. Not on my watch."

His voice rang with such conviction that Sumner couldn't bring herself to argue.

Whom had he seen die? How many?

Suddenly, his loyalty to Batchwell and Bottoms took on new meaning. It wasn't just the job or the silver being wrestled from the ground that was important to Jonah Ramsey. He sincerely cared about his men.

And how could she mount a campaign against that?

Chapter Eight

Thankfully, Sumner was saved from any kind of response because Jonah stopped in front of a large square building.

"This is it."

Glancing up the road, Sumner saw that they'd come a fair distance from the cook shack. In fact, they'd reached the far end of the row of structures that made up the main street of the mine. If she or the other women needed something, they wouldn't be fetching it quickly.

Jonah took the familiar ring of keys from his vest pocket and began to unlatch the padlock. "Don't worry. You can send one of the men to haul back what you need." Then he suddenly grinned. "Send one of the Pinkertons, if you like."

His smile was so real, so unexpected, that it hit her square in the chest and she couldn't help laughing. "I'm sure that would go over well with Mr. Batchwell."

The grin stayed firmly in place on Jonah's face, crinkling at the corners of his eyes and causing them to sparkle in a way that was more blue than brown. "That hasn't stopped you so far."

She wasn't sure if that was meant as a compliment or a

criticism. But as he tugged on a heavy door that seemed more appropriate for a livery stable than a storage facility, she was soon distracted.

Inside, the building was dim and cold. A lantern and a match safe hung from a rack nearby and Jonah quickly lit the wick, then adjusted the flame to give them as much light as possible. Then he held it high and led her into the cavernous depths.

Sumner soon surmised that the huge doors had an obvious function when she saw that crates had been stacked from floor to ceiling, interspersed now and again by narrow aisles. Neat tags had been tacked to each one of the boxes and a shaking script proclaimed the contents: nails, kerosene, sulfur, dynamite.

Dynamite?

"You store your foodstuffs alongside the explosives?" The alarm she felt echoed into the dimness.

"Not exactly. You'll want to avoid that area. Especially with an open flame."

Sumner eyed the lantern in concern, but Jonah was already turning down another aisle. Here, the labels became more mundane—shovels, picks, hammers—then another slight jog where heavy sacks had been piled on wooden shelves—flour, sugar, salt—and even bigger sacks with rice, beans and oats. Farther on, there were barrels of molasses, crocks of pickles and smaller canisters of bicarbonate and yeast.

"We've tried to think of everything—corn meal, wheat, barley." He pointed to another door. "In there, we've hung most of the fresh game as well as smoked and salted meats." He turned a corner to reveal shelves filled with wooden barrels. "In these, you'll find dried apples, cherries, raisins and apricots." On the opposite side, he gestured to huge wooden bins. "Over there, we've got potatoes, turnips and what's left of the squash and pumpkin."

At long last, he stopped. "If you can't find what you need, send for me or Creakle. He has his own filing system. You could also get Willoughby Smalls to help. He works in the livery. Since he helps Creakle store everything, he knows where to look."

Sumner turned a slow circle. She'd never seen so much food gathered together in one place before. But then, she'd never had to consider feeding two hundred or more men through the winter, either.

"Do you have a written inventory somewhere so we know how much is available?"

Jonah nodded. "Creakle is a fanatic about his numbers. I'll have him come meet with you later today." His mouth opened, as if he'd been about to say something, then he closed it again.

Her mood threatened to plummet. Was there something he wasn't telling her? Yet another dire edict passed down from the owners?

"Is there something else we should know?"

"No. I mean…it doesn't concern the other women… but…" Again, he hesitated. "It's just that Creakle won't bring it up himself and…"

Sumner waited patiently, afraid that if she said something, Jonah wouldn't confide in her.

"You might want to ask about his feet."

Her brow creased.

"His feet?"

"His right foot—toe, actually. He rearranged the office a while back and he dropped a filing cabinet on his toe. He was looking forward to having a doctor take a look at it."

A male doctor.

"But I know it's paining him."

The familiar frustration she felt at being compared to her male counterparts seeped away when she realized that Jonah was asking for her help.

"I'd be happy to examine him."

"Perhaps I could have him meet you in the infirmary later today. If he's in the proper setting, maybe he'll agree to take off his boot."

"I think that would be a grand idea."

"Excellent."

As the silence pulsed around them, it was clear that their business together was finished. But he appeared loath to move.

And she was glad.

So glad.

"Do you like your work, Sumner? Being a doctor, I mean."

She nodded. "Very much."

"And your family…they must admire you."

She could have offered a blithe answer or vague platitudes. But for some reason, she couldn't bring herself to lie. Not with Jonah.

Lacing her hands together, she avoided his gaze. "Not exactly. My…father did not approve."

When she glanced up, she saw only an echo of her own sadness in Jonah's eyes. "That must have been difficult for you."

"You've no idea. He did everything in his power to try to dissuade me from pursuing my career. He threatened, cajoled…" She hesitated before trusting him with the worst of it. "He even locked me in my room at one point."

Jonah's eyes blazed. "For how long?"

"Six weeks," she admitted hesitantly.

"His own daughter?"

She offered a dark laugh. "He was worried about appearances. 'No daughter of mine will be seen acting like a man,'" Sumner said in her best impression of her father's deep baritone. She grimaced. "He thought that by locking me away I'd 'come to my senses.'"

"So what did you do?"

"I tried to escape, which didn't work."

"And then?"

Her chin tilted in remembered defiance.

"I refused to eat. Soon, it became apparent that I'd starve to death before I'd give up on my dreams. I guess he decided that the talk of my death would be worse than the talk of my disappearance. So he allowed me to go away—" her voice dropped to a whisper "—as long as I promised that I wouldn't come back."

"Oh, Sumner..."

Jonah's voice held such tenderness that tears pricked at her eyes. But she refused to give in to them. She hadn't cried about leaving her family in a very long time and she didn't intend to start now.

"It's not a Shakespearean tragedy. We both got what we wanted. I began my training in London, then later moved to Bristol to work, leaving him to focus all his time and energies on my half brothers."

Because he loved them more.

He'd always loved them more.

Because they were male.

She didn't know how it happened. One moment she was being pummeled by her inner demons. In the next, Jonah had set the lantern on a keg of dried apples, then drawn her to him, encircling her in the warmth and strength of his arms.

Sumner knew she should draw away. No good could come from being this close to Jonah Ramsey. It would merely rile up the confusing emotions that were already sweeping through her like an avalanche. But her body moved of its own volition, her arms winding around his waist, her head tucking beneath his chin. Beneath her ear, the steady thump of his heart reminded her that she was thousands of miles away from her father. She was in the midst of the Utah wilderness, embroiled in an adventure unlike any that she'd ever encountered before.

And she felt safe.

"He was wrong," Jonah murmured against the top of her head. "Your father should have been proud of you."

The words were a balm to her soul. Sumner didn't bother to analyze why the insight of a stranger had the ability to offer her such comfort. For once, she allowed herself to close her eyes and embrace this man, this moment.

But all too soon, reality intruded when a voice called from the main door, "Boss man, you in there?"

Creakle. Sumner could have recognized his distinctive rusty-sounding voice anywhere.

Jonah didn't immediately speak; instead, he slowly stepped away.

Sumner couldn't bring herself to meet his gaze. Not yet. Not so soon. But she needn't have worried. When she sneaked a peek at his face, Jonah kept his gaze averted, as well.

"Be right there, Creakle."

He reached for his ring of keys, removing two of different sizes. "One of these is for the storehouse, the other is for the doctor's office. I'll see what he needs, then let Creakle walk you back."

"That would be grand. I'll examine him at the infirmary along the way."

His eyes smiled even though his lips remained straight.

"That would be grand, as well," he offered, borrowing her phrase.

Yet, he didn't move. Not for several very long moments.

"Perhaps I'll see you at dinner."

"Perhaps."

She hadn't planned on joining the evening shift, but now she was considering it.

Jonah touched his finger to the brim of his hat and backed away.

"Good day to you, then, Sumner."

"And to you, Jonah."

As soon as she'd heard Jonah's footfalls disappear into the shadows, Sumner grasped the lantern and hurried to meet up with Creakle. To her delight, Willoughby Smalls was also waiting on the boardwalk. As soon as he met her gaze, the large man swept the hat from his head, crushing it against his chest in a gentlemanly greeting.

"Good evening, Mr. Creakle, Mr. Smalls. Jonah has been showing me your storehouse." After locking the door, they began walking toward the center of the mining camp. But midway to the infirmary, Sumner changed her mind about examining Creakle in the doctor's office. The rooms had been shut up for some time. It would be cold and drafty inside—and the previous occupant had left nothing useful in the way of medical equipment.

Shooting a glance at Creakle under her lashes, Sumner said, "Mr. Creakle, I wonder if you would allow me to impose upon you and Mr. Smalls for a favor."

They had been walking in an awkward silence, but at her query, Creakle brightened, finally meeting her gaze.

"It would be our pleasure, Miss Havisham."

Sumner had to bite her tongue to keep from reminding him that her title was *Dr.* Havisham.

"Mr. Ramsey took me to the infirmary to gather supplies last night, and I managed to fill an old crate. But it's too heavy for me to manage. Could you or Mr. Smalls carry it back to the hall for me?"

Creakle grinned and his cheeks grew pink. "Consider it done."

It took only a few minutes to retrieve the crate. Smalls hefted it into his arms as if it weighed no more than a hatbox, then they continued on their way to the hall.

"Are you sure that the box isn't too heavy, Mr. Smalls? We could leave some things, then come back for them."

He shook his head, beaming at her.

But as they closed the last few yards, Creakle's breath came in soft pants and a pronounced limp became apparent. Sumner could see the man wincing with each step, and she was glad that Mr. Smalls was able to handle the supplies by himself.

Sumner quickly ushered the men inside—and the sight of visitors after an afternoon spent cooped up in the hall had the women rushing to help.

Just as Sumner had hoped, they offered the men tea and cookies and insisted they sit near the stove to warm up.

The pink in Creakle's cheeks turned to red, but he appeared to enjoy the fussing. Even Smalls grinned in delight. Sumner waited until the men were comfortably settled before saying, "Are you sure the box wasn't too heavy for you, Mr. Smalls?"

The gentle giant shook his head. A fragile teacup and saucer looked impossibly delicate in his ham-like fists.

"And, Mr. Creakle, I couldn't help noticing that you were limping."

He'd just taken a mouthful of cookie, so he waved dismissingly until he'd chewed enough to say, "I injured my foot some time ago, ma'am."

The other women oohed and ahhed in concern, just as Sumner had hoped they would.

"Would you mind if I took a look at it? As a doctor?"

Creakle's pleasure dimmed, but when he saw that everyone was watching him expectantly, he nodded.

Sumner turned to Willow, saying, "Could you gather my bag from upstairs while I fetch some warm water?"

"Of course."

Willow gathered her voluminous skirts and hurried up the staircase.

Sumner retrieved one of the washbasins, filling it with hot water from the teakettle, and a little from the freshwater basin. Then she carried them back to the table. As she did so, she could see that a group of women had gathered around Willoughby Smalls and plied him with more cookies and fresh tea. It didn't seem to matter that Mr. Smalls didn't speak. Rather, Myra and Miriam seemed to find his familiar face reassuring.

"Mr. Smalls, if you had a bride heading your way, and the train didn't show up as expected, would you wait for the woman in question, sensing that something had happened?" Myra asked.

"Or would you think she'd abandoned the whole idea?" Miriam pressed.

Smalls looked nonplussed for a moment, then awkwardly balanced his saucer in one hand and reached to pat Miriam on the shoulder.

"You see, Miriam. I told you that they'd realize something was wrong. They might even inquire with the railroad."

"Which railroad, Myra? We took three different lines to get this far!"

"Well, they're bound to notice if one is missing."

Kneeling in front of Creakle, Sumner removed his boot and his sock, offering a soft tutting sound when she was able to expose the bruised and infected toe.

"Mr. Creakle. What happened?"

He regarded her sheepishly. "Dropped a filin' cabinet square on the thing."

"Thankfully, you just caught the toe. Something like that could have broken your foot."

At her subtle reassurance that she didn't find his injury inconsequential, he settled back in his chair.

Willow appeared at that moment and Sumner removed a bottle of salts from her bag. "I'd like to have you soak your foot for a little while. Would that be agreeable to you?"

He nodded, his gaze sweeping around the room and the women who were eager to dote on him. He even shot an envious glance at Smalls, who was listening raptly to the twins.

"So I said we should become mail-order brides, and Myra said—"

"We should find ourselves a set of twins!"

"So that's what we did!"

Creakle dragged his attention back to Sumner. "If you think I should."

She sprinkled the crystals into the water. "These are some mineral salts boiled down from spa waters near Bristol. I've found that they have a healing effect, especially with infection."

She gently eased his foot from the floor into the water. Creakle hissed, but when one of the women topped off his teacup, he was easily distracted, allowing Sumner to probe the toe.

"I don't think you've broken a bone, Mr. Creakle, but we'll need to treat the swelling and the infection."

"Yes, ma'am."

"I'll give you a little bag of my special salts. After I've shown you how to soak the afflicted area, I want you to do the same treatment on your own at least twice a day. More, if you have the time."

He nodded.

"Keep the water as hot as you can bear."

"Yes, Doctor."

The spontaneous use of the title brought a jolt of pleasure. *This* was why she'd come to Bachelor Bottoms.

For the first time, she felt a spark of hope. If she could help Creakle, it might encourage others to come to her with their ailments. It would simply take time.

Sumner had never been much good at taking things slow. She tended to race in and try to get things done. But she was beginning to realize that to change the human heart, a person couldn't hurry things.

She smiled up at Creakle and he blinked at her.

"Is that all?" he asked. Obviously, he'd expected direr treatment, perhaps even an amputation.

"That's all. You'll be good as new in no time."

Jonah knew the instant that Creakle returned—how could he have missed it with the man whistling a jaunty tune and slamming the door behind him with enough force to make the windows shudder? Then he called out, "Howdy, boys!"

The murmured responses were too low for Jonah to hear. He glanced at the clock, seeing that it was nearly five. They'd be due at the evening Devotional soon enough.

"Creakle seems mighty chipper," Gideon Gault said. The Pinkerton was sprawled in one of the chairs opposite Jonah's desk.

The man was dressed in his Pinkerton blues for the first time in weeks. Since the man had become a close friend, Jonah was glad to see him up and about. But since Gideon had come to protest the use of his men for "guarding the womenfolk," Jonah was ready for an interruption.

"Hopefully, that means that the man let the doc look at his toe."

Gideon's brows rose. "You're encouraging it?"

"I'm sick of his complaining. I mentioned it to Sumner and suggested she might want to take a look at it."

Gideon's lips twitched. "*Sumner.* Seems you're getting on well with the woman."

Jonah shook his head. "Just being cordial, that's all."

"Uh-huh."

They were interrupted by an uneven set of footfalls climbing the steps. Then Creakle appeared in the doorway. For the amount of time he'd been gone, Jonah had begun to fear that Creakle had refused to have his foot examined at all—or the injury had been worse than he'd let on. But Creakle seemed to be in fine spirits.

"Hey, Gideon!"

"Creakle."

"It's about time you came back," Jonah grumbled. Unaccountably, he was feeling grouchy and out of sorts. The day couldn't pass fast enough—something of a rarity for Jonah. Usually, he found no need to glance at the clock because the job was everything. But today...

"Me an' Smalls helped the doc lug some supplies

back to the hall," Creakle said as he took the seat next to Gideon.

Jonah tossed his pencil onto the desk and leaned back in his chair. "Looks to me like you've been sampling some of their cooking, as well." He gestured to the crumbs sprinkling Creakle's coat.

The man chortled. "They bake some mighty fine cookies. Next time, I'll have to bring you some."

"You're pretty pleased with yourself," Gideon remarked, and Jonah was grateful that the other man had been the one to subtly ply the man for information.

Creakle's expression became positively smug.

"The doc done looked at my toe an' it's feelin' much better."

Jonah tried to look surprised. "That was kind of her."

"T'weren't just kind. She's the company doctor."

"What did she say?"

"T'weren't broken, but it was plumb mortified, just like I feared. She showed me how t' soak it an' gave me some special powder t' put in the water."

Jonah nodded. "Sounds like good advice."

"'Course it is. The woman's a doctor, isn't she?" Creakle slapped the arm of the chair and stood. "Best be getting back to my work." He stomped to the door, but paused before disappearing altogether. "Mebbe you should have the lady look at yer back."

Jonah scowled.

"Couldn't hurt y' none."

"Get back to work," he growled.

It didn't help that he could hear Creakle chortling all the way downstairs.

Couldn't hurt y' none.

But Creakle was wrong. There was nothing she could

do for him. Not because she was a woman, but because there was nothing anyone could do for him.

"He's right, you know. The woman's newly trained—at some fancy place in London, no less. She might have some up-to-date techniques."

Other than Creakle, Smalls, Batchwell and Bottoms, Gideon was the only other person in Batchwell Bottoms who knew about the injuries Jonah had sustained. As an ex-soldier, Gideon understood better than most how the shrapnel pressing against his spine hung over Jonah like a loaded gun. The two of them had actually served together in the same cavalry unit for several years during the war.

"She's a *baby* doctor," Jonah insisted half-heartedly.

Gideon waved that comment away. "She seems capable enough." He laughed. "She's given Batchwell a run for his money." His expression lost its humor. "It might be worth a try. Then you could finally put the past behind you."

Jonah sighed, scrubbing his face with his hands as the old, familiar desperation threatened to overtake him. Unbidden came the remembered horrors of the battlefield.

Though he fought the sensation, his pulse grew fast, thudding against his temples.

And his back.

He had no real recollection of the moment he'd been hit. He remembered ordering a charge and urging his mount into a gallop. Then...

He was in a field hospital, laid out on his stomach, the rough wood of an old door his makeshift stretcher. He'd been pinned there for hours, unable to move, until finally, the surgeon had come to pull the pieces of scattershot from his back with an old pair of pliers.

He'd been shipped home soon after. Spent weeks on his stomach, praying that he'd be able to walk again. And he had, in time. But not before he'd been told that several pieces of metal were still lodged next to his spine. To attempt to remove them would be too dangerous, so the shards of metal continued to plague him, a silent threat to his future.

No. Not just his.

"You can't keep pining after Rebecca," Gideon said softly.

"I'm not pining."

"Maybe that's the wrong word. Maybe it's more like torturing yourself."

Jonah shook his head. "Now you're talking nonsense."

"Am I? Sometimes I think you put the memory of that woman up on a pedestal. And from my point of view, she doesn't belong there. Any woman who would look down on a man for what you've been through—"

"That's unkind."

"Is it? Oh, I'll admit she was a dutiful fiancée. She convinced her parents to take you into their home so she could dote on you. She lavished you with smiles and trays of goodies. For a week or two, she sat by your bed and promised her affection for you was eternal. But then she saw your scars."

Jonah clenched his jaw, wishing that his friend didn't know so much. Gideon had heard it all, right up to that point where Becca claimed she had a maiden aunt who needed a visit. Jonah had never seen her again. Within a week, he'd moved out of her parents' home.

"That's not love, Jonah. That's not even affection. I'd wager that if you thought about it really hard, you might see what the rest of us suspected. Rebecca was a fickle creature. She loved the idea of love, but she didn't really understand it."

Jonah debated several long moments before saying,

"She did what she had to do. Not everyone can live with an uncertain future."

Gideon sighed. "That's a load of hogwash. We all live with uncertain futures, Jonah. That's what makes life exciting." With that, Gideon pushed himself to his feet and headed toward the stairs calling, "Creakle, where can I get me some of those cookies!"

Jonah did his best to return to work, to add up the figures in the ledgers laid out on his desk. But when the numbers became jumbled and his brain couldn't seem to remember how to perform the simplest sums, he stood so quickly that his chair rocked back on two legs before skidding into place again. Grabbing his hat and coat from where he'd left them on the corner of his desk, he stormed from the office, not knowing where he was going, but needing to escape the memories.

It had been years, after all.

He hardly ever thought about her anymore. She'd married someone else.

His best friend.

He quickened his pace, his breath hanging in front of him like a crystal cloud. Mindlessly, he strode down the boardwalk, not seeing where he was going or who might be in his way, until his lungs ached with the cold and his back had begun to burn. It wasn't until he'd reached the storehouse at the far end of the road that he began to slow. His eyes fell on the door and he scowled, seeing that it was ajar.

Finally, he had a target for the anger that swirled within him. The door should be locked at all times, and he had only himself to blame. He should have retrieved his key from Sumner some time ago—or at least checked to make sure that she'd locked it.

The women had only been here a short time, and they

were already having their effect on Bachelor Bottoms. The men were going about their business with mindless grins on their faces, Creakle was giggling like a school-boy and Jonah...

Jonah was forgetting what was important.

No matter what happened, the job would always be there.

It had been the thing that had pulled him through one of the darkest moments of his life, and it would be the only thing that remained. No woman was worth what the job could give him.

So why was that thought suddenly so...unsatisfying?

He was reaching to pull at the handle when the door suddenly widened and Sumner Havisham darted out, nearly mowing him down.

Jonah automatically reached out to steady her.

"Oh!"

One of her hands flew to his chest to keep her from stumbling forward. And even through the layers of his clothing and the red kid gloves she wore, he could feel her warmth.

"Dr. Havisham."

Her laughter was soft and rueful. "So sorry." She held up a cotton sack cinched tight with a drawstring. "I for-got to get the apples for Mr. Bottoms's pie. Could you hold this?"

He automatically took the sack and she turned, lock-ing the door behind her.

In that instant, his anger and frustration fizzled, and he was instantly ashamed. When he'd seen the open door, he'd been quick to assign blame without even considering the fact that there could be a logical reason.

He heard the weighty *thunk* of the lock hitting home, then saw the way Sumner tugged on the padlock to ensure that it had latched properly. Then she held out the two keys he'd given her earlier that day. Somehow, in the intervening hours, she'd tied them with a ribbon to ensure that they wouldn't get lost. The sight of his utilitarian keys being kept in place with a length of blue silk tugged at his heart.

"Do you need these?"

Only moments earlier, Jonah had been ready to demand that she return them, but now, he realized that such measures would be counterproductive. The women would need access to the storehouse, and Sumner had proven to be more than responsible with them.

"No. I've got another set."

She nodded and tucked them into her coat pocket, then reached for the sack.

Jonah subtly moved them out of her reach. "I'll carry them back to the cook shack for you."

"If you're sure?"

He gestured for her to precede him, then fell into step beside her. They walked in companionable silence before he said, "Weren't you supposed to have a Pinkerton with you?"

She wrinkled her nose. "I started out with Mr. Dobbs, but he was needed at the mine, so I told him to go ahead."

Jonah opened his mouth to point out that allowing her guard to go to the mine left her unprotected, but there didn't seem to be much point now.

"Thank you for tending to Creakle. He came back to the office in finer spirits than I've seen in a good while."

"It was my pleasure. If anything, I should thank you," Sumner said.

"Oh?"

Her face seemed to adopt a serene glow.

"I appreciate your confidence in allowing me to tend to one of the miners."

In all truth, he hadn't really thought that far ahead. He'd just wanted to stop Creakle's bellyaching. Too late, he realized that he may have tacitly given his permission for the miners to seek medical attention from the new doctor. Although he doubted any of them would be willing to go to a woman for more than cuts and scrapes, he didn't think Ezra Batchwell would look too kindly on having his mine superintendent undermining his orders.

"Is something wrong?"

"Wha—no. Just a little problem at the mine. Nothing to worry about."

"The women have been told that Mr. Batchwell and Mr. Bottoms will be eating in their homes this evening. We're supposed to have one of the men deliver the food up to their houses." A slight crease appeared between her brows. "Should we take that as a bad sign?"

"Not at all. The owners rarely join the men at night. Instead, they attend the Devotional, then Batchwell takes a brisk walk around the camp and Bottoms retreats to read his books. Neither of them cares too much for ceremony."

"I can't blame them. To eat from a tray near the fire, with a book and a teapot nearby…that's the stuff of dreams."

Jonah smiled at the picture she painted. She had a way with words, creating an image so homey and serene that he found himself longing to experience such a thing.

"You could have all that."

She scoffed. "You mean as a wife and mother." She vigorously shook her head. "Come now, Jonah. Think back to your mother. Did she ever have an evening like the one I described? Or did she spend her meals fetching and fixing for others?"

Jonah couldn't help a rueful laugh. "You've hit the nail on the head, I'm afraid. But…" His mind wandered back to his childhood, to evenings spent in lamplight, a roaring fire in the grate. "My mother had this little metal foot warmer covered in a scrap of woolen carpet. While she finished clearing up the dishes and putting things away, my father would slide open the drawer and place hot coals inside. Then he'd fold a lap quilt on top. By the time my mother joined us, the box and the blanket were warm. She'd settle into her favorite rocker. Then she'd wrap the blanket over her knees and spend the next few hours reading from the Bible or sewing, or asking us about our day."

"That sounds lovely."

Her expression was so wistful he feared that Sumner's childhood had not been so idyllic.

"You must miss them terribly," she murmured.

"Yes. My parents passed several years ago."

"I'm so sorry." She looked stricken. "I didn't mean to be so insensitive."

He waved aside her apology. "The war," he explained succinctly. "I think the worry of having two sons fighting and the burden of the farm proved too much for them."

"And your brother?"

"Killed at Gettysburg."

"Oh." It was a mere puff of sound. "I remember reading about the battle in one of my father's monthly periodicals." She paused, then asked, "Did you have any sisters?"

"No. Just Matthew and me. By the time I returned home…" He shrugged. "The family business was in shambles, the land we farmed all but ruined. I stayed for a time with…neighbors."

Neighbors.

He'd stayed with Rebecca and her family. But when

Rebecca had deserted him, he'd known he needed to move on.

"So what brought you to Bachelor Bottoms?"

"The same as you. I was looking for a new start, a place to make a difference."

He'd accomplished the first, but he wasn't so sure about the latter.

But Sumner must have sensed the thrust of his thoughts because she touched his arm, bringing him to a halt next to the cook shack.

"You've definitely done both, Jonah. Despite the reasons why all these men have gathered here, you've helped to create a thriving community. These men are dedicated and healthy and happy. You should be very proud of your work. I've seen enough coal mines in England to know that Bachelor Bottoms is quite remarkable, despite its stringent rules."

Since they'd arrived at the cook shack, Jonah's excuse for accompanying Sumner dissipated into the cold. She held out her hand for the sack of dried apples and he reluctantly surrendered it. Thankfully, she didn't immediately step inside. Instead, they stood close, but not too close, quiet, but not too quiet.

"Something smells good," he said when a group of miners walked within earshot. He hoped that the men wouldn't see Jonah and Sumner together and draw the wrong conclusions.

"Beans and salt pork, biscuits and oatmeal cookies."

"The men will beat a path to your door."

"That's what I'm hoping." There was a lilt to her tone that warned him she might not be talking about food anymore. But before he could speak, she opened the door. "Until later, Jonah."

Jonah.
She'd used his first name.
And they hadn't been alone.

Chapter Nine

Jonah waited until Sumner had disappeared inside the cook shack before turning back toward the office. But within a few feet, he realized that his conversation with the good doctor had not gone completely unnoticed. Ezra Batchwell stood on the opposite side of the street. He leaned heavily on his walking stick and his face was a study in disapproval.

The man glowered at Jonah as he crossed the street toward him.

"That woman is becoming a problem," Ezra growled.

"She was double-checking your dinner arrangements with me."

"I didn't hire any of them to work in the cook shack. We've got men assigned to that."

"And they'll be back to their jobs soon enough. In the meantime, the miners seem to be enjoying the change."

"Which won't do anyone a bit of good. I won't have them growing accustomed to something that they can't have."

Jonah was pretty sure that Batchwell wasn't referring to the food.

"I want them gone as soon as possible."

"The weather—"

"The weather has been clear for a couple of days. The debris field has had time to settle. Come Monday, if we haven't had any more snow, I want you to send a team of men to examine the pass. There's got to be a way to get those women out before the next blizzard."

Mere days ago, Jonah might have agreed with him. But now, when he thought of any of these women climbing the rugged slopes and walking through the canyon, he balked.

"None of them could make the entire journey on foot."

"Then find a way to get a sledge and team through. Either that, or get them to a section of telegraph wire that isn't damaged. Then we can send a message for a train to come fetch them. The women keep saying that they have people waiting for them. Let them prove it. Monday!"

Jonah watched Ezra Batchwell storm toward the meetinghouse. Due to the shorter winter days, shadows were falling. Soon, the evening Devotional would begin. But how was Jonah going to partake of the Spirit knowing that if his men found a way through the pass, Jonah would have to demand that the women pack up and walk to the nearest railhead? With temperatures hovering below freezing, it would be an arduous trek. Even if Jonah managed to get a sledge through, the women would be tested to their limits.

He knew Ezra was thinking of the welfare of the miners. As much as the owners had tried to ensure that the women disrupted the operation of their community as little as possible, things had changed. Despite their best attempts, a shift in focus was already occurring among the men. True, they completed their shifts and did their work, but an energy shimmered in the air and it was clear that the miners were ultra-aware of the ladies in their midst.

And it had nothing to do with the new menus.

When Monday morning dawned, the sky was cold, dark and quiet as Jonah and his men assembled in front of the livery stable. Since Ezra Batchwell had issued his orders to examine the pass, the weather had remained clear and sunny—so much so that the icicles hanging from the eaves had begun to drip, and slushy puddles were turning the roads from pristine white to a muddy mess. If ever there was a chance to get the women through the pass, this was probably it.

The majority of the men were mounted on horseback, although a few had taken their spots in a sledge being pulled by a team of horses. If they were able to find a way to reach the canyon and the rails beyond, Jonah didn't want to waste time. By bringing the heavy-duty sleigh, they could test the soundness of the snow before ever allowing the women to approach the debris field.

Dropping from the boardwalk, Jonah tugged his gloves more firmly over his hands, then gathered the reins to his horse. "Everyone ready?"

"We're just waiting on Creakle. He's driving the team."

Jonah loosely gripped the reins to his gelding, leading the animal in a wide circuit around the group of miners, checking their gear, their tools, making sure the men were dressed warmly. There were nearly two dozen of them. All had been equipped with rifles—in case they encountered any easy game along their way—and the sledge had been loaded with empty feed sacks, pickaxes and shovels. Even if they found a means of travel clear enough for a man to traverse, a group of women with long skirts may need some clearing in order to make it feasible.

At long last, Creakle toddled toward them, but he wasn't alone. A willowy figure in long skirts followed close on his heels.

"Creakle?" Jonah couldn't help the way that his voice emerged with apparent disapproval. But before he could say anything, Creakle heaved a crate into the sledge, then took his place. When he shifted, Jonah was able to see that it was Sumner who followed him. She placed a drawstring sack in the sledge, as well, then crossed to Jonah.

"You'll be needing food while you're on the slopes. There's biscuits, cold ham, cheese and apple tarts in the crate. In the bag, you'll find some cookies. We'll have hot coffee and a warm meal for you whenever you return."

Jonah felt unaccountably touched. He wasn't sure how the women had discovered the nature of their errand, but he was pleased that his crew wouldn't have to spend the day working on an empty stomach.

"Thank you, Dr. Havisham. And thank the other women in the kitchen. That was mighty thoughtful of you."

Judging by her expression, she was blushing, and Jonah wished there was enough light to see her cheeks grow pink.

"It was no trouble at all. I only wish that we'd been able to find a way to send something hot."

"We'll be fine. Thank you."

She took a half step forward, her fingers lacing together, then she appeared to become aware of the curious gazes fastened in her direction because she directed her words to the entire group. "God keep you safe." Then she lifted her skirts and hurried back toward the cook shack.

Suddenly, the morning was a little brighter, their errand a little less burdensome. Even so, Jonah couldn't shift his heavy mood. He kept telling himself that, rather than focusing on what the community would lose when the women left, he should remember what could be gained. Over and over, the women had insisted that they had destinations to reach and people waiting for their arrival. Although Jonah might have real qualms about the safety of the proposed enterprise, many of the women may be looking for a means to escape the valley. If they were successful today, Jonah might be able to grant them that wish.

Unfortunately, even as he reminded himself of the good that might come of a hard day's work…he couldn't discount the twinge of his gut. He had a bad feeling about the day to come.

A really, really bad feeling.

Throughout the morning and into the afternoon, Sumner tried to keep busy. She'd never been the sort of person who liked to waste the day away. She felt out of sorts if she didn't have things to do—a result, no doubt, from her years of training and working in the women's hospital. She'd grown used to having responsibilities that often overlapped one another.

But since the men had left for the pass, she was having trouble focusing on the tasks she'd assigned herself.

"Any word?" Iona asked.

Much like Sumner, the older woman kept hovering near the window, checking for any sign that Jonah and his men had returned.

"No."

"It's getting late," Willow murmured, her brow creasing. "It'll be dark soon."

As if their concern were catching, the main room of the hall became quiet, and all attention went to the windows.

"Is it a good sign or a bad sign that they haven't come back yet?" Stefania asked.

"I suppose it all depends on whether or not you want to get out of the valley," Ruth mumbled.

Myra and her twin exchanged glances. "We've been praying that they get through." Myra's brow knitted. "I don't want to wish harm on anyone, but…this is our chance to make homes for ourselves. If our husbands-to-be make other arrangements…we have nowhere to go."

Several of the brides nodded in agreement.

Iona sniffed. "Well, I don't mind the delay so much. My sister and her family aren't going anywhere. And since I'm getting on in years, this might be the only adventure I'll ever have in my life."

"What about you, Willow?"

Willow seemed startled to have all eyes turned in her direction. Her cheeks pinkened as she said, "I'm in no hurry."

Sumner wasn't surprised. If Sumner had been destined to marry a man twenty years her senior with a passel of kids, she'd rather put that off for as long as possible.

The room echoed in a companionable silence, broken only by the soft rip of fabric. This afternoon, after Sumner had found a stash of worn-out linens that had been destined for the scrap heap, she'd enlisted the brides' help to boil them in lye soap, then hang them in the whipping wind and bright sunshine. Once the sheets were dry—a feat that took hours in the cold—they tore them into strips and began rolling them into more manageable bundles.

"I, for one, will be glad to get into my own home," Stefania offered.

Sumner was sure that most of the women would agree

with that remark. They'd all managed to settle into their temporary quarters. The hall no longer looked like a male retreat. There were pots of laundry cooking on the pot-bellied stove and articles of clothing hanging from ropes that had been strung from the rafters and the rungs of the banister. Some of the women passed the time by sewing or helping one another to repair items of clothing that had been torn during the avalanche. There was even a pair of women in the corner who artfully mended hats and bonnets by steaming brims and repairing the finery.

But there was no denying that the quarters were cramped. The heat from the stove barely reached the sec-ond floor, so their bedrooms grew chilly and uncomfort-able during the night. During the day, all of the women congregated in the long, narrow room on the main floor. Space was at a premium and seating was limited. The women took turns using the chairs, or made do with upended kegs and weathered crates salvaged from the cook shack.

As much as she feared that moment when the pass cleared and Sumner's fate at Bachelor Bottoms would be decided once and for all, Sumner knew it would be better if the mail-order brides were allowed to continue their journeys. The women deserved a chance to meet with their prospective husbands or waiting families.

On the other hand, if a means of escape proved im-possible or hazardous, Sumner feared the limited space would eventually lead to conflict. The women were with-out privacy of any kind. Nor was there a place for them to keep all of their belongings. Besides their clothing, many of the women had brought trunks and crates full of household goods—dishes, fabric, books, pots and pans—which currently took up most of the back wall and the arch beneath the staircase. And other than the evening

Devotionals and their shifts in the kitchen, they had no real access to fresh air and sunshine, both of which would soon wear on their moods.

Which meant the women were on tenterhooks, wondering what the day would bring.

Sumner was probably the only person who dreaded the moment when the men found a way through the pass. Unlike the other ladies, she had no one waiting for her.

"Is something wrong?"

Too late, Sumner realized that she'd paused while wrapping a bandage around her patient's arm. She looked up to find Lydia Tomlinson watching her curiously.

"No. Just woolgathering."

Lydia didn't look convinced. But then, Sumner had begun to realize that Lydia had an independent soul much like her own. Unlike the other women, she'd sworn off marriage for good. Raised by a pair of aunts who were ardent suffragists Lydia intended to spread the word of temperance and equality up and down the Western coast, much as her aunts had done in Boston.

The door to the rear of the hall burst open, and Emmarissa, Ruth and Greta hurried in, their guards, Dobbs and Winslow, trailing behind them with the last of the sheets.

"Has there been any word?" Ruth gasped.

"No!"

The word was echoed by more than a dozen women, making them laugh.

Sumner's eyes strayed to the window again.

"None that I know of."

The pass wasn't that far away—only a few miles. One would think that it would have been an easy matter to send a runner back with updates.

Unless they'd broken through to the other side.

"How long have they been out there?" Emmarissa asked, unwinding a brightly colored scarf from her neck.

Sumner neatly tied the bandage, offering a soft pat of reassurance to her patient. "They left about five this morning."

It was nearly five in the afternoon.

"There you go," she said with a smile to Nedra. "The gash is healing nicely. We'll keep changing the bandages as least once a day, applying the ointment each time. That should help to prevent some of the scarring."

"Thank you, Dr. Havisham. These miners would be crazy not to keep you on."

As she stood, Sumner's smile was rueful. "If only they shared your views."

"They will. One of these days, someone besides Creakle is going to need your exper—"

A low rumbling shuddered through floor and built to a crescendo.

"Avalanche!" she shouted in warning as she and the other women automatically ducked for cover.

A huge gust of wind slammed into the windows, dirt and debris scratching against the panes, the world turning to a whirl of white.

Then Aspen Valley grew completely silent.

For a moment, Sumner was inundated by memories— the slam of snow against the train car. Tumbling over and over as the carriage summersaulted down the hillside. Only through sheer effort of will was she able to shake the images aside and jump to her feet. She ran to the door, whipping it open in time to see a maelstrom of snow, pine needles and dust spinning in the air.

Sumner didn't need to think twice. She knew what had probably triggered the slide—an attempt to get the women out of the valley. And if Jonah and his men had been caught in the debris, she was sure that some of them could be injured.

She pointed to the nearest Pinkerton, a tall, angular man with a neatly trimmed beard. The man's uniform had been dusted with so much ice that he could have been Jack Frost himself.

"Mr. Kingsley! There's a crate of medical supplies inside by the stove. I need it taken to the infirmary down the street."

He nodded and she gestured to the other men. "The rest of you need to bring me some kindling and firewood. We've got to get that building warmed up and fast."

When the Pinkertons began running toward the rear of the cook shack where a stockpile of logs had been stacked, Sumner dodged back inside.

"I need all of you to gather up anything else that could be of use. We'll need linens and blankets to make up the cots, waterbasins and fresh water."

Lydia made a shooing motion with her hands. "Go. Go! Take your bag, and we'll bring everything else. Then I'll take a group of women to the cook shack to begin making coffee and stew—and some hot broth, in case we have anyone injured. No matter what has happened, the men will be cold and in need of something to warm them from the inside out."

Sumner grabbed her coat and shrugged into its sleeves. "We're going to need light soon, as well. Gather as many lamps and lanterns as you can."

Willow snatched up two hurricane lanterns from the main table. "I'm coming with you. I can help you get things ready."

"Thank you, Willow."

The two women hurried down the street to the infirmary, unlocking the door and swinging it wide. Minutes

later, the Pinkertons arrived and began lighting fires in
the box heaters. Not long after, a brigade of women arrived. Myra and Miriam began cleaning the examining
area, while Nedra, Ruth and Greta made up the cots. Emmarissa, Louisa and Marie arranged piles of bandages
on every table, then began filling pails of snow to heat
on the stoves for fresh water. Iona and Stefania arranged
an army of lanterns brought by the other women, adjusting the wicks so that the rooms were ablaze with light.

By the time the alarm bell near the mine began clam-
oring, Sumner and her feminine recruits were ready. The
infirmary was still chilly, but there was hot water and
a precious cache of medical supplies ready for the first
of the patients.

They didn't have long to wait. Within a few minutes,
a thunder of hooves came from the direction of the mine.
By the time Sumner and her companions dodged outside, men on horseback were already coming into view.

She waved to them, shouting, "Bring the wounded to
the infirmary!"

The men in the lead must have heard her because they
changed direction, their pace unabated until they were
a few scant yards away. Then they brought the animals
to a skidding halt.

A quick sweeping glance assured Sumner that she
would be dealing with minor injuries—cuts, scrapes,
abrasions. One man had tucked his arm inside the front
placket of his coat, which meant a possible broken bone.

Sumner ordered the Pinkertons to help the men inside. Standing near the door, she quickly sorted the injuries. Those that were minor and merely required washing
and bandaging, she directed to the waiting area where
her comrades were ready with hot water, ointments and

bandages. The fellow she suspected of a broken bone, she sent to the examining room.

"How many more men were injured?" she asked as she guided him to a chair, then gingerly began to remove his coat.

"This is most of us but..." He hissed when she tried to straighten his arm enough to slip it from the sleeves of his coat.

"Slowly, slowly," she murmured.

"But there's three men trapped under the snow. They're digging like the blazes trying to get 'em out in time."

Sumner froze. "Three men? D-do you know who?"

The miner shook his head. "I think Pearson Cowan was one, but... I don't know. I was trying to dig myself out so..."

She touched his shoulder. "Don't worry about it. If I hear something more, I'll let you know."

"I'd appreciate that, ma'am."

Sumner laid his coat over the back of a chair. "You'll need to remove your shirt so I can examine you."

The miner's head whipped up so fast he nearly lost his balance.

"What?"

"Your shirt. Do you want to take it off yourself? Or would you like me to help you?"

He shrank away from her. "Oh, no, ma'am. There's been a mistake. I won't be...bothering you with this."

"But, Mr...."

"Fredrickson."

"You may have broken something. I really need to examine it, and I can't do that properly unless you undress."

"No!"

His face leached of what little color had been there. "No, ma'am." He tried to stand. "I won't be bothering you."

"But—"

"I need a *real* doctor, ma'am."

"I can assure you that I'm highly trained and more than capable of tending to your needs."

"No, ma'am. I'll head back to my quarters. Later, I can have Stumpy look at it."

"Stumpy?"

"He's taken to stitching us up until the real doctor arrives. A *male* doctor."

Sumner opened her mouth to argue the point, but more shouting from the main door sent her scurrying into the other room in time to find several men carrying a prone body inside.

She whirled to face Fredrickson. "Go into the kitchen area. I want you to keep your arm up. I'll get back to you as soon as I can. In the meantime, get something warm—coffee, soup."

Fredrickson looked as if he wanted to argue, but when he saw his colleagues, he slid from the table, allowing them to set the prone man on top.

The miner's skin was so pale that she immediately pressed her ear to his chest.

"He's alive."

She pointed to the men who had brought him inside. "Help get him undressed and I'll—"

More shouting came from the waiting room.

"Get him out of his clothes and I'll be right back."

The next patient was conscious, but had suffered a gash across the top of his skull and several broken teeth.

"Kitchen table," she said bluntly. "Get his clothes off. How many more?"

"Just Creakle and Ramsey," one of the men grunted as they moved past her to the doctor's quarters.

"Creakle and Ramsay?" she whispered.

Her stomach flip-flopped—a reaction she hadn't had since the beginning of her training.

Dear, sweet Heavenly Father. Please, please let them be all right.

The door burst open and Jonah staggered inside, bearing the brunt of Creakle's weight.

"I need help!" he shouted.

A pair of men rushed forward to take Creakle just when Jonah looked ready to collapse.

"Put him on one of the cots," Sumner said, pointing. Then she ran to Jonah as he sagged against the doorjamb.

Wrapping his arm over her shoulders, she helped him to a nearby chair. "Are you hurt?"

He shook his head. "No...just winded."

Winded? She'd guess that his back was paining him like the devil—he might have even damaged it further. But she could tell by the glint in his eyes that he wouldn't be accepting her help. Not while his men were awaiting her attention.

She pointed at him with a stern finger. "Don't move," she said.

He nodded—and his agreement to follow her orders had her more worried than ever.

Sumner quickly checked on Creakle, but after ensuring that he was conscious and alert, she asked two women to layer him with blankets and put a hot brick at his feet.

"I'll be back to tend to him as soon as I can."

Then, inwardly girding herself for battle, she headed back to the examining room.

Midnight had come and gone by the time she'd seen to most of the wounded. Mack Epcot, the gentleman whom they'd brought into the infirmary unconscious, had, ironically, been the easiest patient. Before he'd gained his wits again, she'd been able to determine that he had at least three broken ribs. After binding his chest, she'd cleaned and stitched up the gash on his head, then left Willow to sit by his cot with orders to come get Sumner as soon as the man awakened. After that, she had examined Creakle.

He'd shivered from beneath his blankets, insisting that he was right as rain. But after learning that Creakle had been buried beneath the snow for several minutes, she'd insisted that he stay the night in the infirmary. He'd nodded, blinking against sudden tears. Then, obviously embarrassed at the emotions he'd displayed, he'd twisted his head to the side and closed his eyes, feigning sleep. After whispering, "Call me if you need me, Mr. Creakle," Sumner had carefully tucked the blankets around his shoulders, then had gone to the examining room where the other men had finally managed to undress the injured miner.

Pearson Cowan had proven much more difficult, thrashing against the other men when she'd reentered. Much like Fredrickson, he'd refused to let her treat him—or even examine him—until she'd finally been forced to give instructions to one of the Pinkertons on how to give the man a cursory examination. Without being allowed to touch the patient herself, Sumner had been able to determine little more than the man had injuries to his shoulder, knee, and a huge lump at the back of his skull. Unable to do anything more for him at the time, she'd insisted that the Pinkertons carry him to the cot next to Creakle's. Then, issuing detailed instructions, she'd enlisted the Pinkertons' help again to set and splint Fredrickson's arm.

Then finally, with three patients sleeping in their cots, she returned to the waiting room.

Jonah sat exactly as she'd left him. He hadn't even removed his coat. His chin had been on his chest and his eyes were closed, but as soon as he heard her footfalls, he was instantly awake.

He'd told her that he'd once been a soldier. Sumner had seen evidence of such training in the way he led his men, in his efficiency, in his dedication to duty. It was there in the way he held himself and rode a horse. And judging by the speed with which he went from deep sleep to instant alertness, she would hazard a guess that he'd also grown used to resting with one ear trained to his surroundings.

"How are the men?" he asked, his voice gruff.

"They've been examined, treated and are sleeping in the next room. Two of them—Epcot and Fredrickson—have broken bones. Creakle is exhausted and still suffering from the cold, but I haven't found any other injuries. The other gentleman…"

"Pearson Cowan."

"Yes, Mr. Cowan. His shoulder and knee are badly bruised. I don't think they're broken, but they've definitely been banged up. He's also taken a blow to the head. I'll watch him, as well." She grimaced. "Or I'll try. He refused to let me treat him, so I had to make my diagnosis secondhand."

Jonah scrubbed his face with his hands. "I'll talk to them in the morning. Maybe I can get them to—"

"Forget I'm a woman?" She grimaced. "I don't think that your ordering them to accept me will do much good." She sighed. "Indeed, it will probably make things worse. For now, the Pinkertons and I have developed a…system. If I need your help, I'll let you know."

He nodded.

"Now, it's your turn, Mr. Ramsey."

He blinked at her, uncomprehending.

"I need to examine you, as well."

"No. Thank you."

He tried to stand and stumbled.

Sumner whipped her arm around his waist and he hissed.

"Into the examining room, Jonah."

"No, it's really not—"

Her eyes narrowed. "Are you going to argue that I'm not qualified? Because I'm a woman?"

She'd trapped him in a verbal corner. He'd been willing to insist that his men accept her care, yet now, he was the one who was balking.

He must have accepted her bluff because his breath whooshed from his lungs and he nodded. "Lead the way."

The fact that he allowed her to help support his weight told her far more than words that the man was hurting. His gait was unsteady and she could hear his short pants. Her concerns grew.

She helped him to settle onto the table. "I'll need to check your back. Would you like me to leave you alone to undress?"

"What?"

For the first time, she saw something that looked very much like fear in his eyes, but Sumner pushed that thought away. She couldn't imagine Jonah being afraid of anything, let alone an examination. But when she smiled in reassurance, he looked away, clearly upset.

She took a step closer. "Jonah," she said gently, "I can't do my job if I can't see…underneath your clothes. And it's obvious from the way you're moving that you've hurt your back. You may have even aggravated your old injury."

She saw a ruddy color begin to seep up his neck and tint his ears.

Was he uncomfortable?

Or embarrassed?

"Have you had anything to eat or drink, Mr. Ramsey?"

He regarded her blankly.

"No."

"If you'd like, I'll go fetch something hot for you to drink while you shrug out of your clothes." She crossed to the far side of the room to retrieve a blanket. "Are you feeling any pain in your legs?"

"What? No!"

"Then you can keep everything on below the waist. Above the waist" —she handed him the blanket "—you can drape this around your shoulders." She paused before adding, "So you don't get cold."

His eyes narrowed slightly—as if he sensed her amusement. But he took the blanket.

"Ten minutes, Mr. Ramsey. I doubt it will take me any longer than that to fetch your dinner. Then I'll be back."

She was nearly to the door when he called out, "Wait!"

His mouth opened, but he thought over his words, then said, "Have you eaten yourself, Dr. Havisham?"

"I don't know why that matters."

"Have you eaten?"

She shook her head.

"Then fetch us both something hot to drink. After you've finished looking me over—if you're still feeling agreeable—we'll go to the cook shack for dinner. Together." He quickly added, "So we can talk about the welfare of the men."

His words might offer an innocent reason to share a meal.

But those eyes…those eyes conveyed that his motives were far more personal.

And she couldn't resist. Because the warmth of his gaze heated her from the inside out far more than any cup of coffee would ever do.

"Very well, Mr. Ramsey. I'll be back in five minutes."

Chapter Ten

Jonah knew the moment that Sumner returned, even though his back remained to the door. He could *feel* her in some strange indescribable way. An ease spread over him, like sunshine sliding over his body and relaxing him even through the shield of the blanket.

He heard the rustle of her skirts as she rounded the examination table.

"Coffee?" he asked.

"Cocoa." Her eyes crinkled in the corners. "Willow Granger shares Creakle's love for it, and when she found a keg of cocoa powder in the cook shack—" Sumner shrugged endearingly "—she figured the injured needed a special treat. But be warned, Willow likes her cocoa to be more chocolate than milk."

She passed the steaming mug to him, and he was pleased to see that she'd brought one for herself, as well. The fact that she wasn't rushing immediately into her assessment allowed him to relax even more.

He hadn't realized how cold he'd become until his fingers wrapped around the enamelware mug. The heat seeped into his skin, making it tingle and prick as sensation returned to his extremities. He blew on the dark liquid, then took a small sip.

"Hot," he offered needlessly.

"Drink it all. It will help warm you from the inside out."

He took a healthier swallow, closing his eyes and enjoying the sensation as the liquid made a path down his throat. Sumner had been correct. The drink thawed him from the inside out, easing the rash of gooseflesh that pebbled his entire body. Still, it couldn't compare to the way that this woman made him feel, just by being near.

If he were honest, he'd have to admit that he was nervous, anxious—a little scared, even. His back felt as if Lucifer himself had been clawing at it. When the avalanche had been triggered, Jonah had been pushed from his feet and swept down the mountainside like a piece of driftwood. He'd been dragged over rocks and bushes, through tree branches and across icy snowdrifts. At the very least, he knew some of his skin had been chewed up.

At the worst…

He could have dislodged the shrapnel near his spine.

Several quiet moments passed before he looked up again, only to find that Sumner was watching him, her head slightly cocked, her eyes filled with concern.

In the past, he'd shied away from the scrutiny of other people since it was usually the precursor to pity. But with Sumner, he felt no such qualms. At least, not yet. Not until she'd seen the full extent of his scars.

"What happened today?" she finally asked.

"We found a way through the pass."

"Oh."

The word emerged as a bare puff of sound but it held so many emotions: hope, anxiety, regret.

"At first, it was only accessible on foot and the climb

was…difficult." He took another gulp of chocolate, but
it seemed to go down his throat in a lump. "We spent a
few hours with the shovels and pickaxes until we were
finally able to get a team through."

Something in Sumner's eyes dimmed. "A team. Then
the women could be taken out on a sledge."

"In theory."

He waited until she met his gaze.

"It wouldn't be easy. And they'd have to walk the
last stretch through the steepest, rockiest portion of the
canyon."

"How far would they have to go?"

"Five or six miles."

"Oh."

Again, it was a single syllable, but it said so much.
He knew she was thinking of the women, some of them
still injured from the avalanche, most of them unaccus-
tomed to such hazardous conditions. The same thoughts
had plagued Jonah most of the day.

"We'd come prepared. We could have made the entire
trek ourselves, over the next day or two, and cleared a
portion of the path but…"

Her eyes were wide and slightly sad.

"I couldn't do it, Sumner," he admitted, the words
barely audible. "I kept thinking of the women…of *you*…
being forced to make that journey. Maybe it could be
done. *Maybe*. But who knew what other dangers awaited
them—not just on the mountainside, but in the valley
below. The trek wouldn't have taken a few days…it could
have been weeks." His voice grew husky as he remembered the hazards the women would have encountered—
cold, sheer cliffs, slippery conditions. And none of the
mail-order brides would have had the clothing or skills
to endure such hardships. They'd planned on a journey

made entirely by train, not a mountainous hike. "So I called it off."

He knew that she understood the depth of what he was saying. It was more than the fact that he'd determined the trip would be too difficult and had abandoned the idea. No, for the first time, he'd openly defied his employers. Ezra Batchwell had insisted that if there was a way, *any* way, for the women to be evacuated, Jonah needed to ensure that it happened. Immediately.

But Jonah had defied them.

Unbelievably, Sumner took a step forward, placing her cup on the examination table. Then, somehow, their arms were around one another and they clung to each other in solace, comfort and solidarity.

"So how were the men injured?" she whispered in his ear.

Jonah shook his head. "I—I don't know what happened. We were on our way back—we were nearly within sight of the camp. I heard a muffled *boom* and then—" he couldn't prevent the way he held her tighter, drawing from Sumner's warmth, her inner strength "—then a rush of snow came from behind us. We almost outran it. Almost."

He thought Sumner's lips pressed against the top of his head and his eyes closed. He couldn't remember the last time that he'd been this close to anyone—and he found that he was starved for human contact, for the support of someone who understood. It ignited a spark of something inside of him that he hadn't experienced for a very long time.

Hope.

Then, as if he hadn't been blessed enough, he heard her soft murmured prayer.

"Father in Heaven, thank You for all that Thou has

done for us this day, for the way that Thy hand hast blessed these men with strength and safety. Please continue to bless and help them, for they are so dear to us and they have so much yet to offer up to You…"

Maybe he hadn't been meant to hear the words. Sumner had murmured them quietly. They could have been a private expression of her faith and gratitude. But Jonah was so overcome by the action he could barely breathe. He couldn't remember the last time that someone had cared enough about him to pray for him.

The hope that had fluttered within his soul grew stronger, taking wing, inundating his body with a glow unlike any he'd ever known. And he was forced to acknowledge that, for years, his life had been…empty. He'd done little more than exist, going through the motions, focusing on the job and only the job. He didn't regret his work. No, he'd always been a man who had gained great satisfaction from honest toil. But there'd been nothing more.

No true connections.

No joy.

He'd been a hollow shell of a man, allowing the uncertainties of his future and the disappointments of his past to overtake him.

And that was no way to live.

Lifting his head, Jonah met Sumner's gaze. Never in his life had he seen a woman who could relay so much emotion from a single look. He knew without her speaking that she was concerned about him, not just physically, but emotionally. She honestly cared about him. Not just as a doctor…

But as a woman.

There were times in a man's life when a person reached a crossroads, when nothing could ever be the same again. And Jonah knew he'd just encountered one of those points. He could retreat back to the life he'd led up to now.

Or he could open himself up to the possibility of a different path.

There would be no guarantees. He already knew that there were women who wouldn't be willing to saddle themselves to the uncertainty of his old injuries. At any moment, he could become an invalid, or worse. By allowing himself to even think of opening up his heart, he could invite the pain and frustration he'd experienced at Rebecca's desertion to return.

But he couldn't go back.

And he couldn't go forward if he didn't have faith.

Faith in God, who had protected him in so many ways.

And in the woman who seemed determined to look beyond the wounds to the man.

A knock caused Sumner to reluctantly step away from Jonah's embrace. Unable to meet his gaze, she moved to crack open the door. Willow stood on the other side, holding a basin and pitcher.

"Here's the hot water you asked me to bring."

"Thank you, Willow."

"Do you need any help?"

Sumner glanced at Jonah, but he shook his head. Sumner was amazed that the man was willing to let her examine him at all. He'd always been so adamantly opposed when she'd offered in the past. It was a sign that something must be paining him a great deal that he'd agreed to let her tend to him.

"No. I don't think so. But I'll call if I need you."

The young woman backed away—and not for the first time, Sumner found herself wondering about her upbringing. Her speech was that of someone who'd once been employed in service, and her loose clothing and wild Bohemian hair were at odds with her prim manners. But she was so shy and quiet that Sumner couldn't imagine her working as a maid or scullery.

Bumping the door closed with her hip, Sumner carried the pitcher and bowl to a small side table. Willow had looped a cloth through the handle, so after pouring some of the steaming liquid into the bowl, Sumner dropped the square of flannel in to soak.

Then she turned to Jonah.

"How were you injured?"

The moment he opened his mouth, she knew he was about to back out of the examination, so she held up a hand to stop him before he'd even started.

"I know you're hurt." She touched her hand to his forehead. "The fire in the fireplace has made this room blazing hot, and you're cold and clammy. Pale. Something has happened beyond the chronic pain you usually feel."

His head dipped. "When the wall of snow came down, I tumbled down the side of the hill. I might have scratched up my back a bit."

The words were uttered in the same light tone as if he'd gone sleigh riding and had fallen into a drift.

"Then I'd better take a look." She moved around the table, reaching for the blanket draped around his shoulders. "May I?"

He didn't answer her immediately. Instead, he reached to grip her fingers. "Sumner…there are scars on my back. From the war."

She didn't hesitate, merely squeezed him in reassurance. "I know, Jonah. But it doesn't matter. All that matters is that you're well."

She felt him shudder, then relax. Then he nodded and loosened his hold.

Carefully, she helped to expose his back, then had to keep her jaw clenched to keep from hissing at the sight.

There were scrapes and cuts and deep gouges in the skin. Dirt and pine needles had become embedded in the wounds and stuck to the strong planes of his shoulders. But all of the fresh injuries couldn't disguise the web of old scars that ran from his neck to the waistband of his pants.

He'd been hurt so badly. It was a wonder that he was alive. The fact that he was able to walk at all…

That said as much about his character as his determination.

"You really aren't bothered by them—the scars—are you?" Jonah's tone held a note of wonder.

"No. I'm more worried about what's happened today." She made her tone light, breezy.

"There have been…others who found them rather shocking."

The fact that he felt he needed to be so careful in explaining his reticence hurt her heart.

"Sounds like a bunch of ninnies to me."

That comment made his lips twitch, and she was glad.

"I'll be careful, but there's a lot of debris in the wounds. This may sting a bit."

"I'll be fine."

Nevertheless, she could see the way his knuckles grew white as he gripped the edge of the table.

Sumner retrieved the flannel from the water and began to carefully dab it over the exposed area.

He flinched, sucking in a breath, but other than that, he appeared determined to remain stoic, so she tried to think of a way to take his mind off what she was doing.

"So where are you from originally?"

There was a beat of silence, then, "Pennsylvania."

"Did you grow up on a farm?"

"In a way. My father was a cabinetmaker, but we had a little land outside of town. We had a few cows and chickens, a huge garden and some acres that we planted to corn and wheat, squash and beans."

Sumner smiled. "It sounds lovely."

"It was." He sighed. "Until the war came."

"Did you join up right away?"

He nodded. "I had the idea that it would be all brass bands and glory. I was so sure that it would be over in a month or two at most. I'd be back before the harvest for sure."

"And that didn't happen."

"No."

As she wiped his skin clean, Jonah's back told her another story. She could see at least two round scars that could only have been gunshot wounds. And the rest...

"What happened?" she whispered.

"Scattershot mortar. Do you know what that is?"

She shook her head, then realized he couldn't see her. "No."

"It's a type of cannon shot. The Rebs liked to fill them with old nails, pieces of glass and scraps of metal. One hit pretty close as my men and I tried to outflank one of the Rebel strongholds. I don't—" he hissed when she began dabbing at a deeper gash, and she didn't know if the reaction was from the memory or the newer wounds "—I don't remember much after that."

Sumner could imagine. Judging by the extent of the damage, he was blessed to have lived at all.

"So the pain you experience..."

"I have shrapnel wedged near my spine. The surgeon tried his best but—" he shrugged "—it was field hospital medicine."

"And you've been examined since then."

"I tried a passel of doctors, half of whom turned out to be quacks. None of them could offer me much hope. It would be more dangerous to try and take the pieces out than to leave them where they are."

Sumner could understand the diagnosis. The threat of infection was very real. If it should travel to his spine, it could be a death sentence. But the dangers didn't end by ignoring them. The shrapnel could move. Especially after being thrown down the side of a mountain. She tried to probe the area, but he was so tender and raw it was difficult to determine whether the pain ran deeper than those hurts she could see.

She'd managed to clean his skin, so she began to cover the cuts and scrapes with one of her ointments. Then she took a roll of bandages from the shelf and wound them around his chest and abdomen. In the next few days, she would insist on changing the wrappings herself, just to make sure that the area didn't become inflamed. Once the swelling went down, she could focus more on any lingering effects.

"I know your back is feeling raw, but are you experiencing any deeper pain? Near the old injury?"

"I—I don't think so."

"Any numbness to your lower limbs? Tingling?"

His feet moved in slow circles.

"I don't know. My boots were wet and my feet have been cold."

"We need to get you into some dry shoes and socks."

She took a step toward the door, but he reached out to snag her arm, pulling her around the table until she faced him again. Then he took the other hand, as well, holding them loosely in his broad grip. For several long moments, he stared down at her palms as if they held the mysteries to the world.

"Thank you."

"Of course." She offered him a wry smile. "I told you I was a good doctor."

His lips twitched. "So you did. But that wasn't what… wasn't why…" He squeezed her hands. "Thank you for your…tact."

Her brows rose. "I don't know what you mean."

"My back. I know it isn't pretty."

"It will heal."

He looked up and held her gaze. "But the scars won't. They'll always remain."

And in an instant, she understood. Somehow, somewhere, someone had seen his back and reacted badly. Judging by the careful way he'd phrased his words, Sumner would bet that it had been a woman.

What had this unknown female said and done, to make Jonah think that he would be rejected, simply from the sight of a few pinkish lines?

To Sumner, the marks were a badge of honor, a symbol of a man who had fought for his country and had suffered dearly for it. To have endured so much pain—to still suffer discomfort—and live a productive, hardworking existence was something to be lauded.

She lifted one of her hands to touch his cheek, then smooth the rumpled waves of his hair. "I find the whole effect rather dashing, personally. Every woman has a soft spot for a wounded hero. I know I do." She thought she saw a hint of color seep into his cheeks. "Now, I'll go in search of a clean shirt and dry footwear. Then you and I will head to the cook shack. I don't know about you, but I'm positively famished."

* * *

By the time someone had found him some clothes, socks and boots, it was closer to morning than midnight. Jonah knew that he should be tired, but for some reason, he was thrumming with energy. Even more, his senses were heightened. He was aware of the cool kiss of winter against his cheeks, the squeak of newly fallen snow under his boots, the tangy scents of wood smoke coming from the miners' quarters.

As he held the door to the cook shack open for Sumner, he was sure that he caught a whiff of her distinctive scent—orange blossoms—and he wondered if she'd dabbed the perfume on her wrists, her neck or maybe even her hair.

The thought was intriguing. Sumner worked so hard to appear completely professional and competent. She wore severe clothing in dark colors and styled her hair in a way that wouldn't draw attention to her femininity.

Yet, she'd taken the time to apply a hint of scent.

The cook shack had obviously been kept open all night long. Jonah could see a few remaining members of his crew lingering over empty plates and hot cups of coffee. The air was steamy and warm and redolent with the aromas of the meal that awaited them—the deep notes of beef, an accompaniment of yeasty bread and something rich and spicy that reminded him of childhood Christmases.

As they made their way toward the serving area, Lydia Tomlinson rushed to greet them. Where Sumner had tried to disguise her femininity, this woman clearly embraced it. She wore a pink gingham day dress trimmed in lace and ribbons, with more lace and ribbons on her apron. Her hair was arranged in curls and braids and twists upon her head.

But Jonah found his eyes kept sliding in Sumner's direction nevertheless.

"Go on through to the private dining room and I'll bring your food to you," the woman said with a smile.

"Thank you, Lydia."

"We could eat here," Jonah said quickly, gesturing to the other tables, not wishing for his men to get the wrong impression. He wouldn't do anything that could cause even a hint of scandal to be attached to her name.

"No need. The table is set and waiting. Besides—" Lydia leaned closer to murmur "—we've been told to let the owners know when you arrive."

Even with that threat hanging over his head, Jonah's mood didn't dim—and he wasn't sure why.

He gestured for Sumner to precede him, then hurried to reach around her to open the door.

The moment he followed her, he could see that the womanly touch was becoming even more evident at the cook shack. Curtains made of feed sacks had been added to the windows. The table had been dressed with an embroidered cloth and a crock of holly adorned the center. More unbelievably, the places had been laid with real china, shiny silverware and cloth napkins.

Jonah couldn't remember the last time he'd seen a napkin.

He and Sumner had barely taken their places and settled the cloths in their laps before a pair of women entered. One of them plunked a tureen in the middle of the table, while the other brought a tray laden with bowls, a platter of corn bread, a crock of sweet butter and a plate of gingerbread cookies.

Jonah's stomach rumbled as the food was placed on the table. For the first time, he realized that it had been hours since he and his men had eaten the sandwiches that Sumner and the other women had provided. If they hadn't shown that kindness…

"Soup?"

"Please."

She filled his bowl with a steaming stew made with chunks of beef and venison, a thick broth, bits of barley and diced vegetables.

His brows rose and she seemed to read his thoughts because she explained, "We found several sacks of dried carrots and celery in your stores. The hunting party returned this afternoon with more than a dozen rabbits, several deer and elk. We've used the dried supplies sparingly. Just enough to augment the taste."

He couldn't argue with her there. The food was rich and hearty. The cook had been liberal with the pepper, adding another layer of warmth to the fare.

Sumner looked up and her eyes sparkled in amusement. "You have an overstock in spices in your warehouse. Hence, the gingerbread."

Jonah couldn't help grinning in return. Stumpy had never been much of a cook and it didn't surprise Jonah that years' worth of spices had been left unused. Thankfully, they'd provided a boon when they needed it most.

"They smell delicious."

The words had barely been uttered before the outer door flew open and a blast of cold air swirled into the room. Seconds later, Ezra Batchwell strode into the dining room, the capes of his greatcoat flapping around his shoulders like the wings of a giant bird.

"Ramsey."

"Mr. Batchwell." Jonah stood out of respect, even though he wanted nothing more than to ladle hot soup into his bowl. "Would you like to join us?"

Batchwell's eyes glittered in disapproval.

"Miss Havisham."

"*Dr.* Havisham was kind enough to join me for dinner so that I could eat while she gave me an update on the men. You're welcome to stay and hear the news."

The older man's eyes narrowed. "It's nearly four o'clock in the morning."

"And neither of us has had anything to eat since yesterday afternoon."

Batchwell must have realized that he was sounding churlish, because he grunted, then gestured for Jonah to take his chair. "Eat your food," he said gruffly. Then, realizing he would have no answers to his questions until Jonah had satisfied at least part of his appetite, he reluctantly took his seat at the head of the table.

Without looking his way, Sumner unobtrusively pushed the plate of gingerbread cookies toward the older man.

Batchwell grunted. Then he reached for a cookie, oblivious to the fact that one of the mail-order brides had probably supplied the cookie cutter from her trunks.

"Did you find a way out?" Batchwell asked after he'd finished the gingerbread and reached for another.

Jonah spooned soup into his mouth and chewed slowly. He'd never lied to his bosses, and he didn't intend to start. But he also knew what Batchwell wanted: the women out of the valley. Immediately.

"We found a way out. Briefly. But after the second avalanche…there's no way to get them through. Not until the pass melts."

Batchwell's face darkened and he bit the head off the gingerbread man with tremendous force. Then he threw the rest of his cookie onto the plate and stormed from the room.

Jonah waited several minutes before looking up from

his soup to meet Sumner's gaze. To his infinite surprise, she giggled. The stern, controlled Dr. Havisham *giggled*.

And that made him laugh.

Something that he hadn't done in a very long time.

Dropping his spoon into his empty bowl, he pointed to the plate of cookies.

"Would you be so kind as to pass the cookies?"

Sumner's smile was warm and knowing—as if they shared a secret. Which he supposed they did.

"With pleasure."

"Thank you, Sumner."

"You are more than welcome, Jonah."

Chapter Eleven

L͟ater that week, Sumner sighed when yet another miner entered the infirmary under the guise of "visiting an injured colleague." For days now, men had been traipsing in and out of the doctor's office—so much so, that the constant traffic had allowed the chill from outside to infiltrate the rooms. Even worse, the men were more inclined to visit with her voluntary nursing staff, rather than those miners who still needed their rest.

When the change in shifts caused a line to form outside the door, she finally stepped out and said, "Visiting hours are over. For today and tomorrow. All of these men need their rest."

"You heard the doctor," Iona said, rising from a small table where the older woman had set up a temporary registration desk in an effort to control some of the traffic in and out of the building. "Go on now, Mr. Clackett. You've been in here for an hour now, and I daresay, you've spent more time talking to Miss Rousseau than to any of our patients."

The women were met with some good-natured grumbling, but the men retreated—led by Mr. Clackett, whose ears had turned a bright shade of pink. They trudged toward the meetinghouse, since the evening's Devotional would begin in a matter of minutes.

Closing the door behind them, Emmarissa snickered. "You have a beau on your hands, Marie."

Astonishingly, Marie's ears grew just as pink as Mr. Clackett's had been.

"We share an interest in bird watching. That's all."

Emmarissa grinned. "Oh, I'm sure that's his only reason for visiting twice a day."

Sumner tried to keep a straight face, but when Marie suddenly grinned, she joined in with the other women's laughter.

"Despite the…agreeableness of their company," Sumner warned, "if the men continue to flock toward the infirmary, Mr. Batchwell is bound to complain."

Iona grimaced. "I've seen the man pacing past the building at least a half dozen times the last few days. He peeks into the windows, but doesn't come inside."

"For which we are grateful," Lydia said with a sniff. "Judging by his expression, he's spoiling for a fight."

Sumner sighed, moving from window to window, pulling down the bedlinens, which had been temporarily tacked into place until she and the other women could make or obtain more permanent curtains.

"These men are still recuperating. For that, they need some peace and quiet." She shot a glance at Marie. "Which means you might have to go bird watching somewhere else."

Even Marie laughed at that remark.

Iona handed Sumner the clipboard where they had begun to make a list of visitors.

"There has to be nearly a hundred names on this list!"

"And we only have three men under your care," Iona said dryly.

It had taken a direct order from Jonah to keep them there. They still eyed Sumner with suspicion, questioning everything she did, but at least they'd allowed her to tend to them, albeit reluctantly. But then, she supposed it had more to do with the fact that her role had shifted more to nursing them back to health than diagnosis. They had no problem allowing a woman to fuss over them.

As long as she wasn't in charge.

Which is why Jonah had been forced to intervene.

The fact still rankled, but Sumner couldn't allow her own feelings to get in the way of her patients' care.

Once the windows were covered, Sumner walked past each of the cots, ensuring the men were sleeping. Then she and the other women gathered in the kitchen.

Although the personal quarters had only been in use for few days, the area was beginning to adopt a lived-in look. There were dishes stacked on the shelf above the dry sink, a loaf of bread wrapped in a cloth on the table, a teakettle and a pot of water warming on the stove.

The other women moved to the door, donning their coats and shawls.

"Are you going to the Devotional, Sumner?"

"No. I'll stay here."

"You've been here all day," Lydia objected. "Wouldn't you like a change of scenery?"

Sumner waved them away. "I have paperwork to finish."

Lydia looked doubtful. Obviously, the other woman was wondering why Sumner was being so careful with her record keeping when her future at Bachelor Bottoms was uncertain. But Sumner would not be caught derelict in her duties. Even if no one ever bothered to look through her files, *she* would know that she had done the best job possible.

"You all go ahead."

"We'll bring you and your patients some supper afterward," Marie promised.

"That would be lovely. Thank you."

As the others stepped into the cold, Iona hesitated.

"Are you sure you wouldn't like some company?"

"No, no. I'm fine. Willow is sitting with Jenny Reichmann, who's been feeling poorly today. I told her she could find me here if Jenny grew worse."

"I could stay…"

"Go. I'm in my element, you know. I want to enjoy it while it lasts."

Iona's smile was filled with understanding.

"Good night, then."

"Good night."

A stillness settled over the infirmary as soon as the door closed and the women's voices faded into the night. If it weren't for the soughing snores of Mack Epcot, Sumner would have been left in total silence.

She was just grasping a mug from the shelf to pour herself a cup of tea when the front door opened. Sighing, she wondered if she was going to have to lock her patients inside to keep the miners from—

The thought scattered to the four winds when she looked up to find Ezra Batchwell looming in the doorway.

"Miss Havisham."

She knew it wasn't forgetfulness that caused him to omit her title, but she didn't bother to correct him. Instead, she tried to appear unaffected, even though her heart was racing like a freight train.

"Mr. Batchwell. I was about to pour myself a cup of tea. Would you like one?"

"No. This isn't a social call."

She hadn't thought that it was. Anticipating that he

would want an update, she offered, "The men are doing much better. I think we've managed to ward off frostbite. I still worry about the hit Mr. Cowan took to the head, but he's been able to converse coherently when he's awake."

"I haven't come for a recitation of their ills, either," Ezra growled.

Sumner dared to turn her back on him long enough to cross to the stove and fill her cup.

"Really? Because I thought it was the welfare of your men that was always of upmost concern to you."

When she faced him again, she was sure that Mr. Batchwell had caught her unspoken challenge. If he was about to eject her from the infirmary, he needed to think about the consequences. He might not like the fact that he'd unwittingly hired a female doctor. But at the moment, she was the only physician he had.

"I hope that you don't think I'm naive, Miss Havisham."

"I don't understand."

He stabbed a finger into the air. "You and your women have insinuated yourselves into this community!"

"We've volunteered to help, nothing more."

"You think that if you make yourselves...*indispensable*...you'll be welcomed into Aspen Valley with open arms."

Sumner bit her tongue to keep from offering a tart rejoinder. It would do her no good to insist that the women would rather have continued on to their destinations.

"Keep your women away from my men, Miss Havisham."

"*My* women?"

"You know exactly what I mean. Somehow, in this grand...*debacle*...you've become their leader. Whether this came about through accident or machination, I do not know. But things have become slipshod in the past few days, and your women have taken liberties with my authority."

Sumner opened her mouth to insist that the only liberties taken had been by the miners who had subtly begun to bring little tokens of their affection to the women who worked in the cook shack or who had volunteered to help in the infirmary. But she wasn't given the chance.

"You have a week. No more. Then these men will be moved to their own quarters and this infirmary will be locked up tight again. Once that has happened, you and your women will confine yourselves to the Miners' Hall other than to volunteer in the cook shack."

It didn't escape her that she wouldn't be allowed to care for the injured men, but the ladies' efforts at improving the food offered to the camp could continue.

"Mr. Batchwell, I—"

He held up a hand, stopping her before her objections could be made.

"That is all, Miss Havisham."

Then he stormed outside.

Jonah had barely stepped out of the meetinghouse when he found Ezra Batchwell planted firmly in his way.

"I want the women out of the camp within three days' time."

"There's no way through the canyon."

"If you can't get them through the pass, then get them out of the hall. I want them as far away from the mine and its outbuildings as you possibly can."

"We don't have many structures that could house that many people at once."

"Get it done. Three days." He stabbed at Jonah's chest with a bony finger. "The reins of leadership have grown lax around here, and I want them tightened up before we lose so much control that we never get it back again. If they want to continue working in the cook shack, fine. But I want them escorted there and back by the Pinkertons." He stabbed Jonah again. "And tell Gault to put some new men on the job! The ones you've got now are trailing along behind those women like a bunch of lapdogs. I want discipline. Discipline and order. In three days!"

Then he stomped off, snow squeaking in protest beneath his boots.

Jonah sighed, shoving his hands into his pockets.

The task he'd been given was all but impossible. There weren't many buildings in all of Aspen Valley big enough to house all the women, let alone any that could be made habitable in three days. Even worse, it seemed churlish to push them out of the community—especially after all they'd done to help the miners. The daily meals alone entailed hours of work. Yet, they'd volunteered even more of their time when the men had been injured. And for that, Jonah would have to banish them to some unknown location and insist that their "protection" detail become their wardens.

But what else could he do? The owners had given their orders and it was Jonah's duty to follow through.

Even when he didn't like it.

He considered pushing back against this latest edict. But he feared that the women would be the ones to pay the price of Batchwell's ire. So he focused on the fact that, despite his own personal opinions, Batchwell did have the future of the mine at heart.

Because spring would eventually come.

The women would leave.

And the men of Batchwell Bottoms would be left alone again.

He sighed, plunging his hands into his coat pockets, striding blindly in the opposite direction that Batchwell had taken.

Only a few weeks ago, the thought would have brought a wave of relief. But so many changes had come to Aspen Valley. There were wonderful smells in the air, curtains in the windows and the distant sound of laughter. Usually, winter was a dark, gloomy time for the miners. The days were shorter, the weather was harsh and the sun was usually hidden behind a layer of storm clouds.

But this year, things were the same…but immeasurably different. The miners went about their business with a jauntiness to their steps. Rather than stomping from cook shack to mine to Devotional, they appeared to saunter, tipping their hats, offering casual greetings. With Christmas approaching, Jonah had even seen a few of them making tiny carved animals or intricate metal ornaments. Even Jonah had begun to frequent the wood shop more often, feeling a need to take a few hours' break from the job to begin a project he intended to offer to Sumner.

He came to a halt at the edge of the trees, unaware that his pace had increased to a near jog in his efforts to sort through his feelings. Somehow, he'd ended up a few hundred yards away from an old equipment warehouse that was tucked away from the mining camp in a meadow surrounded by tall stands of pines. Although the building was used from time to time, it was nearly empty now. Its location had proven to be too far away from the main buildings to be of much use except for long-term storage.

His breath hung in the air like a silver cloud. He pounded his feet. Sometimes, when he exerted himself, they grew tingly and numb…

"Jonah? You feeling okay?"

He looked up to find Gideon Gault on horseback a few yards away.

"Yeah, I'm fine."

Gault didn't look entirely convinced. He swung from the saddle, leading his mount by the reins.

"What's up? You look ready to chew some iron and spit out nails."

Trust Gideon to sum up his thoughts in such a colorful manner.

"Batchwell's got his dander up again. He wants the women out of the hall and away from the main workings of the mine."

Gault whistled softly in commiseration. "I've never seen the man so riled by anything before. He's always had a temper, but where those girls are concerned…" He followed the line of Jonah's gaze. "Where does he want you to put them?"

"He didn't say, but…" Jonah pointed toward the two-story structure, a plan beginning to form. "What about the old equipment shed there? It's nearly empty."

Gault squinted into the gloom. "I don't know…it's not in the best of shape."

"We'd have to reinforce the siding to keep out the cold, add more box heaters, put up some walls. The women would probably like a little area for cooking. Maybe another place for bathing. And if we put an addition onto that far end, we could even provide a place for Sumner to do her doctoring."

The thought made Jonah smile.

Gideon chuckled softly. "If Ezra Batchwell caught wind of all the improvements, he's bound to blow a gasket."

"True." Jonah met his friend's gaze. "But I don't re-

ally care at this point. After everything the women have
done for us, they deserve a nice place to stay. And judging from all the men I've seen hanging around the infirmary, I'm pretty sure we could get some volunteers who
would be willing to help give a little something back."

Gideon nodded. "I don't doubt that. They've even
managed to charm my men."

"Which is why Batchwell also wants you to change
your shifts."

"As it is, I've got more guys watching the women than
our silver stores."

"Batchwell thinks the ones you've got are being too
chummy. If you aren't careful, he'll probably pull you
away from the mine and put *you* in charge of the women."

Gideon shook his head and held up his hands. "No.
No, no, no. I was raised with five older sisters. The last
thing I need is a day spent with anyone from the fairer
sex. I'll have a talk with my crew. Get them to tighten
things up. But you'd better plead on my behalf if Batchwell threatens to put me on bride patrol."

"I could be persuaded. If…"

"If?"

"If you show up tomorrow, right here, after your shift,
with a hammer, nails and at least six of your men."

"So…all our patients have flown the coop, hmm?"

Sumner looked up to find Iona standing in the doorway to the examination room.

"Yes. They insisted that they were well enough to return to work." She grimaced. "But I'm sure that a visit
from Mr. Batchwell and Mr. Bottoms had more to do
with it than my own doctoring skills."

"Perhaps. Or perhaps it had to do with the work itself.

I heard Mr. Cowan grumbling that time was money and time spent off the job meant no money at all."

"Hmm. I can understand that line of thinking."

Even though Sumner would have insisted that the men take a few more days—or weeks—to allow bones to knit and bruises to fade, she knew more than anyone how the will to support oneself could shift one's priorities.

Iona's gaze grew concerned. "I suppose your thoughts have wandered into similar territory?"

Sumner nodded. "The time will come soon enough when I'll be forced out of Bachelor Bottoms. Mr. Batchwell has been quite clear on that point. Even after showing him that I could handle an emergency situation, he remains…"

"Obstinate."

"Yes."

"So what will you do?"

Sumner shrugged. She wasn't sure why she was being so forthcoming. Normally, she kept her problems to herself. But she was beginning to form strong friendships with so many of the women: Lydia, Willow and Iona in particular.

"I should be establishing contingency plans, I know. I'm going to have to find a new position and a new home."

The thought caused an invisible hand to close around her heart. She'd grown to love this quaint mining community. How she would have loved to test her mettle here a little longer.

But she couldn't stay.

As soon as spring came, she and the other women would be going.

Iona entered the room and sat in the chair opposite Sumner's desk.

"We're in much the same boat, you and I." Iona

smoothed a wrinkle from her all-encompassing work apron. "I never thought I'd say this, but I'm not looking forward to the moment when spring arrives."

"Really? I thought you were originally planning on visiting your sister. Won't you be living in her house?"

Iona grimaced. "I don't mind visiting my sister—we haven't seen each other in ages. It's *living* with her that's the problem."

"Oh?"

"She has a large family—nine children. Her husband's a hard worker, bless his soul, but he and I tend to rub each other the wrong way. I know that they're living hand to mouth—" she sighed "—and I'll be another mouth to feed." Her eyes grew sad. "I don't relish becoming the object of charity."

"I'm so sorry."

Iona waved dismissively. "Don't be. We all have our trials." Her lips twitched in a semblance of a smile. "If I were one of these mail-order brides—and I had a home of my own awaiting me—I'd invite you to stay with me."

Sumner's eye pricked with tears. The offer was so sweet.

"Thank you, Iona."

"Do you have anyone you can go to for help? At least until you can get your feet back under you?"

Sumner shook her head. "No."

She had no kin in the states or the territories. Worse, she had no real money left to pay for passage or even the means to search for another job.

What was she going to do?

So far, she'd spent countless hours on her knees, praying that the Lord would guide her in her decisions. She kept telling herself to have faith. Somehow, someway, the Lord would help her.

Just keep the faith.

Iona took a deep breath and stood.

"Don't give up. When the time comes, the Lord will provide."

Iona's statement was so close to Sumner's own thoughts that she felt a tiny spark of hope.

"I think it's time the two of us headed back to the hall. We'll have a cup of Willow's cocoa and gingerbread, then listen to the other women chatter. It will take our minds off our troubles."

"Yes. That sounds like a good idea."

Even so, at the door to the infirmary, she couldn't help glancing behind her. This time, she'd left the supplies on their shelves and the linens and blankets folded neatly at the ends of the cots. She would never be so callous as to wish for another emergency, but she felt that if a need should arise for her doctoring skills, she would rather perform them in the proper setting.

Straightening her shoulders, she twisted the key in the lock, then linked arms with Iona. The two of them walked slowly, enjoying the weak sun that tried to peek through the clouds. But as they reached the Miners' Hall, a pair of Pinkertons carrying rifles snapped to attention on either side of the door.

Since Mr. Batchwell's visit, the "protection" detail had tightened their stranglehold. They were so rigorous in their duties that none of the women were allowed to leave the Miners' Hall without prior authorization. Once they walked through the door, they were kept under guard with double the men watching them than they'd had before.

"I don't know whether to feel like I'm under house arrest or that I'm so precious I could be stolen from the streets," Iona muttered under her breath. "If it weren't for those sweet miners who still smile at us from across the cook shack counter, I'd begin to think I'd come down with leprosy or something."

Iona's second comment was stated loud enough for the Pinkertons to hear her, and Sumner hid a smile when the two guards exchanged glances.

"Come to think of it…" Sumner glanced around her at the sparkling snow, the mounded drifts and the empty boardwalks. "The camp has been strangely empty lately." She leveled a narrowed gaze on the new guards. So far, they had refused to tell any of the women their names. Perhaps that was considered too *personal*.

"Did Batchwell say something to them?" Iona demanded.

Again, the men exchanged glances, but other than one of them saying, "It's time to go inside, ladies," they offered no explanation.

She shot a glance to the guard at her left, then the one at her right. Neither of them bothered to look her in the eye. They gazed past her, as if expecting a hoard of thieves to appear at any moment.

"Have you been forbidden to talk to us directly?" she asked.

Nothing.

Not even a flicker of an eyelid.

Sighing, Sumner allowed her gaze to stray in the direction of the mining offices. By now, she'd determined that the upper left corner window was the one to Jonah's office. There had been a time when she'd been able to see him standing there, his hands braced on the sill. She'd felt his gaze as she'd moved to the infirmary or the cook shack.

But he had disappeared along with the other men.

One of the Pinkertons reached to open the door to the

hall. Iona stepped inside, but when Sumner moved to join her, she was stopped when a deep voice called out, "Whoa! Hold up there!"

When she turned to find Jonah striding toward her, Sumner's mood suddenly took wings.

"She needs to come with me," he said to the guards. "Dr. Havisham and I have some business to attend to before she rejoins the other ladies."

Jonah led her in the opposite direction. He waited until they were out of earshot before saying, "Walk with me?"

She nodded, her heart thumping giddily against her ribs.

"How have you been?"

Sumner had been so afraid that he would return to the stern manner he'd used the first few days the women had come to the camp that the warmth of his tone took her by surprise.

"I'm well, thank you."

"You've been working long hours at the infirmary."

"I can hardly call doing something I love 'work.'"

He frowned a little. Not in disapproval. More like… regret.

"You're good at what you do."

She couldn't contain the flash of a smile. "Thank you. And how are you feeling?"

"Fine."

This time, it was her turn to frown. He walked stiffly, which meant he was in pain.

"You're sure?"

"Sure enough."

Sensing she would get no other answers for now, she didn't pursue the matter. Later. When they weren't out in the open where anyone could see.

They walked in companionable silence, down the main

street, past the infirmary, past the storehouse, past all of
the established mining buildings, before taking one of
the side streets. No, not really a street. More of a track
that had been formed by the passage of horses, sleigh
runners and boots.

"Where are we going?" she finally asked.

Jonah gestured to a point farther down the winding
road. Although the track soon disappeared into the trees,
she could just make out the corner of a large wooden
structure.

"I need to show you the equipment shed."

Equipment shed?

Were there more foodstuffs there?

Their shoes squeaked in the snow, and when Sumner slipped, Jonah grasped her arm. But even after she'd
steadied herself, he maintained the gentle grip. That small
point of contact warmed her far more than her heavy
woolen greatcoat.

"You've probably noticed that Mr. Batchwell has insisted that the Pinkertons be increased in size. He's also
stated that they are to be more…diligent in their duties."

"Yes. We figured he'd had a hand in the change."

"I know how…burdensome you find their presence."

"It feels as if we've committed a crime."

His head dipped. "I know and I'm sorry for that. But
the owners are adamant. There's to be no interaction between the women and the men beyond the cook shack
and the evening Devotionals."

"So we're doomed to stay indoors like naughty children again?"

Jonah shook his head. "I've spoken to Mr. Batchwell
and Mr. Bottoms, and I think I've been able to come up
with a compromise that will suit you both."

They were rounding the trees now, and Sumner was

able to see that the snow had been trampled down around the building. Ash and sawdust had been trodden into the ice, turning it a dingy gray.

Sumner stopped in her tracks, unsure what huge compromise the cavernous building constituted.

"I don't understand."

"This will be your new home—the home of all the women—until the pass clears."

She blinked, taking in the roughly hewn wood and raw beams. The building had been designed for one single purpose, and that was to hold large pieces of machinery. But as a place of habitation?

From the outside, it looked riddled with knotholes and wide chinks. Judging by its appearance, it hadn't been constructed to keep out the weather. Its confines would be little better than the open air.

Sumner opened her mouth to voice her objections, but before she could make a sound, Jonah squeezed her arm.

"Don't say anything yet. Wait until you look inside."

Sumner held her tongue as Jonah led her forward.

"Out here in the meadow, you're away from the main runnings of the mine, so you'll have more freedom. As long as you don't stray beyond the trees, you can venture outside, go on short walks, tend to your laundry needs from a huge fire pit behind the building."

"But we're still to be...confined. No doubt under the Pinkertons' watchful eyes."

"They'll be farther back, out of your sight."

"But—"

He squeezed her arm again. "I told you it was a *compromise*. That implies some give-and-take from both sides."

So she would have to hold her tongue.

At least until she could see inside and gather more ammunition for her arguments.

Jonah reached out to open the door, swinging it wide.

"My crew and I have been working on this for about a week now."

"*Your* crew."

"I pulled some men off the line to get things in order."

Sumner knew enough about Jonah's work habits to know that such an action wasn't taken lightly.

"Did the men object?"

"No. Most of them volunteered."

His fingers touched her back as he ushered her inside.

The moment the door closed, Sumner was washed in warmth, disproving her earlier assumption that the structure would be cold and drafty.

Slowly, her eyes adjusted from the brilliant sunshine outside to the dimness inside. When they did, she was able to see that she'd been led into a large sitting room complete with two potbellied stoves, a long trestle table and chairs for eating their meals and myriad rockers and easy chairs.

"The men brought some of their own furniture to help you feel more comfortable as well as a few…ornaments."

He pointed to a stuffed moose head hanging from the far wall and a trio of ferrets dressed like clowns positioned on an upright piano.

"Klute Ingraham has a fondness for taxidermy. You can feel free to…redecorate things later if the women find such things objectionable."

Objectionable wasn't the first word that sprang to mind. *Bizarre* would have been a better description. Maybe *unnerving*.

"If you'll come this way…"

Jonah took her through a doorway at the far end.

There, she discovered a kitchen of sorts with a dry sink, a smaller table and chairs and an iron range.

"For your meals should you choose. We figured you women would like a cup of tea now and then." He pointed to planks of wood that had become makeshift shelves. Besides canisters marked Tea and Coffee, she saw a battered coffeepot, a chipped teapot and a collection of mismatched teacups. On a lower shelf were bags of food-stuffs: salt, dried fruits, flour, sugar.

Jonah took her hand, his fingers warm through her gloves. He led her to a staircase near the rear door, taking her up, up, to what had once been the loft.

"We've divided the upper floor into smaller living quarters. A few are private. None houses more than three women."

He opened the doors one by one to reveal neat cots and borrowed dressers.

"Where on earth did you get all this furniture?"

"The men. I don't think there's a soul in Aspen Valley who hasn't brought something."

But it was more than that. There were also crocks filled with untidy clumps of evergreen boughs, bowls filled with pinecones, water pitchers and basins, rag rugs and even an attempt at curtains in a couple of the spaces.

At the last door, Sumner's throat grew tight. "You and your men have gone to so much work, Mr. Ramsey."

"Jonah," he reminded her softly.

"Jonah."

He squeezed her hand. "There's one more."

He took her down the stairs again where they crossed through the kitchen to yet another room beyond. The space looked newer than the rest of the building, and the walls and floors gleamed with newly planed planks. The air was redolent with the scent of pine. She blinked back sudden tears when she saw that the space had been divided in half with a curtain. To one side was a primitive examining table and bookcases to hold her supplies, two cots and a nightstand. To the right was a homier space with a tall tester bed, a highboy, wood pegs to hold a selection of clothes and an elegant rocker.

"Oh."

"This is for you. You can tend to the women's doctoring needs on one side and have your own private area on the other. With only a curtain between you, you'll be able to hear if someone calls out to you."

"Oh, Jonah," she breathed.

He touched the back of the rocker—one that looked like it had hardly been used—sending it swaying.

"Try it."

She quickly sank into its depths, loving the way that the runners caused the chair to lean back.

"It's so comfortable."

"My mother used to call these 'baby tendahs.' They're made to recline ever so slightly so that a baby—or something else—can be balanced on your lap."

She stroked the arms of the chair. "It's beautiful. I don't know if I should borrow something so fine."

"I made it," Jonah blurted, interrupting her. "It's yours. Call it an early Christmas present." He pointed to something else on the floor. It was similar in shape to a loaf of bread, made of metal, with handles on either end. The center section had been wrapped with a section of braided rug. "That's a foot warmer. When you pull on the handle, a metal tray will come out and you can fill it with hot coals."

Sumner found herself speechless—which her father would probably insist was a rare occasion. She remembered how Jonah had once described the way his father had prepared his mother's rocker, a lap quilt and a foot warmer so that she could enjoy her evenings.

"You made these?" she breathed. "For me?"

"Yes. I wanted you to…have something special." He quickly added, "For all the work you did helping my men."

But shivering behind the words was the fact that he'd given her something *personal*.

According to the dictates of polite society, she should refuse such expensive gifts. But…

She'd been rebelling against polite society for a very, very long time.

"Thank you, Jonah."

That familiar secret smile hovered around his lips.

"I'm glad you like it."

"When you said you liked to carve, I envisioned… little animals or small toys, not…" Her fingers trailed over the armrests that ended in a spiral inset with three-dimensional blossoms.

Orange blossoms.

Like her favorite scent.

Or a bridal headpiece.

Where on earth had that thought come from? Sumner had decided long ago that marriage wasn't for her. There wasn't a man alive who would allow a woman to work once they were married. And she'd had enough of controlling males telling her what to do.

But that thought didn't stop the image of spending time with someone like Jonah, someone who regarded her as a partner. An equal. A relationship like that might sway her opinion on the usefulness of men.

"Do you think that the women will find their new home agreeable?"

She nodded. The miners had managed to make a difficult situation bearable.

"As you said, compromises will be made on both sides, but I think that the women will feel more comfortable here."

"The men have volunteered to help with the move. A pair of sledges will be sent to the Miners' Hall tomorrow at midday. My crew will take care of all your trunks as well as anything else you see fit to bring with you from the hall."

"Thank you. That's very kind of all of you."

Jonah nodded, holding out a hand. "Shall we?"

When she placed her palm in his, he pulled her upright, but he didn't immediately release her. Silence spooled between them, warm and silken and sweet as honey. A frisson of gooseflesh ran up her arm when his thumb stroked across her knuckles. Even through the thin layer of her kid gloves, she could feel his strength and warmth.

Strangely, she wanted to wallow in the peculiar new emotions that engulfed her. But she couldn't allow herself that luxury. Nothing could ever come from them. Jonah had already made it clear that he had no desire to ever leave the valley. And she...

She would never be allowed to stay.

As if sensing her disquiet, Jonah's free hand lifted, hovering in the air next to her cheek, before finally, he touched her, briefly, lightly, soft as a butterfly's wing.

In that instant, she felt beautiful. Feminine.

Cherished.

It took every ounce of strength she possessed not to lean into that caress. In another world, she might allow herself the fantasy of a future where anything was possible.

"I'm sorry that Aspen Valley hasn't turned out the way

you'd hoped," Jonah murmured. "But I'm glad I had the chance to meet you, Sumner."

"And I, you, Jonah."

Again, the silence twined between them, binding them together. The air shimmered with possibilities.

Then a door slammed somewhere and a voice called out.

"Boss? You in here?"

Jonah's hand snapped to his side and he released her. Clearing his throat, he took two ground-eating strides.

"Back here, Creakle."

Barely a half dozen heartbeats had passed before the old man joined them. "Hey, Doc! What do y' think?"

"Everything is lovely, Mr. Creakle."

He jerked a hand in Jonah's direction. "This one here demanded nothing but the best. Told us to imagine our own wives or sisters or sweethearts needin' a place t' stay if'n they was stranded. What he said made the men work 'specially hard."

Sumner met Jonah's gaze for only a moment before he looked away, and in that moment, she found her estimation of the man doubled.

"You've all been very kind, Mr. Creakle."

Creakle grinned at her, then turned his attention to his boss.

In an instant, Jonah's eye grew shuttered. Professional. "Did you need something, Creakle?"

"We got a problem in tunnel six. It's fillin' up with water and the men can't pump it fast enough."

Jonah nodded. "I'll be right there. In the meantime, make sure that all crews are accounted for in case we need to evacuate the tunnel."

"Yes, boss!"

Jonah waited until the door slammed before turning to Sumner.

"I've got to go."

"Yes."

But he didn't move. Not immediately.

"I'm afraid I won't be able to escort you back. But I'll send a Pinkerton to come fetch you. It shouldn't take more than twenty minutes for him to get here."

She could have insisted that she was more than capable of walking back to the hall on her own. But…

Compromises need to be made on both sides.

Besides, if she waited for her guard, she would have some time alone to absorb her new home.

"I'll be fine. Go. They wouldn't have sent for you unless it was important."

"It is. I'll…" He grimaced. "I'll check back with you after Devotional, just to make sure that the women have what they need."

"I'd like that."

"If you wouldn't mind, perhaps you could join me in the private dining room for a meal? We could talk more freely there."

"If you're sure you'll have the time."

And there was that ghost of a smile that she was beginning to love.

"I'll make time."

Chapter Twelve

Jonah remained true to his promise. In the days that followed, he made a point to break from his usual routine to spend some time with Sumner.

At first, it had been easy to justify his visits. He needed to ensure that the women were safe, warm and as comfortable as possible in their new home. He oversaw the need for firewood to be stacked against the rear wall and arranged for water and foodstuffs to be delivered. Then there was the matter of a repair to a portion of the roof that was leaking and clearing the paths when it snowed. All in all, he had plenty of reasons to visit the Dovecote, as the men were beginning to call it.

He wasn't the only one who found himself being drawn to the Dovecote. When something needed to be done, there were ample volunteers. Rather than putting the women out of the miners' minds, their new home drew the men like moths to a flame. What had once been an ugly eyesore of a building had become a home. Lamplight glowed from the windows through a filter of lacy curtains cobbled together from old feed sacks and stashes of fabric the women had brought with them in their trunks. Soon, the window coverings were adorned with crocheted trim as fine as a spider's web. Music wove into the darkness from the upright piano, the out-of-tune notes softened by a chorus of feminine voices. And the scents that floated from the stovepipe…since the women had begun to make many of the cook shack treats in the Dovecote, the aromas of cinnamon and apples, ginger and yeast, swirled around the building with their delicious perfumes.

But Jonah knew that even all those elements paled to the warmth and friendliness that flowed from the women themselves. The men used any excuse possible to complete a chore nearby, just to be invited inside to warm themselves by the fire and wallow in a bit of feminine fussing.

Jonah himself had begun to see them all less as a batch of inconvenient females and more as individuals. There was Willow Granger, with her curly hair and voluminous clothing, who always seemed too shy to talk but eager to help; Iona Skye, a motherly older woman who knitted the men mufflers from an endless supply of wool she'd brought with her in her trunks; and Lydia Tomlinson, who had taken over the organizing of the cook shack crews and meals with the efficiency of a master foreman. There were the gigglers: Enid, Molly and Milly. And the worriers: Tilda, Zephronia and Sariah.

And there was Sumner.

Jonah couldn't get her out of his mind. Even in the darkest regions of the mine, he found himself remembering her smile, the scent of orange blossoms that clung to her skin, her laugh.

He wasn't so much a fool that he didn't realize that he was falling under her spell. He may have sworn off women of any kind after joining the Batchwell Bottoms

Mining Enterprise, but that didn't mean he didn't remember the headiness of shared affection.

Over and over again, he tried to tell himself that he needed to take a step back, to remain aloof and to remove himself from temptation. After all, he had absolutely nothing that he could offer someone like Sumner. Even if he didn't live in a community where women were forbidden, even if he didn't know that their time together could only last until the spring thaw, he couldn't erase the more tangible obstacle to any form of relationship.

He was tainted goods.

With the shrapnel in his back threatening his every move, he didn't have anything of worth that he could offer a woman. Even if he might want to consider making her his wife.

His breath hung in the air as Jonah labored to split the pile of logs at his feet. He'd purposely avoided the Dovecote this morning, knowing that it would be best if he started putting some distance between him and the women.

Not just the women.

Sumner.

But here she was again. Haunting his very thoughts.

Dragging air into his lungs, Jonah bowed his head, the ax hanging at his side as he fought the demons that had been plaguing him since the most recent avalanche.

Just when he'd begun to tell himself that maybe he could have a future, that his old injury wasn't nearly the threat that the earlier doctors had supposed, he'd been met with a new host of symptoms. Rather than the ache that had plagued him for years, he was now experiencing a newer, sharper series of pains. Numbness in his toes and feet. Bouts of weakness to his legs. An occasional loss of balance.

No.

Not now.

Dear Lord in Heaven, please help me.

"Jonah?"

He whirled to find Sumner watching him in concern. "Are you all right?"

He nearly laughed aloud. He'd been praying for help and the Good Lord had seen fit to send the object of his torment instead.

"Wha—no, I'm fine."

He couldn't let her see how weak he'd become. Not yet. Not when it might be a phase that could pass.

She walked toward him and he watched in confusion as she reached out to take the ax from his grip, then held up his palms.

Too late, he realized that he'd been so anxious to allow some good, honest exertion to drive the anxiety from his soul that he'd forgotten his gloves and the palms of his hands were blistered and raw.

"Jonah."

This time, her utterance of his name was half sigh, half remonstration. And that British lilt that he loved so much seemed to radiate with concern.

"You have enough firewood here for the entire camp. What on earth made you punish yourself so?"

He wondered what she would say if he replied honestly.

You.

Because I can't have you.

He tried to curl his fingers into a fist, barely feeling the sting to his hands. Instead, he was spellbound by the emotions that swept over her features.

Concern.

Regret.

Tenderness.

For him.

The air seemed to trap in his throat in frozen blocks of ice.

"Come on. We need to see to these or they could become infected."

He wanted to resist. But his body had a mind of its own and he trailed after her as she ushered him into his own home.

No. Not a home.

If there was anything that the women in the Dovecote had taught him, it was that his bachelor quarters were not a home. His rooms were a shelter over his head, a place to keep warm through the darkness of the night.

But they weren't a home.

"Where's—"

"My guard?" Her grin was crooked. Open. Yet somehow private. "Lurking in the trees. I told him that I had a private medical matter to discuss with you and that he could guard me just as well from a distance as he could at my elbow."

"And he believed you?"

Her brows rose. "Why wouldn't he? I was telling him the truth. I might have led him to believe that I wished to discuss someone from your crew, but I came to check on you."

He sank into the chair she'd pulled away from the table, his knees suddenly weak.

She knew.

She already knew there was something wrong.

Jonah swallowed, not quite sure how he felt about that. All his life, he'd fought to appear strong. Whole. He'd sworn to himself that he wouldn't be pitied or dismissed because of his afflictions. There were men who had survived the war who continued to suffer far worse. The last thing he wanted was for others to whisper about him under their breaths. He'd hidden his ailment from most of the men at Batchwell Bottoms, and he would have done anything to have kept it from Sumner, as well.

But now that she knew…

There was a sense of relief.

And fear.

She would reject him. She *should* reject him.

Any other woman would reject him.

He avoided her eyes, praying that he was wrong. Perhaps she was here to follow up on her earlier examination, to check the cuts and scrapes that had all but healed.

Sumner crossed to the stove to retrieve the pot of water that was kept over the dying coals during the day. She tested it with a finger, filled the nearby washbasin, then she returned.

"You need to take better care of yourself," she said as she pushed his hands into the liquid. Even though it was tepid, he hissed at the sting of his battered flesh.

She retrieved a clean cloth from a pile on the upper shelf, then sank into the chair next to him. Scooping his hands from the basin, she began to blot them dry.

"Why didn't you wear gloves?"

"I… I forgot."

Her movements were sure, gentle. Far gentler than he deserved. And with her head bent over the task, Jonah was overcome with a wave of regret.

If things had been different—if *he* had been different—he could easily imagine what it would be like to make his house a home.

With her.

But swift on the heels of that thought came an icy wave of reality.

He couldn't change the past.

He wasn't even sure he could change the present.

She looked up at him then, her eyes dark and warm and filled with concern.

"Now tell me the rest."

The words were enough to cause his heart to thud against his ribs with slow dread.

"The rest?"

She made a soft, disappointed *tut-tut.*

"Something has changed."

One last time, he tried to prevaricate.

"Changed?"

She sighed. "You're moving more stiffly. Your gait is altered. Sometimes you steady yourself going up and down stairs."

He should have known that she would notice. He should have stayed away even more.

"Are you in pain?"

Again, he considered prevaricating. But when their gazes locked, he knew that he owed her the truth. If anything could help to drive a wedge between them, it would be the starkness of his future.

"The pain in my back is different. Sharper."

"Do you have any redness in that area? Swelling?"

He shook his head. "The scrapes and cuts are all but healed. Other than that…nothing."

"Any numbness? Tingling?"

"In my toes. Sometimes farther up."

"So your balance has been affected."

"Sometimes."

He wondered if she was aware of the way her thumbs had begun to move in soothing circles over his wrists. Could she feel even a portion of the warmth that began to spread from that point of contact?

Jonah had thought that by confessing the worst to her, he would feel himself emasculated. After all, what kind of man spoke so bluntly to a woman? His father had taught him that men were to be strong and uncomplaining, never giving any hint of weakness. What lady would entrust herself to a male who couldn't be a provider and a protector?

To his surprise, there was no change of affection in her eyes. In fact, if anything, she grew fiercer in her devotion.

"The shrapnel may have shifted. Judging by the abrasions on your back, you were pushed down the slope with tremendous force."

Again, his throat seemed to be full of wooden blocks that were all pointy edges.

She reached to cup his cheek.

"But it could be nothing at all. There could be some deep swelling that we cannot see, or an injury to the bones themselves."

Did she know how the heat of her hand filled him with bittersweet emotion?

Could she sense the way her attempts at encouragement had the power to rip his heart from his chest?

Because he wanted to believe her.

He wanted to believe that he could have a future.

With her.

She must have sensed at least a small portion of his chaotic thoughts, because her gaze dropped to his lips. He knew what she was thinking.

He should kiss her.

But he couldn't. Not with his confessions hovering in the air around them. He didn't want their first kiss to be given that way—out of fear or concern.

He wanted to give himself freely to her. Heart and mind.

She must have understood, because she leaned back,

her hand dropping into her lap. The curve of her lips became rueful.

"We're quite a pair, you and I," she murmured.

"Oh?"

"You can't give your heart away because you worry about the future. And me? I can't give it away because of the past."

She stood then. "See to it that you wrap your hands with clean, dry cloths until the blisters heal. I won't see you adding an infection to your list of worries."

Then she left in a swirl of skirts.

Leaving the tantalizing scent of orange blossoms hanging in the air around him.

The moment her feet touched the snowy ground, Sumner strode away from the bachelor quarters so fast that her Pinkerton guard had to run to catch up to her. But as he took his regular place at her elbow, she barely noticed him.

What she'd told Jonah was true. His symptoms could be nothing more than his body trying to heal itself. But his own concern over his new symptoms was so palpable that it had touched a frisson of fear within her body, as well. She could sense the emotions and uncertainty that tore at him—and she understood the way he inwardly warred with himself.

Because she was feeling much the same confusion.

Neither of them knew where tomorrow would take them—let alone the next few months. But even those concerns paled in comparison to the emotions that were building between them. They'd begun to care for one another. Deeply.

But their relationship was complicated. Too complicated. There was no denying the fondness blossoming between them. Neither of them could pretend that it was just friendship they shared. Not anymore. No, the tangle of sentiment that ran between them spanned the gamut from attraction to affection to…

Sumner shied away from the thought, knowing she couldn't bring herself to admit that love had entered the arena, as well.

Love was improbable—impossible.

Especially for her.

Her words to Jonah echoed in her brain. *You can't give your heart away because you worry about the future. And me? I can't give it away because of the past.*

What she'd told Jonah was true. It wasn't just the fact that she wanted to be a doctor. It wasn't just that she'd spent a lifetime sacrificing all she'd held dear to bring such a dream to fruition.

The old ghosts of the past still haunted her. As much as she might revel in her accomplishments, there was still a part of her, deep inside, that couldn't believe they were true.

Unwanted tears prickled and stung—against the cold, only the cold. But that still didn't stop her mind's eye from recreating that moment when her father had brought home his new bride and her son.

Jefferson Thackery Newton.

He'd been younger than her, stout and double-chinned, with mean piggy eyes. He'd had an aversion to bathing and a tendency to tease and demean those in his path until tears flowed.

And her father had adored him.

Because he was a boy.

Jefferson had never lost an opportunity to needle her with the fact. Indeed, he'd become her father's toady, echoing her father's sentiments about the proper role of females. But where her father had couched his words in barely veiled criticism, Jefferson had not been so diplomatic.

Her chin tilted ever so slightly.

In the end, she'd shown him—shown them both—that she would not be confined by so narrow a fence. She'd made something of herself—and she'd continue to do so.

Even if a part of her sometimes wished that she could add the role of wife and mother to her list of accomplishments.

But the world didn't work that way. She would be allowed a profession or a relationship but never both. And even if she could have it all, there would still be a mountain range of obstacles in her path. Because she was beginning to believe that she'd met the only man who might be willing to accept her many facets. But in a few months' time, the snow would melt and she would be forced to leave for an uncertain future.

While he would have to remain.

Sumner knew how much he loved his job at the Batchwell Bottom mine—with the men and the employers that he'd grown to respect so much. And since his health was an issue, he might not be able to get work elsewhere.

Not that she would ever ask him to leave.

Sumner would never deny a person the opportunity to work at a job they loved. Not when she herself had suffered such a fate so many times in the past.

So she had to remind herself that they were both better off if they hadn't kissed. They should keep their contact to a minimum and avoid the emotions that twined between them.

"Miss. Miss!"

She skidded to a halt, realizing that she'd walked right past the Dovecote without realizing that she'd arrived.

"You're already home," the man said, gesturing to the door.

Once again, her eyes pricked and she blinked against the brightness of the snow, taking in the V-shaped valley, the dark, spicy pine trees and the glitter of the river in the distance. Here in the Dovecote, away from the mine and its outbuildings, the view was unhindered and spectacular. For a moment, the beauty of the sight was so overwhelming that it nearly took her breath away.

Yes. She was home. This place spoke to the core of her being, reminding her of the beauties of God and the importance of service and devotion.

And love.

So how on earth was she going to survive that moment when she was told it was time to leave?

"I can get that, Sumner. I've already got the hot pads right here."

Not for the first time, Sumner was gently maneuvered away from the range—or the counter, or the worktable. Not sure where she could go to be out of the way, Sumner paused in the doorway of the cook shack, her gaze roaming over the miners who were bent above their meals.

Normally, she tried to help during the morning shift, but after her encounter with Jonah, she hadn't wanted to spend the evening alone with her thoughts. And since she lacked patients to fill her little infirmary at the Dovecote, she'd decided the heat and steam of the kitchen would give her the diversion that she needed.

But she was beginning to believe that she'd become an extra wheel in a well-oiled machine.

So, she needed to find something else to do. Something where she wouldn't be in the way.

Grabbing a cloth, she retrieved a pot of coffee from

the stove. Rather than filling the mugs of the men who made their way down the line, she moved into the dining room itself.

She knew there would be the devil to pay if Batchwell or Bottoms came into the room. The women had been allowed access to the kitchen, but had been strictly forbidden to talk to the men without the pass-through counter between them. Even then, their conversations were supposed to be contained to yes, no and the food.

But Sumner didn't care.

"Good evening, Mr. Cowan."

Cowan jumped when she hovered over his shoulder.

"Miss… *Dr.* Havisham." His gaze glanced guiltily to the door, then to the other miners seated at the same table. A hush settled over the room. Even the sound of cutlery stilled as the men waited to see what happened.

"How have you been feeling since you returned to work?"

"Fine." The word was a statement, but emerged as a slight question.

"Wonderful. Could I warm up your coffee for you?"

There was a beat of silence, two, each of them accompanied by the blink of his eyes. Then he seemed to shake himself loose.

"Yes, ma'am?"

This time, his response was a definite question, but Sumner didn't give him a chance to change his mind. She topped off his mug and turned to the next man. "Mr. Smalls, how about you?"

Smalls eagerly nodded his head.

"I heard that you have a small herd of goats near the livery that you keep for their milk?"

He grinned.

"Are any of them angora goats?"

He nodded again.

"I'll be sure to tell Mrs. Skye and the Misses Claussen. They are very fond of knitting, and they've mentioned that they are nearly out of wool." She turned to the next man. "Mr...."

"Ingraham," he supplied quickly, holding his mug out, even though it was still nearly full.

"Klute Ingraham?"

"Yes, ma'am."

"Thank you so much for the stuffed ferret clowns you donated to the Dovecote. The women have found their addition to our home delightful."

By the time she moved from that particular table to the next, the men had lost their reserve. They welcomed her arrival with broad smiles and raised cups, offering her their names without being asked.

"Cliff Cooper. I work in the shop."

"Peter Rundel. I'm part of the blast crew."

"And Mr. Wanlass," she said, recognizing the lay preacher. "I've enjoyed your sermons at the evening Devotionals. Thank you."

"Thank you, Miss Havisham."

She paused with each man, asking about his day, inquiring whether he liked the food, discussing the weather. As conversation went, there was nothing scintillating about her topics or her methods. But with each encounter, the men began to stand out in her mind as individuals, rather than just a group of employees for the mine.

Again and again, she returned to the kitchen, filled the coffeepot, then ventured out into the dining hall. When the coffee ran out, she returned with plates of cookies. To her immense satisfaction, the interaction helped to remind her why she'd become a doctor in the first place. She loved helping people, loved making them feel better, physically and mentally. So she smiled and laughed, her spirits lifting with each conversation.

Something of her mood must have translated itself to the men, because the dining hall—which had always echoed with low, hushed tones—grew loud and boisterous with laughter. The men seemed less on guard.

Sumner wasn't sure when she became aware of being watched. She turned, fearing that the owners had stepped into the room, and inwardly, she braced herself for a confrontation. But when she looked up, it wasn't Batchwell and Bottoms who stared at her from the archway leading to the kitchen.

It was Jonah.

Her heart lurched into her throat. She might have been willing to defy the owners, but she didn't want to do anything to make Jonah think less of her. But as she met his gaze and wondered if she'd strayed too far from the rules, his lips lifted in a smile—one that crinkled at the corners of his eyes. Then he touched a finger to the brim of his hat in silent salute.

The breath nearly left her body altogether. How could such a simple gesture of support affect her so deeply?

She wasn't given enough time to analyze the sensation. Just as quickly as he'd appeared, he was gone.

"I do believe he's smitten with you, Dr. Havisham."

She whirled to find that the table nearby held a single occupant. A tall, slender gentleman dressed in the familiar Pinkerton uniform. But as she studied his face, Sumner was sure that she'd never seen him guarding the hall.

He reached for one of the cookies on the plate she held.

"I'm afraid you're mistaken, Mr...."

"Gault. Gideon Gault." He took a bite of the cookie, chewing slowly, peering at her so intently that she feared the heat beginning to creep up her neck might give her true feelings away.

"I don't think so. Ramsey and I...we go way back."

His gaze was piercing, his features blank—and in that instant, Sumner knew why she'd never seen him as one of her guards. This was a man who was used to being in charge, who regarded each assignment as a battle campaign to be fought. There's no way Batchwell would have moved such a keen employee away from his silver to watch over a passel of "no account females."

"Mind you, I don't have anything against it, if you and Ramsey take a shining to one another."

"But?"

Gault's brown eyes glittered with something akin to ice and he leaned forward slightly. When he spoke, his voice was so low that only Sumner could hear him.

"But the man's been hurt."

"I know about his—"

"I'm not talking about his back. I'm talking about his heart. So if you can't accept him the way he is, flaws and all, then I'd appreciate it if you'd keep your distance for the next few months."

Sumner stiffened. "I really don't think that any of this is your concern, Mr. Gault." She couldn't help the way her voice adopted the pinched, high-clipped tones of her childhood governess, Miss Primble. "But you may rest assured that I need no such warnings. I have found my interactions with Mr. Ramsey to be beyond reproach."

He watched her with eyes narrowed, and then, to her infinite astonishment, the man grinned. And with the speed of lightning, his expression changed and the starch fled from his posture. Lounging back in his chair, he took another bite of his cookie, then shook the remaining half in her direction.

"I like you, *Dr.* Havisham. You've got some backbone to you." He nodded, then ate the rest of his cookie in one bite and stood. "I think you'll do. I think you'll do very well indeed."

Then, before she could say another word, he swept his hat from the table and tipped his head in her direction. "Good evening to you, ma'am."

Jonah strode from the cook shack into the frigid, snow-driven air, but even the bite of the mountain air in December couldn't douse the warmth that had settled into his chest. He supposed he should be out of sorts at finding Sumner interacting so freely with the men, but he wasn't. If anything, he'd found the episode endearing. When one spent so much time with a group of men, they became a person's family. He'd been pleased to find the men laughing and relaxed. For weeks now, they'd tiptoed around the women, not wanting to do anything that might give the girls a bad impression. But Jonah had known that such restraint was wearing on them, and he'd feared that their efforts in the cook shack would lead to frustration and short tempers in the mine.

Sumner had shown, in a simple act of kindness, that she accepted them, totally and completely—even if their clothes were muddy or their manners needed some polishing. In an instant, the brittleness had been broken and the cook shack was back to normal.

His men were back to normal.

Jonah supposed that Ezra Batchwell would have something cutting to say about the whole event. But Jonah was touched.

"Jonah, wait up!"

He turned to find Gideon jogging toward him.

"Hey, Gideon."

"I got a chance to talk to your girl, Sumner."

Jonah opened his mouth to insist that Sumner wasn't his girl, but for some reason, the words wouldn't come.

"I like her."

Jonah wasn't sure what he'd expected his friend to say, but the simple statement would have been far from his wild guesses.

Gideon's eyes twinkled. "She's no shrinking violet, that one. She'd catch the tail of a tiger and give him what-for, if she had a mind to do so."

Jonah shook his head in confusion. He couldn't remember the last time he'd had a full night's sleep and his weariness was making it difficult to understand what Gideon was trying to tell him. But before he could ask, Gideon pointed a finger in his direction.

"You'd be crazy to let that one go without a fight, I'm telling you here and now."

"Gideon, Sumner and I are just…friends."

"Then you're a bigger fool than I ever took you for—and I've never taken you for a fool." He jabbed with his finger again. "That woman is the first girl I've met who's worthy of you." Gideon's voice grew oddly husky. "So don't wait too long, you hear? God's sent you a gift, so don't let someone else snatch it away from you."

Then, before Jonah could gather his wits about him, Gideon turned on his heel and strode away.

Leaving Jonah standing on the stoop to his house, his hand wrapping around the doorknob, his body thrumming with pain and weariness and Gideon's words shimmering in the darkness like cracking ice.

God's sent you a gift, so don't let someone else snatch it away from you.

But even as the words wrapped around his heart, the pain in his back was nearly overwhelming.

Help me, Heavenly Father. Help me to know what to do.

He stepped inside, closing the door behind him, knowing that he'd be better off on his knees than praying on the doorstep. But his back was on fire and his feet were so wobbly he feared that, once down, he wouldn't be able to get up again. So he dropped into his mother's rocking chair and closed his eyes. Breathing deeply, he murmured, "Please, Lord. I'm lost and alone and I don't know which way I should turn."

Then he sat in silence as his mother had taught him to do.

He waited, becoming intimately aware of the sough of the wind and the *tic-tic-tic* of snow being thrown against the windows. Gradually, a peace began to seep into his chest, bringing a warmth and heat that had nothing to do with the tepid box stove. Muscles he hadn't even known were tense began to loosen.

Have faith, Jonah.

The words weren't spoken aloud; they weren't even whispered in his heart. He *felt* them. *Felt* the hope that they brought. And even though his mind railed against their sentiment, his soul latched on to them like a drowning man being thrown a rope.

He stayed with his head bowed, reveling in the emotions that blossomed within him, allowing them free reign in a way he never would have allowed before. Then he added his thanks to God, who had once again come to his aid.

Jonah didn't know what to make of the path that had been shown to him. But he'd never been a man to turn his back on inspiration.

Standing, he winced when his muscles seized up before finally allowing him to straighten. With the last ounce of energy he could summon, he climbed the stairs and went into the sparse room he called his own.

In truth, it looked more like a prison cell than a sanctuary. There was a cot, a trunk and hooks along the wall to hold his clothes at night.

Lifting the lid to the trunk near the foot of his bed, Jonah hissed at the stabbing pain in his back as he bent enough to dig into the far corner of the tray. There, he found a small, faded velvet pouch.

His heart thudded in his ears as he loosened the drawstring and reached inside, retrieving the delicate gold ring. A deep red ruby glowed at him from the shadows.

His grandmother's wedding ring. Even Rebecca had never seen it. She'd frowned on anything old, wanting to be surrounded by new, glittering things. Soon after she'd rejected him, Jonah had tucked it away in the recesses of his trunk, knowing that he would never have need of it.

Until now.

His pulse pounded even harder, filling him with terror and anticipation, peace and exhilaration. Then he slid it back into the pouch, and the pouch into one of the pockets of his vest. As he carefully buttoned the flap, he saw the way his fingers trembled.

There's no need to fret. Not yet. You might not have need for it, after all.

But the moment his inner naysayer issued the warning, Jonah pushed it aside.

Have faith, Jonah.

The nervousness he'd felt vanished as swiftly as it had come. Straightening, Jonah glanced at his watch. He could fit a few more hours of work in before bedtime. He knew that he hadn't been sleeping much lately. For the past few weeks, he'd found it so difficult to nod off that there hadn't been much point turning in at all.

But as the sound of snow shifted to the rustle of sleet, his eyes strayed toward the bed.

Maybe he'd put his feet up. Just for a minute.

He gingerly sat on the edge of the cot. Then stretched out. Then sighed as his muscles throbbed, then loosened.

Then all conscious thought fled, and he slept.

Chapter Thirteen

Jonah woke feeling more at peace with himself than he had in years. He'd slept deeply, dreamlessly, and it wasn't until the late-morning sunshine hit his face that he became aware of his surroundings at all.

Unaccountably, he took his time getting ready. He polished his boots, found a freshly laundered shirt at the bottom of his trunk, and a new pair of trousers that he'd been saving for a special occasion. After laying everything out near the bed, he glanced into the mirror over his pitcher and basin. Darned if he didn't look like an old mountain man with a too-long beard and hair. He'd have to stop at the barber shop sometime this morning and see to that, as well.

It was noon by the time he stepped into the mine and headed down the tunnel toward the lean-to office. A trim and some proper grooming by Anson Pettibone left him smelling of bay rum and feeling like a dandy. Even more pronounced was the sensation of hope that permeated his whole being. The glow centered around the circlet of gold still tucked in his pocket for safekeeping. At odd moments, he found himself patting his side as if to reassure himself that somehow, someway, he'd find a way to make Sumner a permanent part of his life.

He was whistling under his breath as he opened the door and stepped inside. But it wasn't until the latch clicked back in place that he found he wasn't alone.

Phineas Bottoms waited in the chair behind the desk.

The melody died from Jonah's lips. He was late for work—especially by his own standards—but he refused to feel guilty. He'd more than put in his hours over the last few months—*years*. He didn't need to be ashamed of running a personal errand.

"Mornin'," he offered as he settled his hat on the coat tree and shrugged out of his jacket.

"Good morning." Phineas had been reading one of the production reports and he tipped his head so that he could look over the spectacles he wore for close work. "You're looking mighty chipper this morning."

Jonah didn't bother to comment—after all, what could he say?

As Jonah settled into the only other chair, Phineas removed his glasses and carefully folded them before placing them in his pocket.

"It's nice to see you taking some time for yourself."

Jonah grimaced. "I'd grown shaggy as a bear, so I figured I'd better head to the barber shop before the rush."

The man nodded, and Jonah hoped Phineas accepted his explanation on face value.

Jonah wasn't really sure what had led to Batchwell and Bottoms becoming business partners. All he knew was that the two men had worked together as boys in the coal mines of Scotland. After a youth of toil and hunger, they'd decided to band together in business—first by providing cheap goods for the miners, then investing in bigger and bigger enterprises, until they'd decided to set sail for America and the opportunities to be found there.

Jonah could understand the business relationship between the two, but Ezra and Phineas were so contrary in nature that their relationship should have remained cool and professional. Where Ezra Batchwell was hot-tempered, cantankerous and drove a hard bargain, Phineas was meditative, pragmatic and quiet. But there was a shrewdness to Phineas that most people overlooked. If a business enterprise needed to be analyzed or an employee's effectiveness examined, it was Phineas who saw to the heart of things. Sometimes, Jonah wondered if the man could peer through walls.

Unfortunately, it seemed as if Jonah had captured the man's attention.

"You've been feeling a little poorly lately," Phineas remarked.

It wasn't a question.

Jonah didn't bother to lie or prevaricate. It wouldn't have done any good.

"That second avalanche didn't do me any favors."

The older man frowned. "It was a fool's errand sending you and your men to the canyon. I tried to get Ezra to change his mind, but…sometimes he gets an idea stuck in his craw and there's no dislodging it. I'm sorry that you all ended up getting hurt."

Jonah waved aside the apology. It was an act of nature, something over which Bottoms had little control.

"Have you injured your back again?"

Other than Batchwell, Bottoms, Gideon and Creakle, no one else at the mine knew about Jonah's condition. But when Jonah had interviewed for the position, he'd been up front with his employers. And he was indebted to them. If they hadn't taken a chance on him, he wasn't sure how he would have survived the last few years. For that, they deserved his continued honesty.

"I don't know. I've had some numbness and tingling in my feet. Dr. Havisham isn't sure if it's due to the old injury or the fall down the hill."

Phineas nodded, those pale blue eyes narrowing as he ruminated over the information. But when he spoke, he took a slightly different tack than Jonah expected.

"She knows her stuff… I'll give her that. I didn't think a little thing like that would ever be able to keep up with the needs of a mining community. But she's handled herself well."

Coming from Phineas, that was high praise indeed. Jonah made a mental note to pass on the news to Sumner.

"It's too bad so many of the men don't take too well to a female doctor." For a moment, Phineas's gaze moved to the windows that looked over the juncture leading to the various tunnels. He ruminated a moment before saying. "Still, she's proven to be a good leader with a level head on her shoulders. A person like that could be a valuable member to a community."

"Yes. Yes, she could."

"I'm glad to see that you've let her see to your back. You do what she says."

"Yes, sir."

Phineas stood and moved to the door, then paused yet again. "You still got that piece of property…north of here, wasn't it?"

"Yes, sir."

His first few years in the territory, Jonah had used his wages to register a homestead on the other side of the river, right on the border of the mine's property. It had been difficult making the improvements and cultivating the land while keeping up with his duties at the mine, but he'd been determined to have something that belonged to him. Just in case. In the past few years, he'd spent little time at the cabin he'd built. There hadn't been much point once the row houses had been finished. But during the spring and summer, he'd still visit the place a few times a week to make sure everything was secure.

"It's a pretty little spot, if I'm remembering right. A place like that would be the ideal location to raise some cattle or horses someday." He made a soft, chortling sound. "I'd do it myself if I were a little younger."

Then he disappeared, leaving a stillness in his wake.

For long moments, Jonah sat in his chair. There was something to the older man's words, something that Jonah couldn't quite piece together. But it seemed…important.

"Boss man, we've got trouble in tunnel six again!"

Creakle's bellow pulled him from his reverie and he looked up to find Creakle striding toward the lean-to.

Later. He'd mull it over then. But for now…

He had work to do.

Sumner finished smoothing salve over the back of Iona Skye's hand.

"Are you sure you don't want me to wrap it with a bandage?"

Iona shook her head. "No, dear, I'm fine. I should have been watching what I was doing. When I poked the coals, I turned to talk to one of the other women and hit the stove door with my hand. That's what happens when you get old and forgetful."

Sumner shook her head, making a tutting noise.

"Nonsense. You're in your prime, Iona."

Iona couldn't be much older than sixty and with everything she'd done to help Sumner at the infirmary, she'd proven that her mind was sharp as a tack.

"Perhaps." A wistfulness settled over her features. "But I have to admit that I'll miss all this when it's over." She used a hand to gesture to the Dovecote.

"You're still thinking about the arrangements with your sister, then?"

Iona shrugged. "I can't help but think about it. I worry that once I'm there…I won't be needed. There's nothing on earth that makes a person feel old than not being needed."

Sumner reached out to squeeze her uninjured hand.

"I wish you had a better option. I wish we both had better options."

"Have you thought of what you'll do, Sumner? Will you try to stay in the territories? Or will you go back to your home in England?"

Sumner shook her head. "No. I won't go to England."

"But won't your family be worrying about you?"

"No. My family…my family doesn't want to see me again. It was one of the conditions of my becoming a doctor."

Iona's eyes grew moist. "Oh, my dear. How awful for you."

Sumner's throat grew tight. "That's why I came here. To make a new start." She squeezed Iona's hand again. "It's too bad the two of us couldn't team up and pool our resources." Her smile was rueful. "Maybe if we put our heads together, we can come up with something that would help us both."

Iona winked. "Wouldn't that be something."

Sumner helped Iona to wriggle off the examination table and began putting her medical supplies away. She would need to go through her trunks to see if she had enough ingredients left to make another batch of burn salve. She had less than a third of a jar left.

"Would you be up to helping me make some medical concoctions today, Iona? I'm running low on a few of my cures."

Iona's eyes sparkled. "With pleasure. Anything to beat the boredom away."

Now that they'd moved to the Dovecote, the women were allowed more freedoms. They'd begun taking the air outside—at least as far as their Pinkertons would allow them to go. Some of the younger ladies had begun fashioning a family of snow people that populated the tree line. A laundry station had been set up in the clearing outside of Sumner's office and the women kept themselves busy washing, ironing, sewing. Some of them had even begun taking in mending for the miners. But there were times when the sameness of their days grew tiresome.

The outer door creaked open and both women turned. Sumner expected to see one of the other mail-order brides carrying in a basket of laundry frozen into odd angles. But it was Jonah who stepped into her office.

Immediately, Sumner was overcome by an odd excitement and her pulse leaped into an irregular gallop. She barely heard Iona offer a murmured greeting, then leave the room.

Sumner's cheeks grew hot as she realized that Iona must have sensed her charged emotions to leave so quickly. But even that thought flew from her head almost immediately.

Something had changed with Jonah, something dramatic. At first, she thought that it might be the fact that he'd trimmed his hair and his beard. The effect was startling, highlighting his sharp brow, high cheekbones and razor-square jaw. But she soon realized that it was more than that. There was a color to his cheeks and a lightness to his expression that she'd never seen before.

He closed the door behind him and swept his hat from his head. Sumner's fingers twitched to smooth the new springy waves back into place. Idly, she wondered if his newly cut hair would feel as soft and silky smooth as it looked.

"You must be feeling better today," she said with a smile.

"Yeah. I slept well last night."

Even his eyes appeared lighter, more blue than brown.

"Listen, I've got to get back to the mine. We're having trouble shoring up one of the tunnels. But… I wondered if you were going to be busy tomorrow afternoon."

She shook her head. "No. I should be done in the cook shack by eleven."

"Great. Do you think you could rustle up a few sandwiches for a picnic of sorts? I've got something I'd like to show you. It's several miles off company property, so we'll have to take a sleigh. Dress warmly. If things go well," he said, spots of color appearing in his cheeks, "we might be gone for a couple of hours. I'll pick you up at noon."

Mystified, she nodded. "That sounds wonderful."

His smile was soft and gentle and filled with meanings she couldn't begin to fathom.

"I hope so."

From deep in the Dovecote, a chime sounded, and he grimaced. "Wish I could stay…"

"I understand."

He settled his hat onto his head. "I'll see you tomorrow."

Then, before she realized what he was about to do, he bent forward and pressed a kiss to her cheek.

"Bye, Sumner."

As he left in a swirl of snow and cold air, her eyes unconsciously flickered closed as she absorbed the lingering scents of bay rum and hair tonic, wood smoke and the outdoors. And she knew that she would forever associate those scents with Jonah Ramsey and that kiss.

Her hand lifted to touch her cheek. And much like Jonah, she felt different somehow. Special.

She wasn't just a "girl" anymore.

She was Jonah's girl.

No. She mustn't think like that. To even entertain the possibility of a relationship would mean the end of her wish to become a doctor.

Her chest suddenly felt as if it were made of stones and she was filled with a sinking premonition. Tomorrow's outing...could it be that Jonah wanted to formally ask to court her?

No.

Although she cared for the man—deeply—there could be no future for them. Not without giving up so much. Jonah would be left without employment. And she...she would never be allowed to pursue her career. Could any marriage survive such disappointments?

No. Not even the strongest of bonds could endure the death of one's dreams.

The joy that had so recently bloomed within her completely withered away when she realized that she would have to cancel her outing with Jonah. It would be easier to stop things now, before they'd ever began.

So why, then, did she feel like such a miserable coward?

Sumner rolled in her bed, frowning as the wisps of sleep melted away like fog. Blinking, she discovered that it was still dark, the moon high in the sky outside her window. Which meant it could only be two or three in the morning?

She sighed, pulling the blankets tighter around her neck as she became aware of the chill touching her skin. The coals in the infirmary stove would have died down, which meant that she should try to go back to sleep.

Her head whipped to the side and her gaze scoured the darkness as she tried to pinpoint the unfamiliar sound.

Bells?

Sweeping the covers back, she grasped for her robe, already running through the Dovecote to whip open the outer door. The sound came louder now. From the camp.

The alarm bell.

A few of the women must have been awakened by the same noise, because they huddled on the stairway, trying to peer into the darkness.

"What is it, Sumner?" Myra whispered loudly.

"Get everyone up," Sumner called out. "Something must have happened at the mine. That's the alarm bell."

As Sumner rushed back to her own quarters, she could hear the knocks and calls as the news was spread throughout the building.

Sumner paused at her washbasin to splash cold water on her face. Then she dressed as fast as she could. As she buttoned and combed and pinned, she offered a silent prayer to Heaven.

Dear Father of all that is great and good in this world, please bless the men in the mine and those above, whatever the dangers might be.

By the time she returned to the main room, her bag in hand, there were several women waiting. She didn't even need to offer instructions.

"Stefania, Marie and I will get the cook shack opened and fires laid," Lydia said as she buttoned her coat. "The mine is cold and damp and wet and if there's been an accident there, the men will need somewhere warm to go."

"We'll have coffee and hot water on as soon as the coals can be revived," Stefania added.

The three women headed out into the cold.

Iona came hurrying down the steps, Willow trailing close behind her.

"Willow and I will head to the infirmary. We can get the fires going and the lamps lit, just in case."

Myra and Myrna were already striding around the Dovecote. "The rest of us will wait here. We'll get the fires roaring and the lamps lit. If you need more help, you can either send the minor problems to us, or let us know where you need us to go."

Sumner blinked for several minutes, amazed at how much they'd all learned to help one another over the past few weeks.

"Thank you. Thank you, all. If we have men who require some bandaging, I'll send them to you and the women in the Dovecote. Make sure that you thoroughly clean any cuts and scrapes. Then slather a little of my homemade ointment on the wounds before applying the bandages."

"Yes, ma'am."

She pointed to Ruth, Emmarissa, Greta and Louisa. "Why don't the four of you come with me. Maybe this is a false alarm…" But as she paused, it was clear that the bell hadn't stopped. It continued to ring in such a hectic pace that it caused her own pulse to pound with urgency. "The five of us will see what information we can obtain at the mining offices first. Then I'll send a few of you back to inform the others and gather supplies if necessary."

"Yes, Dr. Havisham."

Plunging her arms into the sleeves of her coat, Sumner

didn't even pause for her bonnet. Instead, she draped a scarf tightly around her neck and hurried into the night.

None of them said a word as they rushed out into the newly fallen drifts, funneling into a single-file line until the snow could be broken enough to form a trail. Ironically, when they needed them most, their Pinkerton guards were curiously absent. Not that Sumner would have expected them to be on guard night and day. But...

If they'd been in attendance, maybe they could have offered them some information.

Overhead, the sky was inky and clear and cold, the stars glittering like chips of ice, the moon hanging like a sad crooked smile. Leading the way, Sumner shivered as the snow began to seep over the tops of her boots and cake on the hems of her skirts, weighing her down.

Something had happened.

Something horrible.

She could feel it in her very bones.

Finally, finally, they managed to reach the boardwalks of the main thoroughfare.

As she drew closer, Sumner began to see a knot of people ebbing and flowing around the office steps. Ezra Batchwell stood at its top, issuing orders and pointing. As the women closed the distance, he finally noticed them. Without hesitation, he pointed to Sumner shouting, "This is your doing! All of you! I warned you women about the consequences of distracting the men from their jobs, but you all kept pushing and pushing the boundaries you'd been given. Now you may have killed them with your carelessness!"

Phineas Bottoms emerged from the offices and rushed to Ezra's side. Tugging on his arm, he tried to pull him inside, but Ezra wouldn't budge.

"I want you all out of here, as soon as humanly possible. I won't have you endangering their lives further. I won't have you ruining what we've worked so hard to build here!"

"Enough, Ezra!"

Sumner had heard Phineas Bottoms speak only a half-dozen times—and never in anger. The shock of hearing him do so now cut through the confusion on the street, bringing a startling silence.

"You've spoken your piece, Ezra, now move on back into the office and let the men get back to work. This isn't the time for a confrontation or an argument. Once you've calmed down—"

"Those chits will still be here! The problem will remain!"

"Get inside, Ezra!"

The words boomed through the valley and echoed off the mountains themselves.

Still red-faced and seething, Batchwell stomped inside.

Bottoms waited a moment, before turning to the crowd.

"All of you get to the mine and see what you can do to help. And you—" he speared a finger in Sumner's direction "—get that infirmary opened up. We'll be sending the injured men to you as soon as we can reach them."

Injured *men*.

The stark words sent a shiver down her spine.

She touched a nearby man on the shoulder, asking, "What happened in the mine?"

He glanced at her impatiently but said, "A bump. An explosion. Gases can sometimes build up, and if there's a spark…" He gestured with his hands, conveying the resulting explosion. "The fire blew itself out as soon as it started, but one of the tunnels collapsed and there are men trapped."

Sumner's mind immediately scrambled into gear.

Explosion.

That meant burns.

Tunnel collapsed.

There would be broken bones, lacerations, internal injuries.

She didn't bother to say another word, simply turned and ran in the direction of the infirmary.

Once there, she found Iona and Willow on the boardwalk. Too late, she realized that she no longer had a key to open the door. She doubted that she had the time to find Jonah—even if such a feat would be possible in all the confusion. Closing her eyes, she rued the fact that she could once again be incurring Mr. Batchwell's wrath, but it couldn't be helped.

"We need to get in somehow."

Greta shouted something in German and motioned for the women to get out of the way. Then, without warning, she ran full force into the door, hitting it squarely with her shoulder. The flimsy lock gave way—along with part of the threshold.

"Well done!" Sumner said with a grin, then she and the women rushed inside.

Orders didn't need to be given. Remembering what they'd done the last time the infirmary had been used, they began rushing to ready the rooms. Louisa and Ruth carried in firewood while Greta unrolled mattresses and covered them with linens and blankets. In the meantime, Iona and Willow stoked the fires and gathered buckets of snow to melt for hot water.

When the preparations were just about finished, Sumner pointed to Emmarissa. "Go back to the Dovecote and explain what has happened. Divide everyone into two teams. Leave one group at the Dovecote and send the rest back here."

"I'll hurry," Emmarissa promised as she ran out the door.

The woman had barely disappeared around the corner when a stream of men began carrying the wounded inside.

Seeing a familiar face dressed in Pinkerton blue, Sumner pointed to Dobbs. "Stand on the boardwalk. Send those with minor injuries to the Dovecote, and the more severe cases in here."

"Yes, ma'am."

"Iona—"

"I'll stay near the door and direct the most grievous injuries your way. If it's something that can wait, I'll have Willow and the other girls begin washing and bandaging things until you can get to them."

"Thank you."

Sumner hesitated only a moment, overcome with a wave of déjà vu. But those sensations passed when she realized that what she had seen after the avalanche was nothing compared to the wounds she was witnessing now. The miners being ushered inside were filthy, wet and cold. They had broken bones and burns on their hands, faces and shoulders—and there were so many men. As she began to examine them, she heard snippets of conversation that, combined with the injuries, gave her a clear picture of what had occurred.

...*tunnels gassy*...

...*stray spark from a pickax*...

...*ball of fire*...

...*timbers collapsed*...

...*men still trapped*...

Then there was no time to ponder on what was hap-

pening belowground. She couldn't have said how many
of the injured had been sent to the Dovecote, but every
available cot in the infirmary was filled within minutes.
Then the chairs. Pallets on the floor.

Sumner moved from person to person, instructing the
women on how to clean and tend to the burns. It wasn't
the first time that she had been exposed to so many severe wounds. She'd been present at a hospital in London
when factory workers had been brought in after a boiler
had exploded. But she'd been allowed to do little more
than watch since such injuries would "insult her delicate
sensibilities."

Delicate sensibilities or not, Sumner was fiercely determined to help these miners. She ordered more buckets
of snow be brought in to take the heat from the wounds,
and removed slivers and chunks of wood from their skin.

Even so, there was a part of her that listened for a familiar set of footfalls and the low rumble of Jonah's voice.

She knew it was silly. He was probably down in the
mine, helping to free those who were still trapped. There
was no reason on earth why he would come to the infirmary just to check on her—and the fact that he hadn't
proved that he'd come to trust her abilities.

But even with those inner assurances, her gaze skipped
to the windows after each patient. Bit by bit, she watched
the sky ease from black to gray to pink as night gave
way to morning.

The door burst open and she looked up again, endur-
ing the same wave of disappointment when she found it
was Miriam carrying a pail of snow into the infirmary.

"Have there been any updates?" Sumner asked as she
approached.

"From what I've heard, they've managed to punch a
small hole through the debris to get air to the trapped

men. There are about a dozen or so miners still trapped with Mr. Ramsey."

Sumner's head snapped up. "What? Mr. Ramsey is trapped in the mine?"

"That's what I was told. He and that nice Mr. Creakle."

Her fingers began to tremble and she turned away from her patient under the guise of washing her hands in a nearby basin of water. But the trembling didn't cease. Instead, it swept through her whole body until she could scarcely stay upright.

Not Jonah.

Not Creakle.

Although she'd known there were men trapped, having names made things so much worse. Instead of imagining hazy silhouettes caught behind a wall of rock and shattered timbers, she now had faces.

An icy fist clenched around her chest, making it difficult to breathe.

Fragmented thoughts raced through her brain like runaway horses. Could Jonah breathe? Was he injured? Had he been burned?

Was he alive?

In an instant, all of her hopes and fears coalesced around a single thought.

Please, please, Dear Lord in Heaven...let him be safe. Let them all be safe.

As she blindly reached for one of the rolls of bandages, she felt her whole body vibrate with a sense of regret. In that instant, she realized what a fool she'd been. She had grimly clung to her preconceived notions of how her future should unfold without ever bothering to see that perhaps God had offered her a new path. She'd been so sure that her love of doctoring and her love—yes, *love*—for Jonah couldn't coexist. She'd foolishly doubted her

Creator and pinned her hopes on her own stupid pride. In doing so, she'd failed to see that, where love is concerned, there are no absolutes. True, it might not be possible for her to practice medicine *here*. Especially if she and Jonah were to live together as man and wife. But that didn't mean that such a future was unattainable. In order to be together, she and Jonah would have to make sacrifices and compromises, to be sure, but she'd never even given him a chance to talk things over.

And that might be the worst mistake that she'd ever made.

"Dr. Havisham? Are you unwell?"

Sumner's head jerked up, and she glanced over her shoulder at the man who still waited for her to bind his wounds. She knew him. She'd talked to him the other night when she'd been pouring coffee at the cook shack.

Mr. Ingraham. The wizened little man who loved taxidermy and had made the stuffed ferret clowns. Clowns that the women had originally found appalling, but which had become quirky, endearing mascots within the Dovecote.

Blinking against the burning of her eyes, she tried to paste a bright smile on her lips. Her efforts must have looked as hollow as they felt, because Ingraham still regarded her with open concern.

"I'm fine." Her voice was sandpaper rough, so she quickly cleared her throat. Then, knowing that nothing but the truth would do, she offered, "I'm worried about the men who are still trapped. They've been down there a long time."

Ingraham reached out to touch her hand, his grizzled beard twitching as he made a soft *tutting* noise. "Don't you fear none, Dr. Havisham. Those men are tough, you hear?"

Her lips trembled at the way Ingraham offered her comfort when she had none—and the gesture caused the tears to well behind her lashes. How she'd come to care for these men. These brave, upstanding, hardworking men.

"I'm sure you're right, Mr. Ingraham."

"And they've got the Lord on their side, as well. That's why the men go to Devotional twice a day. It was something we started all on our own. Mine work is dark and dirty and dangerous, and a body needs a little divine intervention now and then." He offered her a sweet Father Christmas smile. "That's why this is such a special place to work, even if it means we have to be away from our families for a little while."

Suddenly, she realized what Jonah had been trying to convey to her when the women had first been marooned Aspen Valley. Over and over again, he'd tried to impress upon her that the women would cause problems, remind the men of the loved ones they'd left behind. And in this instant, when she didn't know when—or *if*—she would see Jonah again, she had a small taste of that exquisite agony. She couldn't imagine the heartache of waiting *years* to see a loved one again.

"Do you have family waiting for you, Mr. Ingraham?"

The man's whole face lit up. "Yes, ma'am. I have a wife and three sons. My oldest son is married and I have three little grandbabies waiting for me near Aberdeen." His forehead puckered. "They're probably not so little now. When I left them, they were wee bairns toddling around the yard. But *ach*…they'd be strapping lads." He tapped his head. "But up here, they're but wee things, y' know?"

"Yes. I do know."

She thought of her stepbrother. He would be eighteen?

But in her head, she always imagined him as that mean-spirited little boy who'd been brought home so abruptly and had stolen what crumbs of her father's affection that she'd ever managed to obtain. Time had probably changed him. It had certainly changed her. She knew the way his brash statements had spurred her on whenever she'd even thought of giving up her goals. She'd been driven to prove that he'd been wrong when he'd insisted that she would never be good enough.

Because she was a girl.

But she wasn't a *girl* anymore. She was a *woman*. And he was probably well on to being a man.

Which meant it was high time she put those inner demons to rest. They were nothing more than ghosts of her past, and from this moment on, she refused to allow them to have the power to sting. She'd learned that *she* was responsible for her future. And with help from God and a good measure of determination, there wasn't anything she couldn't do.

Sumner hadn't realized how much bottled-up resentment she'd held within her until it began to seep from her body in that moment of forgiveness. A forgiveness that had been too long in the making. With it came a peace and a certainty that she would be writing a letter to Jefferson to make that forgiveness complete. It was the only way to move forward.

Please, Lord. Give Jonah and I another chance to make this right.

Realizing that Mr. Ingraham was still watching her closely, she smiled and began wrapping the gash on his forearm that she'd stitched closed.

"Tell me more about your family, Mr. Ingraham. I would love to hear all about them."

Chapter Fourteen

Jonah knew he was in trouble. He lay on his stomach, in much the same position as he'd been when the explosion and cave-in had thrown him to the ground. He could feel the water rising around him, chilling him to the very bone. It wouldn't be long now, before the wetness would reach his face.

Creakle's face swam in front of him and Jonah tried his best to focus. The man was a gray fuzzy shape in the darkness. Behind him, Jonah could see that the workers on the other side had managed to punch a hole through the debris. In the glow of their lanterns, he could see that the opening was nearly large enough for the men to crawl through.

But not Jonah.

He panted softly as waves of searing pain radiated through his body from a point low on his back. He was finding it difficult to breathe.

"As soon…as you can make it through…you get out…all of you…"

Creakle shook his head.

"We ain't goin' nowhere without you, boss man."

Jonah tamped down a sound that was half moan, half sob.

"I'm not…going anywhere… Creakle…" He swallowed against the nausea that rolled in his stomach. "Can't move…can't feel my legs…"

"Don't you fear none, boss. We'll have you out in a jiffy. Then that nice doc'll fix you up right as rain."

Jonah couldn't prevent the desperate laugh that shuddered through his throat. "She can't fix this, Creakle."

Creakle bent close, so close that his nose all but touched Jonah. "Now you listen to me, and listen good. There ain't nothin' wrong with you that a few days in bed won't cure. That beam that landed on you…well, it cut off the blood flow, that's all. That's why you're feelin' a bit numb. Willoughby Smalls is waiting on the other side of that wall. As soon as they've got a hole big enough for him to wriggle through, he's gonna lift that beam up— an' you know he could lift an ox with a single finger, if'n he had a mind t' do so. An' he'll get you out."

Jonah shook his head. For years now, he'd lived with those little pieces of metal pressing against his spine, but this time he knew they'd shifted. He'd tried to move his feet, his toes, all to no avail. He'd known that this could happen. But somehow he'd thought that he'd go quick.

Dear sweet Heaven, let him go quick.

But not until he'd seen Sumner one more time.

He could feel himself slipping. Though the voices of the miners were growing more excited, he was having a hard time seeing the glow on the other side of the wall of rocks, rubble and shattered timber. Jonah reached out, flailing his hand in the darkness until he found Creakle's gnarled fingers.

"If I don't make it, I need you to do something for me."

"Yer talkin' nonsense. Just a few more minutes. Then we'll have you out of here."

"Tell Sumner that I'm sorry."

"Sorry? Y' don't have anythin' t' be sorry for."

"Yes. Yes, I do. For the longest time, I didn't trust her enough to…to tell her how I really felt…how I… I should have told her…sooner…" He could feel the seeping water against his chin now and he coughed.

"Don't you fret none, y' hear? You can tell her yerself."

The tunnel appeared to dip, sway. Jonah's stomach heaved.

"Tell her I love her," he whispered.

Or he thought he'd said it aloud.

It might have only been his heart echoing the words that Jonah had tried so hard not to accept.

The doors to the infirmary burst open, letting in a swirl of cold air. Sumner turned to chide the person responsible, but the words died in her throat. Several men were carrying a makeshift stretcher fashioned from a ladder covered in blankets. The moment she saw the familiar profile of the man on the stretcher, she waved them into the examination room.

"In there. Quick!"

The men staggered, maneuvering the tight spaces until they could set the ladder on the floor. Then each of them grabbed a handful of wool in their hands and hoisted him up onto the examining table.

Sumner turned to the closest man saying, "I need hot water, lots of it." She turned to the others. "The rest of you, start getting him out of his filthy clothes."

Sumner had been told that the affected mineshaft was wet and damp and cold, and she could believe it when she saw the state of Jonah's clothes. He was covered in mud that began dripping onto the floor. If she didn't know the shape of his face as well as she knew her own, she wouldn't have recognized him.

The men glanced at one another uneasily, and they were so caked in mud Sumner wasn't sure if she knew any of them by name.

"He was hit by a beam and fell facedown in the mud." As soon as the apparent leader spoke, Sumner recognized the low tones of Gideon Gault. "We brought him to you the way we found him. Before he passed out, he was saying that he couldn't feel his lower limbs."

A cool finger of dread slithered down her spine, but Sumner pushed the sensation away. He was here. He was breathing. She wouldn't borrow trouble before she had a chance to uncover the facts. Crossing to a nearby table, she retrieved a pair of shears, which she slapped into Gideon's hand.

"Cut him out of them if you have to, then cover him in blankets. As soon as you're finished, call for me. I'll be gathering up a few hot bricks as well as some water to wash him. We've got to warm him up as quickly as possible."

If the men thought it untoward that she, a *female* doctor, would be about to examine their boss in the all-together, they gave little indication. Rather than fulfilling the dire prophesy uttered by Ezra Batchwell mere weeks before and running her out on a rail, they appeared grateful for her no-nonsense orders.

Nevertheless, as she hurried to the stove to retrieve the bricks that had been stacked there for warming, her legs were trembling so badly that she had to pause. Planting her hands flat on the table, she bowed her head, knowing that she would need every means of help that she could summon. The infirmary had only the most rudimentary supplies and equipment, and even without a detailed exam, Sumner knew that Jonah was in mortal danger.

Dear Lord in Heaven, Creator of all, Giver of life...

She didn't have a great deal of time, but she prayed from the depths of her soul, asking for guidance and strength and wisdom. When she finally lifted her head, she was feeling calmer.

Have faith.

She quickly wrapped a pair of bricks in flannel.

"Do you need help?" Willow asked as she entered the room with a handful of bandage rolls. They'd already run out of those that they'd prepared earlier and a team of women was ripping sheets and making more.

"If you could bring a few more bricks into the examination room?"

"Of course."

Clutching a pair of hot blocks against her chest, Sumner reached the examination room just as the door opened.

"He's ready."

"Put these near his feet. We'll have more soon."

Gideon nodded and hurried to comply.

As Sumner approached the table, she was alarmed by the pallor to Jonah's skin. She touched his forehead.

Icy.

Clammy.

But there was a hint of warmth.

She leaned low, pressing her ear against his back. After a moment, she was able to hear the *thump* of his heart. Slow. So slow.

Willow swept into the room. "I've got the bricks you needed."

"Thank you. Tuck them next to his legs and feet please."

Although he'd been covered by a blanket from his shoulders to his toes, Sumner glanced over Jonah's frame, taking in the dirt and grime, then glancing at the pitcher and basin that had been brought in for washing. If he was as dirty beneath the blanket as above…

"Willow, could you bring more water and cloths? We've got to get him clean before I can see what needs to be done."

"Of course. I'll be right back."

The men had stepped back and now stood uneasily, watching as she worked.

"Gideon, you and your men can go to the cook shack and get yourself something to eat," Sumner said, not even bothering to look up.

"If it's all the same, Dr. Havisham. We'll wait here. Just in case you need us."

She opened her mouth to refute such a statement, then stopped herself. She would not let pride get in her way.

"Thank you. I appreciate that. You said the beam struck his back?"

"Yes, ma'am. He was pinned for a while."

Her heart lurched in its cage of ribs before settling back into place. Carefully lifting the blanket, she hissed. An angry red-and-black bruise ran diagonally across his back. Even worse, shards of wood had embedded themselves in his skin, one of them right near the base of his spine beneath the tangle of old scars.

Sumner glanced up, meeting the worried gazes of Gault and his men.

"You were right. I'm going to need your help. I can't pull these larger bits of wood out. They could leave slivers behind that could cause infection. I may need to make sure that they haven't caused more internal damage. That means I'm probably going to have to operate."

Gault's expression became grave, but he didn't shrink from the news. "What do you want us to do, Doc?"

"I need one of you to run back to the Dovecote. Tell them I need the box marked Ether. Be careful on the way back—we don't want to break the bottles. Make sure you bring the whole box. I'll need the face cones, as well."

One of the men dodged out of the door.

"The rest of you wash up. I want you scrubbed head to toe and dressed in the cleanest clothes you can find. I may require your help in holding him down."

The men wasted no time vacating the room—even Gideon disappeared after only a quick look at his friend. And for a moment, Sumner was alone with Jonah.

He was suddenly racked with shivers and she covered him again with the blanket, tucking it around his shoulders. Then, unable to resist, she reached out to stroke his cheek. Her fingers brushed away the tangled curls, finding them as soft as she had often imagined.

Leaning down, she continued to stroke his hair, whispering for his ears alone.

"I love you, Jonah. Be strong."

The door opened again and Iona Skye rushed in with a pitcher of water. Several cloths had been looped through the handle.

"I told Willow to stay in the other room. Figured you needed a widow woman who wasn't about to faint at the first sight of a man's bare back."

She set the pitcher down and dipped one of the cloths into the water. When it emerged, steam seeped into the air around the flannel.

"Thank you, Iona," Sumner said, more relieved than she would have thought. She was beginning to realize that there was no more shame in asking for help than in offering it.

"How are you at the sight of blood?"

The older woman laughed. "My father owned a butcher shop."

"Good. I can use someone with a steady stomach." She folded the blankets down. "We need to work quickly. The moment the men return, we may need to operate."

"Just tell me what to do."

Day faded to night and back into day again, and Sumner had her training tested over and over—but never so much as with Jonah's surgery. Just as she'd feared, the shards of wood had driven deep into his muscles and had required a scalpel to remove them—a fact which had turned out to be a blessing. If she hadn't opened him up…

Arching her back, Sumner stood from the bedside of a miner with badly burned hands. The man was sleeping now—thanks to a precious dose of laudanum taken from her cache of supplies. At this rate, Sumner would run out of her supplies before she left Aspen Valley.

With the infirmary calmer than it had been the day before, and the patients well-supervised by her impromptu nurses, Sumner felt that she could check on Jonah once again. Entering the examining room where they'd kept him quarantined from the other patients, she glanced at Iona, who had been calmly sitting in Sumner's rocking chair, which had been brought from the Dovecote for that purpose. She'd been knitting for most of the day and a pile of hats and scarves lay in a basket at her feet.

"I'm going to run out of wool soon," the woman said. "Then what will I do with myself at the Dovecote?"

Her eyes twinkled, making it clear that she'd find something to occupy her time.

"There's always Mr. Smalls's angora goats."

"Yes, but I suppose they'd object to being sheared in the dead of winter."

On the examination table beside Iona lay Jonah, still lying on his stomach, his body swathed in blankets.

"How is he?"

"He's holding his own," Iona murmured. "His color is looking much better and he's trying to rouse. He's been mumbling in his sleep for the past quarter hour." Her eyes crinkled as she smiled. "Sometimes, I think he's trying to say your name."

Sumner felt the warmth seeping up her cheeks, but Iona didn't pay much attention. Instead, she stabbed her knitting needles into the ball of wool and she stood somewhat gingerly.

"These creaky old bones don't take too well to the winter weather anymore," she said. Then she gestured to the chair. "Why don't you sit here for a spell? It sounds awfully quiet in the other room, and I'm sure someone will find you if they need your help. In the meantime, if you don't mind, I'll go get a bite to eat."

"Of course, of course. Take as long as you need. Most of the other injured men are sleeping." Sumner sank into the chair that Iona had just vacated. As soon as she settled into the rocker that Jonah had made for her, she offered a soft, slow sigh. She was glad to be off her feet. She hadn't had time to sit for more than a moment or grab anything but a cup of tea since the alarm bells had sounded.

Iona spread a blanket over her lap. "You've been working nonstop and you need to keep your strength up. The brides and I can take charge for a little while." She gestured to Jonah. "In the meantime, I think you're needed here."

The woman's smile was soft and knowing. After donning a cape and bonnet, she said, "I'll bring you a tray when I come back. I don't think you've eaten anything since the accident. You need some nourishment. Maybe a hot bowl of soup and some bread?"

"Thank you, Iona. That would be nice."

Iona paused again at the door. Glancing over her shoulder, she said, "You know, Mr. Batchwell had no cause to say those things to you—to any of us. He might not be willing to admit it, but this place is better off since we came, and most of that's due to you. These men have been living in an emotional desert. They're starving for something better. It just may take some time to get them to admit it."

Sumner was so tired that she was barely able to summon a ghost of a smile. "Maybe. But somehow I think Mr. Batchwell likes the desert."

Iona chuckled. "That may be…but soon enough, he'll be outnumbered. Especially after all you've done for the miners the past few days."

The door closed behind Iona with barely a *snick* from the lock. Even so, her words reverberated in the room. In her heart.

But finding a way to force Ezra Batchwell to honor her five-year contract as company doctor had faded in importance compared for her love for this man.

She reached out to touch his cheek with the back of her hand, and she was relieved to find that it had lost its clamminess. He had a fever, but a mild one—not unusual for someone who had suffered through an hour's worth of surgery. The next few days would be critical. As with any procedure, infection would be her chief worry. He would need nourishment as soon as he'd completely roused from the effects of the ether. But he'd had some laudanum for the pain and his sleep was more natural than the last time she'd had a chance to check on him.

As if sensing her concern, his brow knitted in a frown and a soft moan escaped from his throat.

Sumner leaned close whispering, "Shh, shh. You're going to be fine."

With her lips so close to his ear, she could not keep from pressing a fleeting kiss against his temple.

"Be strong, Jonah. Be well."

As if he'd heard her, his eyes flickered open. He stared at her for the longest time. Then his mouth twisted into a ghost of a smile. His lips parted, and she could have sworn that he said, "Sum…ner. Am I…dying?"

Then his lashes flickered closed again.

She stroked his cheek with the backs of her fingers.

"Not yet, Jonah. With the Good Lord's blessing, you've got years and years before you have to worry about that."

Fire.

Jonah felt it raging deep in his core and he fought to open his eyes, to move. The explosion must have caused more damage than he'd feared, reigniting behind the rubble.

He couldn't move.

He couldn't…

Cool fingers touched his cheek, his forehead. Then a wet cloth was pressed to the back of his neck, easing the flames, forcing them down to a fierce ache that centered at his back.

He struggled against the darkness, needing something, *someone…*

At long last, he was able to open his eyes, but as they focused, he couldn't account for what he was seeing. He wasn't in the tunnel anymore. Bright sunlight streamed through a pair of windows that were crazed with frost.

An older woman sat in a chair nearby, knitting a strip of bright red yarn.

He must have done something to alert her, because she bolted to her feet and hurried away.

No.

Don't go.

Too late, he realized that he hadn't said the words aloud.

He closed his eyes in frustration, swallowing against a throat that seemed dry as dust.

Just when he feared that the blackness would return and he would find himself back in the tunnel, he heard the swish of skirts and a gentle hand touched his shoulder.

"Jonah?"

His eyes sprang open, and he prayed that this wasn't a dream. He knew that voice. Knew it as well as his own. But when he tried to turn, the hand on his shoulder stopped him.

"No. Stay there."

He heard chair legs scrape against the floor, then the shape of a woman.

Sumner.

Unmanly tears pricked at the backs of his eyes and he tried to blink them away. He didn't want her to see him this way, so vulnerable. Hurting. Unable to move.

But rather than being repelled, she leaned closer to place a kiss against his forehead. The gesture was so fleeting, so tender, so whisper-soft, that it could have been made with the wings of a butterfly. But the depth of meaning that it held was like a balm to his battered spirit.

She accepted him as he was.

He wasn't a fool. As his wits began to gather and his heart stilled from its galloping beat, he knew where he was. He knew why he was here.

And he was numb from the waist down.

The tears gathered again when he realized that he could be that way for the rest of his life—whatever life remained.

Yet, she still accepted him.

Somehow, she must have sensed the path of his thoughts, because she stroked his hair, whispering, "Shh, shh. You're fine. You're fine."

And in that moment, he *was* fine. Because he could see in the warmth of her gaze, in the answering sheen in her own eyes, that she loved him.

She kissed his forehead again, his cheek, and he'd never felt anything so wonderful. A warmth spread from those tiny points of contact, flowing through his entire body, filling him with a glow that radiated from his heart.

He couldn't prevent the words from bubbling free.

"I love you…Sumner."

He could see in her eyes that she didn't completely believe him, that she thought it was his illness talking. Knowing that it was important that he convince her the sentiment was true, he reached wildly for her hand, finally finding it and grasping it like a lifeline.

"Love…you…"

She stroked his cheek.

"Shh. Sleep now."

He shook his head, knowing that this moment was important. He'd learned all too well that the future could be precarious. What mattered was what a person did with the present.

"Get…my clothes…"

Her brow creased in confusion. "You aren't going anywhere."

"No…need…my vest."

"Jonah, you don't understand. You were wounded. I had to—"

"I need...my vest," he interrupted firmly, his wits growing stronger by the minute as he focused on one of the most important things he would ever do in his life.

She sighed, but was willing to humor him. He heard the rustle of her skirts again as she crossed the room, then returned to the chair.

"Reach...in the pocket."

She removed the little velvet pouch that he had been carrying around for days. It had seemed to burn a hole in his skin, goading him, urging him to find the courage to take action.

Have faith.

"Open it."

She tugged the drawstring loose, then shook the ring into her palm. She gasped softly—in pleasure, he thought—but when she met his gaze, her brow knit in confusion.

"It's...my grandmother's."

"It's beautiful. But why do you need it?"

His heart was pounding so hard it felt as if it were rapping against the hard surface he lay upon. "I've... I mean..."

Why did the words desert him now?

"Marry me?" he suddenly blurted.

As proposals went, it wasn't grand or romantic. There had been no carefully prepared speeches, no bended knee. He knew how much store women put in such things, but he couldn't bear another moment with his declaration unsaid.

Her brow creased. "Jonah...you've been injured and—"

He grabbed her hand, ring and all.

"I've been carrying that around with me...waiting for the right time. But I've learned there *is* no right time... if that means delaying things another minute." He swallowed, searching for a way to convince her. "I love you, Sumner Havisham. I love *all* of you. I love who you are... what you do. I love your heart...and your head and your endless capacity for giving. I don't want...to spend another day longer than I have to...without you by my side. If you'll take me as I am, half a man and—"

She placed a finger against his lips, stopping him before he could completely utter his greatest fears. Then, in a very un-Sumner-like fashion, she burst into tears.

"But your job," she whispered.

"Sumner...no job is worth being without you."

He thought that he'd been reassuring, but she began to cry even harder. When he tried his best to comfort her, she seemed to laugh and weep at the same time before she leaned close to whisper against his lips.

"These are happy tears, Jonah. Nothing on earth would please me more than to be your wife. Even if I have to give up my doctoring."

He squeezed her hand.

"No!" He jerked, his foot kicking out, hitting a small table laid out with Sumner's tools.

Sumner's gaze was rooted to the table, but he forced her to look at him with another squeeze. She'd begun to tear up again, so he insisted, "Neither of us...is giving up. We'll find a way. With God's help, we'll find a way." Then, before she could offer any more objections, he took the ring from her palm and slid it over her finger. "I don't know how much of a husband I'll be."

Again, she pressed a finger to his lips. "Stop, Jonah. Stop. You don't understand. You were injured in the tunnel collapse when a beam struck you. Several large splinters of wood were driven into your back and I was forced to operate to remove them."

She twisted to retrieve a small bottle from the nearby table. Holding it where he could see the contents, she shook it so that three jagged pieces of metal rattled against the sides.

"The accident loosened the shrapnel embedded near your spine. I was able to retrieve them. It will take some time for the incisions to heal…but, barring infection, you should recover soon."

"I'll try not to be a burden to you."

"No, Jonah. You don't understand. I think you'll make a full recovery."

He knew he couldn't allow her to entertain false hope.

"My legs are numb, Sumner."

Her smile spread from her lips to her eyes, making her whole face glow with joy.

"But you kicked the table, Jonah."

"What?"

"You *kicked* the table. You may feel numb—it's understandable with everything you've gone through. But you moved that foot all on your own. You're going to be okay. It will just take time."

Then she was kissing him. Not a butterfly kiss, but a real kiss—albeit brief—that left him in no doubt of her feelings or her love. And he knew then what it meant to be truly accepted, in sickness or in health. She had been more than willing to accept his infirmity, and she'd been equally willing to celebrate in his recovery.

Because she loved him.

As he loved her.

The rest would be left up to God.

* * *

It was more than a week later when Sumner answered a knock at the rear door of the Dovecote. In that time, her patients had begun to heal rather nicely. She had only a handful of men who still required around-the-clock care, so rather than tending to them at the infirmary, they'd been moved to the Dovecote, where Sumner and the other women could spoil them shamelessly. In the meantime, Sumner had moved her personal belongings upstairs where she shared a room with Lydia and Iona.

Even so, the last person Sumner had expected to see was Phineas Bottoms.

"Mr. Bottoms, what a surprise!"

"A pleasant one, I hope." He stepped inside, stamping his boots on the braided rug. Then he allowed Sumner to help him shrug free from his coat. "I heard Jonah was up and about, and I figured I'd better see for myself."

Sumner beamed with pride. After all he'd been through, Jonah was recovering even more quickly than she'd expected. Although he still required a cane for balance, he'd been able to walk the length of the Dovecote and back.

She led Mr. Bottoms behind the curtain where Jonah sat propped up in the tester bed. Her fiancé's face brightened when he saw Phineas, but he held out a hand for Sumner, lacing their fingers together. Sumner knew the gesture was meant to provide her with much-needed support as well as to make it clear that the rumors flying through the mining camp were true. The two of them would be married. Although there was no official clergy in town, one of Gideon Gault's men had the power to serve as justice of the peace and that would have to do for now.

"It's good to see you, sir."

Phineas waved aside Jonah's formal tone. "No need to be putting on airs. This is more of a social call than anything else." He settled into the rocking chair next to the bed, and before Sumner could go in search of another, Jonah pulled her onto the bed beside him.

"You're looking good, Jonah. Really good."

Jonah squeezed her hand. "Thank you, Phineas. I'm already feeling better than I have in years."

Phineas pointed his hat in Sumner's direction. "I think the little lady here has a lot to do with that. In more ways than one."

The man's gaze was piercing as he met Sumner's eyes, but the sensation wasn't unpleasant. To her surprise, he didn't appear upset with the fact that Jonah and she had broken the rules by becoming engaged. He appeared… pleased?

No. She couldn't be interpreting things correctly.

"I suppose you've heard that I've asked Sumner to marry me," Jonah said, choosing his words carefully.

"I did catch something to that effect."

This time, it was Sumner who squeezed Jonah's hand in support. Knowing that neither of them would be able to make a living in Bachelor Bottoms, they'd already determined that they would live in Jonah's cabin on his own property for the rest of the winter. Come spring, they would try their hand at finding work somewhere else.

"That means I'll have to tender my resignation."

But Phineas appeared confused. "Why's that?"

Jonah's gaze bounced from Bottoms to Sumner, then back again. "Married men aren't allowed in Bachelor Bottoms."

Phineas's brows creased. "What on earth do you mean? We've got plenty of married men here at Bachelor Bottoms."

"But, sir, the rules specifically state that all employees are to refrain from having any contact with women."

"On mine property," Phineas inserted before Jonah could finish. "What they do on their own time, on their own property…" He shrugged, a definite gleam entering his eyes. "Well, that's a matter between them and their Creator." He pushed himself to his feet. "Seems to me, the two of you have what they call a loophole."

Sumner couldn't be sure, but she thought Mr. Bottoms winked.

"Now, where can I find the other men?"

Sumner jumped to her feet. "They're in the main room. The women have been making cookies for the Christmas Devotional, and the men decided to watch."

When she took a step, ready to show Phineas the way, he held up a hand. "Don't bother yourself. I can follow my nose to the source of those delicious aromas. Meanwhile, you set yourself down and enjoy this man's company. We'll be needing him back at work as soon as he's able. This place just doesn't run right without him."

Phineas strode from the room, leaving the curtain around Jonah's bed swaying to mark his progress. As soon as it was clear he was gone, Jonah began to chuckle.

"He's a sly one, isn't he?"

Sumner returned to Jonah's side. "What do you mean?"

"Didn't you hear? He's just told us that we can stay *and* keep our jobs."

Sumner shook her head in confusion. "I didn't hear anything of the kind."

"Don't you see? As soon as we're married, we'll be living on my homestead, off company property. I can still go to work every day, still follow the rules when I'm there. But my wife will be only a few miles away." His voice became deep and soft and oh-so-tender. He stroked her cheek with the backs of his fingers. "Waiting for me."

She nodded. At least Jonah could continue working at the job he loved so much.

Jonah must have sensed a portion of her melancholy because he tipped her face up.

"That means you can work, too."

"But how?"

He grinned. "It shouldn't take much to put a spare room on the back of the cabin. Then again, you'll probably be needing a separate building altogether. You can set out your shingle and do your doctoring." His voice deepened meaningfully. *"Off company property."*

Hope fluttered in her breast, soft as a dove's wing.

"But the men…"

"There will be some who might not come to you, but there's more that will. With everything you've done for them—for this community—they trust you, Sumner. You're one of them now. You might not have an official office on the premises, but you're their doctor." He tipped his head toward the voices coming from the other room. "Phineas knows that, and one of these days Batchwell will come to his senses."

The fluttering in her chest grew and strengthened until a whole flock of birds whirled around her heart.

They could stay.

Here, where she'd grown to love the people, the community…

And this man.

As if he'd heard her thoughts aloud, Jonah pulled her close. "I love you, Dr. Sumner Edmund Havisham. You are the most dedicated, talented, beautiful woman I have ever known, and that day we exchange our vows will be the happiest day of my life."

How blessed she was to be able to share all her accomplishments with a man she loved more than life itself.

"I love you, Jonah," she whispered. "More than anything."

Then the distance between them dissolved as they sealed their happiness with a kiss.

* * * * *

Dear Reader,

I hope you enjoyed reading *Accidental Courtship*, the first book in The Bachelors of Aspen Valley series. I had such fun with Jonah and Sumner's story. For years, I've been wanting to write about the challenges faced by some of the first women in the medical profession, and Sumner's journey to Aspen Valley seemed tailormade for the opportunity. I also enjoyed using the rugged setting of the Uinta Mountains, located in my own home state of Utah. Although I've travelled all over the world, there's something about the craggy mountains, glittering rivers, and fragrant stands of pine that speak to me of "home."

Be sure to watch for future books in the Bachelors of Aspen Valley series to discover the romantic fates of many of the characters you've come to know. Aspen Valley will never be the same after such an eventful winter!

I love to hear from my readers, so if you'd like to contact me or stay in touch with release dates and information, please feel free to join me at lisabinghamauthor. com, Facebook.com/lisabinghamauthor, or on Twitter @lbinghamauthor.

Best wishes,
Lisa Bingham

COMING NEXT MONTH FROM
Love Inspired® Historical

Available February 6, 2018

SUDDENLY A FRONTIER FATHER
Wilderness Brides • by Lyn Cote
Mail-order bride turned schoolteacher Emma Jones no longer
wants a husband. But when the man she planned to marry
returns to town after being called away for a family emergency,
can she resist falling for Mason Chandler and the two little girls
he's adopted?

THE RANCHER'S TEMPORARY ENGAGEMENT
by Stacy Henrie
When he hires a Pinkerton agent to investigate sabotage on his
horse ranch, Edward Kent doesn't expect the agency to send
a female detective. Even more surprising is Maggy Worthing's
suggestion for her cover story: a fake engagement to Edward.

HONOR-BOUND LAWMAN
by Danica Favorite
When Laura Booth's ex-husband escapes from prison with the
intention of coming after her, former lawman Owen Hamilton
must come out of retirement to keep her safe. But can the
widowed single father protect her without losing his heart?

AN INCONVENIENT MARRIAGE
by Christina Miller
Widowed reverend Samuel Montgomery is excited to start over
with his daughter in a new town—until he learns he'll lose his
job if he doesn't marry. His only solution: a marriage in name
only to local heiress Clarissa Adams, who needs a husband to
win her inheritance.

———————

**LOOK FOR THESE AND OTHER LOVE INSPIRED BOOKS WHEREVER
BOOKS ARE SOLD, INCLUDING MOST BOOKSTORES, SUPERMARKETS,
DISCOUNT STORES AND DRUGSTORES.**

LIHCNM0118

Get 2 Free Books,
Plus 2 Free Gifts—

Love Inspired HISTORICAL

just for trying the Reader Service!

YES! Please send me 2 FREE Love Inspired® Historical novels and my 2 FREE mystery gifts (gifts are worth about $10 retail). After receiving them, if I don't wish to receive any more books, I can return the shipping statement marked "cancel." If I don't cancel, I will receive 4 brand-new novels every month and be billed just $5.24 per book in the U.S. or $5.74 per book in Canada. That's a savings of at least 13% off the cover price. It's quite a bargain! Shipping and handling is just 50¢ per book in the U.S. and 75¢ per book in Canada.* I understand that accepting the 2 free books and gifts places me under no obligation to buy anything. I can always return a shipment and cancel at any time. The free books and gifts are mine to keep no matter what I decide.

102/302 IDN GLWZ

Name	(PLEASE PRINT)	
Address		Apt. #
City	State/Prov.	Zip/Postal Code

Signature (if under 18, a parent or guardian must sign)

Mail to the Reader Service:
IN U.S.A.: P.O. Box 1341, Buffalo, NY 14240-8531
IN CANADA: P.O. Box 603, Fort Erie, Ontario L2A 5X3

Want to try two free books from another series?
Call 1-800-873-8635 or visit www.ReaderService.com.

* Terms and prices subject to change without notice. Prices do not include applicable taxes. Sales tax applicable in N.Y. Canadian residents will be charged applicable taxes. Offer not valid in Quebec. This offer is limited to one order per household. Books received may not be as shown. Not valid for current subscribers to Love Inspired Historical books. All orders subject to approval. Credit or debit balances in a customer's account(s) may be offset by any other outstanding balance owed by or to the customer. Please allow 4 to 6 weeks for delivery. Offer available while quantities last.

Your Privacy—The Reader Service is committed to protecting your privacy. Our Privacy Policy is available online at www.ReaderService.com or upon request from the Reader Service.

We make a portion of our mailing list available to reputable third parties that offer products we believe may interest you. If you prefer that we not exchange your name with third parties, or if you wish to clarify or modify your communication preferences, please visit us at www.ReaderService.com/consumerschoice or write to us at Reader Service Preference Service, P.O. Box 9062, Buffalo, NY 14240-9062. Include your complete name and address.

LIHI7R2

If you loved this story from
Love Inspired® Historical
be sure to discover more inspirational
stories to warm your heart from
Love Inspired® and
Love Inspired® Suspense!

Love Inspired stories show that
faith, forgiveness and hope have the power
to lift spirits and change lives—always.

Look for six new romances every month
from **Love Inspired®** and
Love Inspired® Suspense!

LISTLIH0118R

SPECIAL EXCERPT FROM

Love Inspired HISTORICAL

Mail-order bride turned schoolteacher Emma Jones no longer wants a husband. But when the man she planned to marry returns to town after being called away for a family emergency, can she resist falling for Mason Chandler and the two little girls he's adopted?

Read on for a sneak preview of
SUDDENLY A FRONTIER FATHER
by Lyn Cote*, available February 2018*
from Love Inspired Historical!

Mason turned, startled when he heard his name being called. "Miss Jones. What can I do for you?"

"I'm glad to see you are walking without your crutch," she said, not replying to his question.

He didn't have to think about why this lady had come. Colton had repeatedly told him that Miss Jones wanted the girls in school. Evidently Emma was a woman to be reckoned with. His irritation over this vied with his unwelcome pleasure at seeing her here, so fine and determined. "I can guess why you've come. But I wasn't ready to send them to school yet."

"Your girls are ready. Do you think you are helping them, keeping them out?"

"I'm keeping them from being hurt. Children can be cruel," he said.

"And adults can be. Do you think keeping them out protects them from hurt? Don't you realize that keeping them home is hurting them, too?"

"I can teach them their letters and numbers."

"That's not what I mean. Isolating them is telling them that you don't think they can handle school. That they are lesser than the other children. Are you ashamed of Birdie and Charlotte?"

"No. They are wonderful little girls."

"Then bring them to school Monday." She turned as if to leave. "Have some trust in me, and trust in the children of this town."

She left him without a word to say.

The girls ran to him. "Did the lady teacher say we could come to school?" Birdie asked.

He looked down into Birdie's eager face. "Do you want to go to school?"

"Yes!" Birdie signed to Charlotte. "She says yes, too. We can see Lily and Colton. And meet other children."

He wondered if Birdie was capable of grasping the concept of prejudice.

"Some children will like us and some won't," Birdie said, answering his unspoken question. "But we want to go to school."

He hoped Miss Emma Jones knew what she was doing. He wanted everything good for his children. But he knew how cruel people could be.

At least no one knew the dark secret he must—above all else—keep hidden.

Don't miss
SUDDENLY A FRONTIER FATHER by Lyn Cote,
available February 2018 wherever
Love Inspired® Historical books and ebooks are sold.

www.LoveInspired.com

Copyright © 2018 by Lyn Cote

LIHEXP0118